Mit 2 0

LINE OF SIGHT

LINE OF SIGHT

JAMES QUEALLY

The following is a work of fiction. Names, characters, places, events and incidents are either the product of the author's imagination or used in an entirely fictitious manner. Any resemblance to actual persons, living or dead, is entirely coincidental.

ISBN 978-1-947993-89-1
eISBN: 1-978-1-951709-03-7
Library of Congress Control Number: 2019953455

First hardcover edition March 2020 by Polis Books, LLC
221 River St., 9th Fl., #9070
Hoboken, NJ 07030
www.PolisBooks.com

POLIS BOOKS

To Jenny, for saving me from thinking I couldn't do this

*To Newark, for teaching me that the way the world looks depends
on where you're standing*

PROLOGUE

They always said don't run. Don't resist.

As Kevin Mathis sprinted down South 11th Street, lungs burning from the cold air and too many "I'll only smoke two each day" cigarettes, he wished they could have seen what he was running from, and why it doesn't always matter what you did or didn't do.

He chugged along, fists balled up, elbows swinging toward his hips in violent motions. Punch the midget, like the track coach said, that whole week he actually went to practice freshman year.

Back then, 14-years-old with less mileage on his airways and fewer two a.m. drive-thru meals padding his stomach, he might have been able to open a lead on his pursuer. But as the footfalls got closer, echoing through the spaces between the apartments and birdcage homes that you couldn't tell apart even when the sun lit up Newark's West Ward, he knew his legs weren't what would keep him alive.

Kevin spun left, away from the few working street lights, into the vacant lot of a Family Dollar, hugging the chain link fence that separated parking spaces from row houses, looking for the hole he'd cut in it however many years ago, the shortcut he still used from time to time.

The shouts came in spurts, profanity tucked in-between authoritative commands. Cop-speak, but he wasn't sure the guy was a cop. The way he'd walked up to his porch, no uniform, way more confident than anyone roaming the neighborhood at 1 a.m. should have been, made him think the guy might have been hiding a gun or a badge.

But Kevin had been arrested before, knew the steps to that dance. Besides, with everything that had been going on, the cops that knew where to find him also knew it was best to steer clear. For their own sake.

Still, the only people who came to Kevin's door that late at night were fiends or friends. This man was neither, which meant he was trouble, which meant Kevin needed to move.

He let his hands run along the fence until a sharp edge bit one of his fingers. The hole was narrow, ragged. They'd done a shit job with the bolt cutters back in high school, when he and a few friends had made this little escape route in the first place.

Metal scraped his forearm, leaving the kind of chalk color scratch that won't draw blood but hurts like hell in the moment. Something stalked off under foot as he crept through the dead grass and litter. A stray disturbed from its slumber, rushing through the November cold in search of somewhere else to hide.

Maybe they'd both get lucky.

Kevin stumbled, hands out in front of him like he was just learning to walk. There was a hole in the fence at the other end of the block, cut on the same day for the same reason, which led out toward Woodland Cemetery.

He heard a high-pitched yelp from behind him. His unwanted friend had found the hole, and the fence wasn't interested in letting him through. The metal rattled like a set of keys in a drier, and the annoyed howls faded as he found the space slashed into the end of the alley.

He exploded into the street, adrenaline surging into his legs as he imagined the man and his gun wrestling with his shortcut. Woodland was in sight, the old oak trees with the shaggy branches waving hello in a winter gust.

Some people liked to think you'd find more bodies in Woodland with a flashlight than a shovel. The cemetery wasn't the ideal place to run if you wanted to keep breathing, but unless one of the neighbors decided to fling open their doors and offer Kevin a hiding spot with a space heater, it would have to do. The old cemetery, with its ornate mausoleums and half-filled granite crypts, was a little too upscale for the neighborhood residents who usually ended up planning funerals a generation before any mother should have to think like that. Most of the people buried at Woodland had gone to ground in recent years, their lives ending on nearby Springfield Avenue, one of Newark's main drug corridors.

Anyone in Woodland at that time of night was at risk of becoming a permanent resident. Likely to get carried out in an ambulance, leaving their grieving family to wonder how the hell they're gonna afford to bring them back in a hearse.

Kevin's mother wouldn't have to stress that. She'd smoked away any responsibility to him, living or dead, before those freshman track practices. Dad though … he didn't wanna think about that. Kevin had to at least make it to his 21st birthday, let his father live out the fantasy of buying that first legal beer even though they both knew he'd started sneaking them years ago.

He ducked behind a stone structure with a tiny angel sitting on top. A naked baby dancing to an unheard song. Kevin never understood why people put those angels anywhere near headstones. They were just dead kids with wings.

Kevin hunched over, bending his knees, trying to shake the fire out of his chest. His heart rate fell slightly from jackhammer to bass drum as he tried to figure out who was chasing him and why. He thought about the last time he was in court. His last pickup from Levon and the one before. The officer with the zig-zag scar. The video on his cell phone.

He leaned back against the stone, breath returning to normal, nothing but darkness between him and where he'd run from.

He was safe until he turned his head the other way, found the shadow peering out from the stone condo full of dead people to the right. An arm came up, a familiar shape where a hand should have been.

He didn't run.

He didn't resist.

It didn't matter.

CHAPTER 1

"And you're sure this will work?"

No.

"Of course it will," I said, peering through the dirt specks on the windshield of my never quite clean Chevy Impala, scanning the sidewalk outside the Newark Police Department's 3rd Precinct for the guy Officer Anthony Scannell was so worried about.

"This just seems a little … out there," Scannell said, rapping his fingers incessantly against my dashboard. "What happens if he says no?"

Well then, Officer Scannell, you'd be fucked.

"He won't say no," I replied, watching someone round the corner leading up to the precinct's limestone steps, pretty sure it wasn't the guy we were looking for. But I couldn't be entirely certain, because Scannell's nerve-addled stammer was distracting me and making me wish I'd never quit smoking.

"How the hell can you be sure?" he asked.

I couldn't.

"I am," I said, tongue far out ahead of my brain as usual.

"Goddamnit man, this is my career on the line. My ass," Scannell said, like I didn't already know that. "I could use a little explanation."

The whining was driving me nuts. Scannell was a big enough guy, probably went 230, six-foot-plus. I'd heard him speak before, years

11

earlier, when we'd both been in the same room but he had no reason to notice. He was a natural baritone, the kind of guy who used profanity in place of cleverness to make it seem like he had something to say. Scannell's voice was bred tough until a boot got anywhere near his throat, then it turned into a mix of helium and worry. A little kid with a bad report card.

I gritted my teeth, thought about a smoke, and gritted more. Forty-seven days without a cancer stick. In forty-seven days, I'd run at least twenty miles, saved nearly five-hundred bucks and managed to look slightly less than spastic in a pick-up basketball game.

Scannell wasn't sending me back to zero. But I needed something in place of a nicotine buzz.

Berating my client seemed like the next best thing.

"You're not exactly in a position to ask questions," I said.

"I hired you, didn't I?" he asked.

"Yeah, to keep your ass out of the jackpot, not to pat your head and tell you everything's gonna be fine."

Scannell sat up straight, crowded me a little.

"You know what happens when someone talks to me like that on the job?" he asked.

"If I had to guess, I'd say you'd beat their ass in the middle of a drug bust, tuck about six grand in your vest, then turn in a weak-ass case that doesn't even get you past a grand jury, freak out when said suspect goes to pick up his personal property and finds it light, then run to someone who sent you to me for help."

His face froze, jaw slack and stupid, and he shrunk back to his side of the car.

"Allegedly," he said.

Allegedly. The useless word I used to type in sentences like "allegedly shot six people" or "allegedly sexually assaulted his stepdaughter." A legal term I had to write to protect monsters because libel lawsuits are

12

like lower back tattoos.

With Scannell cowed, I went back to staring at the sidewalk, hoping to catch sight of Antonio Rice before he got anywhere near the precinct's front door. The Third was on Market Street, north of Ferry, close to the city's Ironbound section. The neighborhood was all Hispanic and Portuguese, but we'd been here for close to an hour and I hadn't seen a black man anywhere. Unless I'd missed Rice while debating the facts of life with Scannell, he should have been here by now.

I turned to the officer, who was staring out the window and plotting his revenge against me.

"A thought," I said. "How are you so damn sure Rice will come down here to file a complaint? You can do that over the phone."

"That skel doesn't know that," he replied.

"And you're certain that Rice isn't smarter than the average skel?"

"No, I'm certain that I've done a solid for the desk sergeant in the Third, and when someone called trying to feed me to the rat squad, he told him they didn't take complaints over the phone. Then he did me the courtesy of giving me enough time to find you."

God bless the Blue Wall.

On cue, a tall, skinny black man wearing a camouflage jacket rounded the corner at the back of the precinct, hop-stepping with a determined gait and a slight limp. His hair was done up in twists, just like the mug shot I'd seen on the state corrections website.

"That's him," Scannell muttered, sitting straight up.

I waited a few seconds and let Rice get closer to the precinct, watched Scannell freak out a little. A small part of me wanted to stay in the car, let the universe take out its trash. But I needed the money more than the department needed to be rid of an oaf like Scannell, who sure as shit would cost me business when he inevitably bitched about losing his job in every cop bar between here and Montclair.

13

November greeted me with an icy blast as I got out, forcing me to tuck my jacket close as I marched across the street and into Rice's path.

"Excuse me," I said, nearly breaking into a jog to catch up to him. He ignored me.

"Yo man," I tried again, earning a half turn of his head but nothing else.

"Yo, Tonio," I shouted. "Slow the fuck down."

He stopped. Turned.

Abrasive was Newark's native tongue.

Antonio gave me the once-over, trying to figure out if he knew me. If I was cop or criminal. Friend or foe. Fifty feet from a police precinct and even then he didn't feel safe. It was the kind of practiced skepticism that kept predators from turning into prey in Newark's West and South Wards.

At least for a little while.

"I don't know you," he said.

"You do not."

"But you know my name."

"Sort of. Know why you're here too," I said.

Antonio took a step back, hand traveling toward his waist on instinct.

"It's not there, Antonio. We both know you're not gonna walk into that precinct and lodge a complaint against a police officer while carrying a concealed weapon," I said. "Besides, I just wanna talk."

"Then talk. Start by telling me how the fuck did you know I was gonna be here and why I came? Actually, hold up, first off, who the fuck are you?"

"My name is Russell Avery," I replied. "And I think this will go a lot easier for you if you don't walk into that building."

"That a threat?"

I ran a hand through my hair and craned my neck. The hell was

14

everyone always so defensive for?

"No man. I don't do threats. I'm all about mutual benefit. See, you going in there doesn't get you any closer to your missing money," I said. "You not going in there, things could go another way."

"And what if this ain't about money, huh?" Antonio asked. "Maybe I just wanna see that fat fuck swing for this, do my civic duty, ya know?"

"It's always about money, Antonio. But I'll play along, if you wanna pretend it's not," I said. "So, you walk in there, right? File your complaint. Meet with a detective from the vaunted Internal Affairs bureau. Then the 'fat fuck,' as you so eloquently put it, comes down here to fight the charges with a union lawyer. Then there's an administrative hearing. You know how often that ends with the cop getting in trouble? Carry the one, round down to zero, and it's right around never. That's no spin, by the way, that's math. This department got something like 200 of these kinds of complaints last year. Cop went down for it like five times. You like those odds?"

"You're just talking man," he said.

"Oh, I'm not done. So, he gets off, because of course he's getting off, and then you become public enemy numero uno for him and all his bunkmates in Major Crimes. Which means the next time they come looking for you, it's not gonna be a possession rap. They'll trump some shit up. They'll tune you up in the process. Or, since you'll have really pissed off the good ol' boys by going to IA , they might just decide they saw you reach for something. Decide their lives were in imminent danger."

He kept his hard stare, but my eyes were already following the tapping sound to his foot moving every which way. It was cold, but it wasn't that cold.

"In case you were wondering, that was the threat," I said.

I highly doubted Scannell or his friends would ever try to kill this kid. Or anyone, for that matter. But it was plausible. To Antonio.

15

Probably to a lot of people in the city. I didn't know if that said more about them or the department.

Antonio jutted his chin out a bit, chewed his lip, kept up the "don't fuck with me" glare like it made a difference.

"So you gonn' tell me the other way this could work?" he asked.

"Yeah. I'm gonna hand you eight grand. You're gonna pretend you never met me."

"Eight?"

"Interest, for your pain and suffering."

"You think you can just buy me off like that?"

I wanted to lecture him on the insanity of a drug dealer seeking the moral high ground, but then I remembered who I was working for and what I was doing.

"Money's in my jacket pocket Antonio. Just saying."

His eyes wandered to where my hands were tucked. We stood there like that for a minute, keeping up the pretense that he needed time to think about this.

But we both knew the way the world worked.

I waited outside my car after it was over, making sure Antonio didn't double back and suffer a crisis of conscience. In the span of five minutes I'd helped a dirty cop keep his job and likely financed a month of cocaine sales for Antonio.

At that moment, a little conscience might not have been the worst thing.

***

My conscience had her eyes trained on the newspaper I no longer worked for, using an elbow to keep the page trapped on a table while fishing at a soup bowl with her free hand. She was sitting in the back of a place called Heaven's Delight, an old brick building that didn't have a sign out front, so you knew it was good and it was cheap. They made one hell of an Oxtail soup.

16

She was muttering to herself, either reading the article in an incoherent whisper or providing a running commentary, when I sat down across the table and banged my knee on the underside.

A splash of soup leapt for freedom, clearing the rim of the bowl and turning a used car advertisement into a soggy puddle.

"Asshole," Key said.

"Sorry about the paper," I replied.

"That's not why you're an asshole."

"Well there's long list of reasons…"

"Don't start with the jokes," Key said, picking her saucer wide eyes up from the paper and training them on me. The woman really needed to switch to tea. Her pupils were stuck halfway between the Lincoln Tunnel and the moon.

"I checked in with Antonio," she said. "Sounds like everything's handled."

"Are you surprised?" I asked.

"Also said you threatened him."

"That's a pretty strict interpretation of the word," I replied. "I simply advised him of all the possible ramifications of his choices."

"Sounds like a fancy way of saying threatened," she replied.

"Hey now. As the ordained writer of the two of us…"

She cocked her head to the side and cut me off before jabbing one of her unpainted, unmanaged fingernails at the newspaper.

"You a writer? That's funny," she said. "I don't see your name in here anymore."

"That's cold, Key."

"So's what you did to poor Tonio," she said.

"I kept Tonio out of a lot more trouble then he'd normally get himself in and made him enough money to commit felonies to his heart's content. Poor isn't the right word."

Now she smiled. I loved making her smile. It was the only thing

17

that kept her from slapping the shit out of me.

For as long as I'd been bouncing around the Brick City, Keyonna Jackson had been my advisor, guide, friend, source, and when I needed it most, reality check.

We'd met back when I was a reporter, or as I like to remember it, that point in time when I actually mattered.

My first year on, the city saw a crazy surge in homicides. Ten days. Ten bodies. Chicago or Baltimore might do those numbers in a weekend, but Newark could fit inside either of those places twelve times over.

When a city's big, but not huge, people tend to know the dead and dying as more than just names in the police blotter. They're cousins, neighbors, that guy who owned the bodega on Elizabeth Avenue or that kid who couldn't keep his mouth shut in your son's math class.

Like most of her city, Key knew at least one of the people who fell that week. Unlike most of her city, she decided to do something about it.

On a particularly sweltering Wednesday that August, Key and a few others blocked traffic near Meeker Street. The week after that, the number grew to 30. Then fifty. A couple dozen more tacked on the next month. The department started sending details to monitor the protests, and the news cameras followed like they always do.

It wasn't long before Key's bullhorn-aided screeds found their way to YouTube. Videos of her wild charcoal hair and way too large black tee-shirts – usually made up at a local print shop that week and lined with the names of the city's most recent dead -- racked up a healthy amount of views. Every now and again she'd go way off-script, suggest they arrest the Mayor for negligence or something. Sounded crazy to me, but then again, I didn't live in the South Ward. If I had coin-flip odds of making it home unharmed every night, I might've been out there with her.

The city's homicide total dropped the next year. A little bit more the year after that. People stopped following Key into the streets, and my tribe got distracted by a State Senator using campaign funds to cover-up the fact that he was sleeping with someone who wasn't his wife.

The protests died off, but people kept right on dying, just at a pace the city could sell as progress. Time heals exactly no wounds, but it helps you get used to the scars.

Key still sent out text message blasts every week, announcing a new demonstration in a new intersection. Wednesday. 5 p.m., a bullhorn leading the loose collection of die-hard activists who considered themselves the city's Anti-Violence Coalition. They spoke, but nobody came who needed to listen. The city only rallied around people like Key when it was angry, and at that moment, Newark was hovering around its normal standard of shitty, but tolerable.

"So, you come all the way up here just so I could yell at you?" Key asked, eyes lost in the newsprint again.

"Just curious if you had anything else for me right now."

Most of my work came from the cops, mostly in the form of playing fixer for officers like Scannell who had jammed themselves up. Technically, I was a licensed P.I., but I didn't do a whole lot of investigating. I was more like a problem solver, negotiator, arbitrator, maybe a referee. Whatever job title you wanted to affix to it.

I cost less than an attorney, and the kinds of cops that came knocking were more than happy to pay me to prevent an internal probe when I could. I had enough street contacts from my reporter days, people like Key, that I could usually broker a peace with whoever wanted to lodge a complaint before anything ever got on paper. As long as one side paid a commission.

"You can't possibly be hurting for work, Russ," she said. "I mean, the way you keep bailing those Major Crimes boys out, you're gonna put that union lawyer out of business."

"Remind me why I like you again?" I asked.

"Because I might have something for you that doesn't make you wanna throw up when it's over," she said.

"I like you again."

Key spun the page she'd been staring at, jabbed a finger at a two-column wide gray rectangle filled with text that jumped from bold to italic to regular.

Her talon was hovering over the paper's Law & Order briefs, a short item about a murder. I looked at the byline underneath, saw a name that put a phantom pain in my chest.

The story was about someone named Kevin Mathis who "was shot and killed in Woodland Cemetery shortly before 1 a.m. Wednesday. A police spokesman declined to comment on a motive, and a suspect had yet to be identified."

"And?" I asked.

"And a boy's dead," Key replied.

"And a boy's dead on the west side, in Woodland no less, at that hour? You know exactly what that is."

Key made a futile attempt to narrow those cartoon eyes. I knew what I sounded like. I also knew I was probably right.

"You just assume it's a gang thing?" she asked.

"No, I just assume it's a drug thing," I replied. "The bangers here are just dealers with dumbass code names, you know that."

"Well, this boy's father seems to think otherwise," she said.

"Oh, fuck me, Key. You let some good-hearted parent actually believe their own nonsense?" I said. "You know how this ends. I used to get these phone calls once a week. Nobody wants to believe their kid died because of some shit they got themselves into."

"Man says he can prove it," Key replied, leaning back in the chair and folding her arms. She hit me with the disappointed Mom stare I'd come to loathe and fear in the six years we'd known one another.

"Prove it?" I asked. "He got a signed confession from the shooter? 'Dear Mr....'"

I had to look down at the paper to remember the dead kid's name.

"Dear Mr. Mathis," I continued. "I aced your son because I am actually human garbage. He was a really good kid and he didn't deserve it."

I stood up from the table.

"What are you gonna tell me next Key? The kid was gonna turn his life around?" I asked. "Get a job at Home Depot? We've been at this way too long to trip over day one stuff."

She stood up, the glare on high.

"You just hit me with every assumption and stereotype there is," she said.

I went to say something back, but my tongue was out of ammo. She was right. She knew it, and I knew better than to throw bad after worse when arguing with her.

"Just talk to the man. In private. Investigate," she said. "That's your job ain't it?"

"I don't really have time for this Key," I replied.

"Way I see it, you got all the time in the world. I don't have any other jobs for you," she replied. "Unless of course, you wanna do more of what you been doing all day."

I stared at Key, but the harsh lines under her eyes gave way to Scannell's fat face and his coffee breath and his "please save my incompetent and borderline corrupt ass" whine. I thought about him collecting a pension while I paid off my student loans just in time to start take on a mortgage.

I didn't wanna do anything for the cops or this grieving Dad who refused to believe his drug dealer son died for drug dealer son reasons.

But the cops never stared at me like Key did.

CHAPTER 2

I've spent more time than I'd care to think about around the relatives of Newark homicide victims, and through each sad and infuriating conversation, one thing stayed the same. By the end of the interview, you might tell them more about their fallen son or daughter than they tell you.

It's not that they lie. There was nothing nefarious about the wrong answers provided by each widow, brother or mother that I'd spoken to in the past. They just didn't know. Maybe they didn't want to. I can't blame people for not going out of their way to find out why Johnny was face down in a stairwell at the Meeker homes, why Denise might have been a familiar face at the Hotel Nile, one of the city's oldest and cheapest flophouses.

From what Key told me about Austin Mathis, he seemed like a good enough man, a bus driver whose only brushes with the legal system came in the form of a few parking tickets. He worked nonstop, left to raise Kevin and his two sisters when Mom followed the needle to oblivion too many years before. He was the kind of client that still made this job worthwhile.

Unfortunately, a quick glance at his son's background also made me think I was right when I told Key this was a waste of time. With one parent gone to work all hours and the other just flat out gone,

Kevin Mathis was conscripted to the street before he was old enough to know what that would mean. Dad barely around to help with your homework one year eventually leads to Dad not being around to drag your ass back inside when trouble comes the next.

He had priors for drugs, but his known associates didn't set off any alarms in my head. No gangland players that I knew of, and he hadn't been tagged for anything violent.

But the arrest locations were right on top of one another. The dots were too close on the map to mean anything else. He was dealing regularly in his own neighborhood.

A kid who dealt in his neighborhood, shot dead late at night in that neighborhood in a graveyard stacked three deep with dealers. And Key wanted me to help prove it was something other than what it was.

But she was right. It wasn't like I had anything better to do. At the least I could convince her she was wrong, end my long losing streak in our never-ending arguments.

I stepped out of the Impala and into the parking lot of the Family Dollar near the crime scene, pulling my gray pea coat close. The lot was empty except for a few cars that someone must have been too lazy to tow, but I saw a small crew of what looked like teenagers out beyond the concrete dividers. They were leaning against a rusted green fence at the edge of Woodland, all huddled around a collection of mylar balloons and white poster board with crudely scrawled farewells in acrylic marker. A rainbow of votive candles formed a semi-circle at the base.

A dollar store memorial: the hallmark of a homicide. When Newark grieved, it did so on a budget. It had to.

A thought about the teens being dealers crept into my head, one bolstered by the sour marijuana scent that hit me as I came closer. But I felt Key's specter staring at the back of my neck again. Even if my assumptions were right half the time, I knew they came from a place that wasn't.

A stream of leaves and withered cigarette filters swirled along the sidewalk as I walked up to the group, the wind making a rustling sounding like a bag of potato chips being used as a punching bag. I stopped moving when I reached the edge of the sidewalk adjacent to them. In the days when I had a press pass, this was the moment where I'd light a cigarette, pretend to take a phone call, and let the locals size me up. You don't barge in on people when they're grieving.

But I didn't smoke anymore, so I knew what I was in for.

The six of them stopped talking, stopped moving, as I crept into their half-circle. Three of them were just done being babies, 14 at best, and their hard stares were all poker faces and no cause for concern. The one in the black hoodie leaning against the fence was about my height, hands jammed far into his pockets like they always belonged there. Two others milled around the edge of the frame, down coats and long jeans, halfway grown between the kids and the man who'd locked onto me as I approached.

"You lost?" Hoodie asked.

"Why would you ask that?"

"You know why I asked that," he said.

I didn't like the glares, but they were deserved. People of my complexion didn't come here unless they wanted something.

"First off, my condolences," I said, the line coming out rehearsed from the hundred times I'd said it before.

"Condolences?" Hoodie shot back. "We look sad to you?"

"Your friend, Kevin."

"I don't know anybody named Kevin," he replied, poking his head out and looking to his audience. "Y'all know a Kevin?"

They snickered, little sputtering laughs. The hard ass routine was as well practiced as my feigned grief.

"Hey, I know him," said one of the two mid-size kids, pointing at me but staring at Hoodie. "Seen him around here before. Work for the paper, right?"

"Nah man, we met the girl from the paper yesterday," one of the freshmen chimed in. "In the black skirt. How could you forget that? I was thinking about it all night."

Dina's portrait entered my mind, followed by the thought of this 14-year-old figuring out how puberty worked, chased by the thought of me dribbling a 14-year-old's head off the concrete.

"Oh yeah," Hoodie said, shooting a disapproving glance at the kid, like he'd spoken out of turn. "Least when she was here, it was worth my time to get a look."

"Sorry, I know she's got a better ass than me," I said.

"Like you," Hoodie started, but whatever insult he had coming was overtaken by the kid.

"Like you ever seen it," the 14-year-old spat.

The rest of the teens in their down jackets had their eyes shot down the street, uninterested in laughing like the rest of the hyenas. I followed their stares and found the source of their concern, realized I could play this a little looser.

The 14-year-old was cackling, giving skin to one of the others, when I stepped to him. Hard as he thought he was, the realization that he'd just insulted someone who had six inches and sixty pounds on him caused his jaw to snap shut.

"Let's just say I know a guy who used to date her," I said. "He's got a problem with mouthy kids whose dicks barely work talking about her like that."

Dina's not-so secret admirer didn't say anything. The others were still laughing, now at him instead of with him. I looked to Hoodie, who let a little smile slip as he moved his heel off the cemetery fence.

"That was good," he said, pulling one hand out of his pocket to show it was empty. "But I can't let you talk to my friends like that."

25

His left hand abandoned its hiding spot next, but it didn't bring a gun with it. He didn't need one. Hoodie waved and the rest of the pack formed a tight circle around me. The older ones sneered like they'd done this before, while the others mirrored what they'd seen on TV.

One of my old sources, a veteran Newark homicide lieutenant, had taught me a few self-defense moves back when I still spent most of my time in bad neighborhoods after the sun went down. I'd hoped to use them in a situation like this, where I could square up and slap down some mouthy asshole. Land enough punches to earn a good war story, and, more importantly, stay out of the hospital.

But my amateur repertoire wouldn't keep me conscious too long in a 6-on-1 beatdown. Thankfully, I'd noticed a few potential witnesses to my pending ass-kicking while I was walking up.

"We can do this if you want," I said. "But that's not gonna make our friends leave any quicker."

Hoodie was visibly confused.

"Crown Vic, seven or eight cars down, opposite side of the street," I said. "Jumping a citizen at a crime scene with the cops in the front row probably isn't your best move. Maybe you call your boys off, and we handle this in a less stupid fashion."

He looked around like another option was going to present itself before shaking his head "no" toward the others.

"The fuck you want from us man?" Hoodie asked.

"Same as I said before. I want to talk about Kevin. You help me a little bit, and I'll find a way to make them leave."

Hoodie brushed himself off and went back to leaning against the fence like nothing had happened. He even placed the same heel against the metal, as if he could hit rewind and reclaim his "fuck you" aura.

"He's dead. It sucks. The end," Hoodie said.

"Anybody in particular who might've wanted him gone?"

"Not that I heard."

"Well, he was dealing right?" I asked.

He didn't speak, move or even twitch.

"Listen man, I'm not with the cops or the paper. What you say here doesn't go past me," I said. "Besides, I don't even know your name. What are you worried about? That I might tell someone that some black kid somewhere on the west side told me something? In case you didn't notice, you don't exactly stick out around here."

"You really gonna make those cops leave?" Hoodie asked.

I nodded. He shrugged his shoulders, probably figuring the only way he was getting rid of them was to get rid of me.

"He moved some shit. But the real players around here were OK with it, that's what I heard."

"Which set?" I asked.

"C'mon man," he shook his head. "You wanna know who runs shit around here, it ain't hard to figure out. But I ain't going that far. Just know that Kev was alright by them. Whatever he got killed behind, it wasn't no drug shit."

"I know what you're saying but … where he died, how he died. You could see why I'd think otherwise."

He stepped off the gate and pulled his hood back, revealing short cropped hair and a face older than I expected. His left cheek had an indentation, maybe a scar, and there was a 973 tattooed in tiny numbers on the upper part of his neck, just below the ear. Newark area code.

"Man, why are you even asking me questions if you're gonna tell yourself the answer. If you already made your damn mind up about what happened then why don't you leave us the fuck alone?"

"I was just saying…"

"You was just saying what they always say. Like how he lived just had to be why he died," he said, his voice creeping closer to a roar now. "You know what? I'll tell you one more thing I did hear, and not cause I'm trying to help you, but maybe so I can educate your dumb ass.

People been saying some people walked up on Kev, not long before he fell. One or two people, depending who you ask. White boys. Ain't too many white drug dealers out here, you know?"

I knew what he was implying, and nodded, figuring they'd done all the talking they would, and turned my back.

I might have learned a lot and I might have learned nothing. Either way, now I had to deal with the cops. Not because I felt any obligation to honor my deal with Hoodie, but because a post-budget cut police department wouldn't have officers sitting on a drug murder this long after the body dropped.

Unless, of course, it wasn't a drug murder.

Two crushed QuickChek coffee cups and what looked like a sandwich wrapper were nestled against the Crown Vic's driver-side tire, the leavings of at least two cops who'd been left sitting somewhere too long. They were gonna be really happy when I knocked on their window.

The glass slid down to reveal one half of a salt-white chin strap beard and a set of crow's feet stacked like a stepladder. The face turned slowly, bringing the matching features on the other side into view, all anchored around browned lips that were always puckered into a coiled spring.

Lieutenant Bill Henniman raised his head just enough to meet my surprised stare, his lips parting slightly to let out a sigh as smooth as someone blowing smoke.

"You lost?" he asked.

Henniman and Hoodie would've had a lot to talk about.

"Me? Not at all. Just enjoying the sights and sounds of the West Ward. Did you know they opened an IHOP just a few blocks from here? I'm partial to the Smokehouse combo," I said. "Are you lost? This seems like a strange place to find a Major Crimes lieutenant in the middle of the day."

"Homicide is a major crime, Avery," he replied, voice in its permanent croak. "We tend to solve those."

"One internal affairs complaint at a time."

"Christ, Avery. You know, when you started this new job, I actually convinced myself you'd smarten up, understand who the good guys were," he said. "I heard about the garbage you pulled with Scannell, by the way."

Henniman folded his hands atop his chest, let another breezy sigh escape. The lieutenant was the kind of guy who just seemed exhausted by everything and everyone, almost like he was too tired to get upset. He was an old dog. He'd bark at a car every now and again just to keep up appearances, but if he had his way, he'd watch the world from inside his house. It was less upsetting that way.

"What do you want from my life, Avery?" he asked. "Scannell paid you, didn't he?"

"Yeah, standard fee. I'm not here about money. I wasn't looking for you, certainly didn't expect you here, it being a little over 24 hours after a routine drug murder and all," I said. "But here you are. Maybe wondering if someone like me was going to show up, making me wonder if coming down here wasn't such a waste of time after all."

"If you wanted to write stories, Avery, you should've stayed at the paper. This is what it looks like. Dumb kid deals dope, dumb kid gets done in because of it. That little crew you were playing paddy cake with has two people we've collared before in it. We were doing surveillance, before you came over here and screwed it up," Henniman replied. "I'll call you when your services are required again. Until then, go fuck yourself."

I could've just left. Henniman's presence and Hoodie's rant were enough to tell me Key's suspicions were, at the very least, not completely insane. But a deal was a deal.

I fell back against the car, just hard enough to make Henniman

29

angry, and pulled out my cellphone, dialing some combination of digits that didn't matter.

The window rolled down behind me.

"What are you doing, Avery?" he growled.

I turned and shook my head, feigning confusion.

"You're still here?" I asked.

"What are you doing?"

"Just making a phone call. Ain't talked to Dina in a while, heard she was down here too."

"Dina Colby?" he asked. "The reporter?"

"You know her? Oh, that's great. She's probably going to want to interview you about the case. I'll let her know you're down here," I said. "You know how it works right, gotta win points with the ex when you can."

Henniman stared a hole through me as he reached for the keys and stirred the engine to life. It whined and sputtered for a minute like every ancient department car did before surrendering and turning over.

"I don't know what crawled up your ass today, Avery, but I think you need to remember who your friends are," he said. "You got that investigator's license of yours pretty fast if memory serves, and a lot of clients right after. That whole business is built on relationships. Like ours."

He rolled the window shut and drove off, leaving me in a cloud of exhaust and standing in a pile of trampled slush. I turned back to Mathis' discount memorial and saw Hoodie and his boys were gone.

***

The Lieutenant had a point.

I let the radio on the Impala flip to a band called Cloud Nothings, hoping the raw guitar rock would help clear my head or at least create enough space up there to list all the bad places Henniman's involvement could lead.

The Lieutenant was a career cop with no exit plan. After twenty-five years, most people made their peace with Newark's police, moved onto a private security gig or a cushy supervisor's spot with the prosecutor's or sheriff's office. Not Henniman. He liked the sway he'd built up over the years, the agency-wide influence that came with it. He loved that badge with the kind of passion most people reserved for spouses. Henniman hadn't had one of those in at least a decade.

The unit had been bequeathed to him by Frank Russomano, the former lieutenant who'd retired two years earlier. Since Frank was one of my sources, Henniman's cell phone number was bequeathed to me the same way. But my relationship with the two men couldn't have been more different.

Where Frank was a person first and cop second, the kind of guy you could drink with and debate the shortcomings of the NPD without entering into a screaming match, Henniman was what they called a true believer. The kind of cop who thought a badge was akin to Superman's cape, the kind of cop who thought criticizing police meant you hated police.

The squad room was Henniman's church, the detectives who worked under him and the allies he made through the job his apostles. I fit into the second category, back when I had a press pass, though I always tried to remind Henniman that the source on one story could be the subject of the next. It never really took, and the distinction rarely ever mattered. Henniman wasn't dirty, as far as I'd ever known or cared to look, just moody. Desensitized from years spent wrist deep in the city's dead, unconcerned about the way he treated the living who weren't part of his tribe.

He'd shout down reporters he didn't like at press conferences, badmouth them around the agency so they couldn't get info beyond the choppy releases typed up by the public information office. Cops who didn't fit his unit, or god forbid, challenged the Major Case lieutenant's aggressive tactics, found themselves transferred to the 5th Precinct. The South Ward. The part of Newark I didn't like going after dark unless I knew the cops would be on a scene in full force.

Henniman's threat played on loop in my head as I drove back to the central part of the city, crossing Broad Street and into the slightly safer environs of the Ironbound.

I'd never really thought about what life might be like outside of Henniman's circle, and now I remembered why.

Sure, I'd made a crack about his unit being a client farm, but all good jokes have a dash of truth. Cops were the majority of my business, a business they'd helped start when I quit the job I'd loved one year earlier.

The newspaper had mutated from the place that raised me, the place that held the city accountable, to an awkward appendage that waived around and counted clicks, using some impossible calculus to determine news.

I needed to leave, so I did, but I still needed work.

I'd always joked about becoming a P.I., but in New Jersey, it's tough to snag a license unless you're an ex-cop or an ex-soldier. Otherwise you need to spend five years working under a registered Shamus, and the money isn't great when you're doing surveillance work and other gofer tasks at someone else's behest.

But if you've got cop friends, and they have State Police friends, then there's a chance some of them will gladly attest to the years you spent training under a private investigator from Red Bank named Mark Mueller.

Whoever the fuck that was.

Of course, no one does anything for free. The kind of cops who might be willing to fudge a few forms to get me a private investigator's license were the same kind of cops who might benefit from having a P.I. in their corner. That was how it started anyway. Representing cops who weren't exactly clean, but nowhere near filthy either. The dirt under the fingernails kinds of corrupt: second job overlapping with shift hours, hidden assets to avoid alimony. Whole lot of vice detectives who claimed their wives were cheating and asked me to follow them. Most just wanted me to keep tabs on their beloved so they could sneak off with their own side pieces.

It wasn't the Lord's work, but it was palatable. Right up until my reputation as a cop's P.I. sprinted ahead of the reality, and people with real, indictable problems started coming to me. People like Scannell who were about to run face-first into a termination hearing or a grand jury.

I'd like to tell you I said no when these cops came into my office and asked for help, but it turns out people with real problems have real money.

Henniman's guys couldn't stop finding reasons to pay me. He chalked up the high number of internal affairs complaints to the fact that his squad regularly went at it with the worst Newark had to offer: dealers moving felony weight, heavies armed with rifles or worse, legit jumped-in gangbangers, not the play actors who just claimed sets because they liked the name.

Sure, a routine drug murder would warrant the Major Crimes unit's attention. They responded to all shooting incidents in the city. But it wouldn't warrant a personal visit from a boss, from someone like Henniman. If he was sitting on the scene of the Mathis homicide, then that probably meant the dead kid was connected to something unsavory for the unit. And if Henniman thought I was in pursuit of said unsavory fact, then my business would disappear faster than a case of Pabst in a fraternity basement.

Of course, that was all hunch. This wasn't the first time Key came to me with a case like this that amounted to a column of smoke with no fire. The money Henniman's guys paid me I could reach out and touch, even if it left my hands grimy.

I parallel parked on Congress Street, lucky to find a spot within walking distance of my office. Every apartment on the block was a multi-generational household, grandparents on down to at least two adult grandchildren, and each one seemed to own a car. Even in the middle of the day, I sometimes wound up using the pay lot near Newark-Penn Station.

Why couldn't the dead drug dealer just be dead for typical dead drug dealer reasons? Newark averaged between 90 and 100 homicides a year, and three-fourths of them were over the kind of penny-ante bullshit disputes that people used to resolve with their fists. Someone steps on the wrong corner, sleeps with the wrong girl, argues with the wrong guy, and winds up dead. Did they deserve it? No. But they weren't the kind of slayings my readers asked too many questions about either.

I reminded myself I didn't have readers anymore, just clients, as I trudged up the steps to my apartment and flicked the lights on inside my three-room fiefdom. The front door led into a sparse living room. Couch, coffee table and a television I didn't use enough to justify the cable bill. There was a kitchenette beyond there and a hallway jutting out to the left of the fridge that led to my office/bedroom. I slipped off my shoes and turned the lights back down, deciding the few sun rays creeping through the blinds were enough lighting for 3 p.m.

The exception to my usual opinions about Newark slayings was framed above my desk, and I tried not to look at it as I fell into my rolling chair and stared at the black phone next to the computer. The newsprint was starting to curl and yellow behind the glass, but I didn't even need to look at the words to remember what I'd written at the top.

Deon Whims didn't want to be remembered as a statistic. But, in his world, it might have been better than dying a snitch.

34

Deon was a high-level player in the Sex, Money, Murder Bloods set, the faction that won Newark's brutal version of king of the hill more often than not. He was just coming out of prison during my third year on the cops beat, and he'd pumped out a book about his life while sitting in a federal lockup in Pennsylvania. Handwritten, on loose leaf. It caught on as something of a scared straight text in the city. I'd been talking to him about a profile in the weeks before he was shot and killed at a gas station on the McCarter Highway, the main thoroughfare in or out of the Bricks. A few cop sources warned me that, despite his reformed image, Deon was still a shot caller inside Sex, Money, Murder. He'd just gotten smarter about doing the street shit that got him sent away the first time.

His friends told a different story, about how the F.B.I. had turned him informant on the inside in exchange for early release. Supposedly they'd hinted that his girlfriend was being threatened by members of a rival Bloods set, and he wanted early release so he could look out for her. The story was horse shit, but it got Deon to comply. Sooner or later, word of his arrangement got out, and someone put him down.

If I'd gone off the NPD press releases at the time, Deon's murder would have been something forgettable, another drug dealer dead for drug dealer reasons. Six inches on page nine that no one read.

He deserved better than that. Maybe the Mathis kid did too. Maybe he didn't.

But I wouldn't know if I didn't ask.

***

I spent the ride to Shish Kebab House blasting At The Drive-In, ripping down Route 1 out of Newark toward Elizabeth. The band's "Enfilade" was one of several pump-up tracks I used to play on the way to crime scenes back in my reporter days.

I pulled into the restaurant's parking lot, a two-window hole-in-the wall nestled between a nail salon and a tattoo parlor. The sonic boom of a jetliner replaced the raw howls of Cedric Bixler's voice when I exited the car.

The reporter skin felt right again, at least for a little while. Shish Kebab House was just outside of Newark, serving forgettable food at the foot of the layover motels near the airport. It was the place I took sources I didn't want to be seen with, close enough for a cab without being somewhere anyone who mattered would look.

My adrenaline was up. It had been a while since I felt like I was chasing something I wasn't supposed to catch.

Then I walked in, locked onto the sad and confused eyes of the man sitting next to Key, and remembered there were parts about clutching a notepad that I didn't miss.

Reporters are, by trade, egomaniacs. We can be sympathetic, empathetic, careful and concerned about the people whose stories we tell. But part of the drive to uncover some amazing tale is knowing your name might be synonymous with the story. It's an easy feeling to subdue when you're doing it every day, but this was my first taste in a while, and I felt a little ashamed at my own exuberance.

I was excited to be inside this dingy restaurant swapping tales about the dead. Austin Mathis looked like he was wondering what he'd done to wind up in that room. It was something an editor taught me back when I was an intern, thinking the late-night crime shift was my chance to play detective.

"Remember," she said. "Half the people you're gonna talk to are having the worst day of their lives."

Broad-shouldered with black hair blossoming into silver tufts, Mathis' head picked up as soon as I stepped through the door. He had his elbows on the table, hands folded, and he looked away as soon as we saw one another. He whispered something to Key, shaking his head as his eyes dropped down.

"Mr. Mathis?" I asked, plopping onto the ripped cushion of one of the restaurant's beat down chairs.

He nodded. Didn't talk. His face didn't betray a reaction, leaving me nothing to gauge as I wondered how I'd react if I was meeting a man I didn't know to discuss my recently murdered son.

"Austin, this is Russell, the man I told you about," Key said, placing a hand on his shoulder, giving that maternal rub then leaving it there. He wasn't the first grieving father she'd helped keep it together and he'd be far from the last this month, maybe even this week.

"My son wasn't a bad kid," he whispered, eyes still down.

A waiter, an older man who seemed to recognize me from when I was a regular, walked up to the table, read the scene, and decided this wasn't the time to describe the lunch specials.

"Never said he was," I said.

"Yeah, but you probably thought it," Austin replied. "Key told me you used to be with the paper. That means you probably looked up my son's cases and formed some opinions. But I don't want you bringing them in here."

"Russ is one of the good ones," Key said, clasping Austin's hand. I wasn't sure if she meant reporters or white people. I'd known her long enough to think it might be both. "Just tell your story. He'll listen."

He finally looked at me, eyes slightly wet, bulging a little. If he'd slept lately his face didn't know it. Wrinkle lines marked his cheek bones, and one of his eyelids had a purplish hue. Maybe a sty.

"The police seem to think your son's history had something to do with … what happened," I said.

I always resisted the urge to say dead, killed, slain. As if the phrasing could change reality.

"Of course they do," Austin replied. "Nobody looks twice at a drug murder on the west side."

"Alright, then tell me why they're wrong," I said.

"For starters, they might have had something to do with it," he

37

replied.

Fuck.

The "cops did some nigh unprovable shit" interviews were the worst. I'd sat through sob story after sob story that sounded plausible but was always unprintable. Next, he was gonna tell me…

"I can prove it," he said.

I looked at Key. She knew the levers being pulled in my head and shot me a "don't you dare" scowl. Out of complete terror of my Newark spirit mother, I sat up straight and gave Austin Mathis my best "I totally believe your bullshit" face.

"Alright," I said. "Why do you think that?"

"I'll just show you," he replied. "It's easier that way."

Austin produced an iPhone and placed it flat on the table. He struggled to navigate the device. Eventually, a video player opened.

"This was taken about four days before Kevin died," Austin said.

A grainy stream came to life with no sound. Austin tilted the frame so I could get a better look. He turned away, like it was something he didn't need to see again. Key did the same.

The feed showed what could have been one of a hundred back alleys in Newark, a non-descript streak of concrete running between a chain-link fence overrun with ivy and a row of apartment windows with bars on them. It seemed like the home movie was being shot from behind the fence, parallel to the alley itself. A vaguely human shape, a man upon closer inspection, was running alongside the lens, fists balled up and knees jutting forward in a dead sprint.

His form was breaking down from exhaustion, body slumping left or right. He was out of shape. The guy leaned against the fence for a minute as the people he was running from came into focus. There were three of them, all at the edge of the frame, but they were getting closer while the man who had been running tried to recover.

The gap closed. I waited for some kind of exchange or a hint as to

38

what was going on, but heard nothing. I jammed the volume button on the side of the phone.

"No sound," Austin Mathis said.

As the trio got closer, a lens flare shot from one of their hips, something glinting in the streetlight's halogen bath. Badge? Gun? Both?

They looked like they were talking, maybe shouting. Without the dialogue, the story was hard to follow, but this seemed to check all the boxes of a basic foot pursuit. The guy who had been running still had his back to them. He was still panting. The cinematographer was too close to his subject, and I could only see the man from the waist up. His hands appeared to be near his belt.

The man half turned, hands clearly empty from my perspective, apparently not from the officer's.

I didn't need to hear the gunshots to know a volley of bullets had caused the fleeing suspect's body to jerk, seize and twist before it spun to the ground, either already lifeless or soon to be.

"When did you take this?" I asked.

"I didn't," Austin Mathis replied. "My son did."

CHAPTER 3

Key and Austin Mathis had invited me into a world I wanted no part of.

That video wasn't evidence of anything. It was an implication, not a link. It was also a time bomb, and I wasn't sure I was ready to risk getting caught in the blast.

I'd left the paper about a month before anyone could point out Staten Island, N.Y. or Ferguson, Mo., on a map, back when they were places that just happened to be near bigger cities, not the epicenters of a nationwide battle over public safety and whose lives really mattered.

Austin didn't know the name of the kid who had been shot and killed in the video, or why his son was in the position to film his last breaths. Kevin apparently wasn't carrying his phone when he was gunned down near Woodland Cemetery four nights later, and he wasn't very creative when it came to passwords, according to his father. Austin had punched his son's birthday into the device while going through his kid's belongings, not sure what he was looking for, but very convinced that what he'd found was the motive behind his son's death.

If he'd been hoping I'd share in his eureka moment, he was wrong.

I'd nodded politely, told him I'd be in touch, then shot Key a disapproving glare as I left.

She'd called me four times as I drove back to the city. I didn't answer. She'd find me in time, and hopefully by then, I'd lose the urge to strangle her.

40

I wasn't panicking because I thought Austin Mathis was crazy. I was panicking because I'd seen this fight play out before and knew the win-loss record of the side without badges.

Sure, they'd take the first few rounds. The controversial video would breed outrage, and outrage would breed relentless news coverage. But that was the part that played out on the street, where the aggrieved had home field advantage. Once it moved to the courts, where change could happen, it rarely did. The status quo almost always earned a technical knockout.

I knew what Austin was suggesting by showing me the clip, saw how that line of thinking dovetailed with what I knew. The timing of his son's death, less than a week after he filmed that video. Henniman's presence at the crime scene when I'd dropped by. The street punk telling me Kevin had carte blanche to do business in that area, making it at least plausible that he hadn't been dropped by a rival dealer.

It was tenuous, but troubling, a plausible alternative to the all too familiar drug murder scenario. Dots far from connected, but at least in each other's orbit. Still, I wasn't anywhere near ready to believe the cops had killed one minority to cover up the fact that they'd killed another, and I really wasn't looking forward to the consequences of asking around about it.

When I was a reporter, I rarely had to do penance for posing questions to power, because that's what I got paid to do. When you pissed off one source or agency, you buttered up another. Made friends with Sheriff's investigators or assistant prosecutors, cuddled up to the city council members who had taken a hard line on police issues. I had options then, enemies to play against one another until the cold thawed.

Now? I had clients instead of readers. Pissing off Henniman could put my bank account and client list in a freefall, and I had loans and a half-decent apartment to pay rent on. Going after the cops was someone else's job. Dina's, in fact. I could tip her off. But if Austin's hunch was right, and someone with a badge had dropped his son over that video, I couldn't put her in that position.

Which meant my only other option was to forget what I'd just seen. Forget about the video that could go public and be analyzed a hundred different ways by a hundred different people who might all be right based on their life experiences. Forget about Austin Mathis' helpless stare, his blood in the teeth insistence that his son didn't die as a result of some corner heroin deal.

The phone rang again. Key, for a fifth time, asking me to take a stand with her.

But the last time I did that, went up against the paper's decision to defile itself and corrupt my old job, I'd lost my weekly paycheck, lost Dina, and fallen into my current station, the one I was less and less fond of each day. I didn't want to know what the next rung below that looked like, but if I pissed off Henniman for the wrong reasons, there was a good chance I'd find out.

I'd probably end up in public relations, and then I'd probably end up shooting myself.

If I was going to put those kinds of chips on the table, it wasn't going to be a snap decision. I needed some advice, some goodwill high up in the department, and in the event things were about to go as sideways as I feared, maybe some cash.

I looked for Colleen's number, hoping her ex-husband was still enough of a dick that she might be willing to offer all three.

***

Normally, I stayed away from divorce cases. Too messy, too time consuming, and frankly, a little beneath me. I had no love for my reputation as a police problem solver, but the idea of collecting checks by sitting in my car and using a long lens to snap people slipping in and out of truck stop motels along Route 1 wasn't much better.

It took a little bit of desperation, and a special breed of dipshit, to get me involved in a client's love life. Unfortunately for him, Colleen Quinn's ex-husband was an exemplary asshole, the kind of man who not only treated a great woman wrong but also took some kind of sick pleasure in it.

Colleen had worked a number of posts throughout the Newark Police Department in a 20-year career, but she'd been with Internal Affairs for the past five. In spite of that, most cops smiled when you mentioned her name. Colleen was warm, fair. She'd taken the promotion to captain without contracting the amnesia for patrol life that drove a wedge between supervisors and rank-and-file in most cities. She wore her long red hair tied back, draped down to her upper spine, swinging right in the center of the police blues she sported even though it wasn't required.

Captains normally wore business attire, but she hadn't adopted the Wall Street look as she climbed the ladder. I was never sure if that was a tactical move to keep herself one of the boys, but knowing Colleen like I did, I assumed she was only wearing the clothes that fit. She cut across the space of Newark's lone sushi house, greeting me with a wider smile than I deserved.

"Gotta say Russ, I was more than surprised to see your number pop up on my phone," she said.

"I can't take an old friend out for lunch?" I replied.

"Didn't you used to tell me sources couldn't be friends?"

"That was back when I had the notepad," I said. "And even then, I was just covering my ass. We were always friends."

"Friends don't take friends to Japanese restaurants in Newark," she said.

"They do when they want to have private conversations."

Newark wasn't exactly home to a thriving Asian community. If you wanted soul food, some of the better Jersey diner fare or an incredible

43

pastrami sandwich, you came to the Brick City. The people who opened Nori on Central Avenue two years earlier, however, must have gotten lost on their way to a different part of the state. The place didn't get a lot of repeat customers, probably because most of its rolls were more mayo than fish. .

"How's Nathan? Still making those alimony payments on time?" I asked.

"That would imply he started making them at all," she replied. "What do you care? I asked you to look at this when you first got your license. You were always too busy."

"My dance card is suddenly empty."

"Not what I hear," she said.

"Oh?"

"I'm an Internal Affairs captain, Russell. Half your clients should be on my list.".

"I don't like what you're implying, Colleen."

"I'm not implying anything, just stating facts. I know you're not here because you need business, and I'm damn sure it's not out of the goodness of your heart," she said. "We've always been straight with one another. All I'm asking is you don't change that now."

A waiter came over and babbled about specials I wouldn't feed to strays. I ordered us two Miso soups and took the menu out of Colleen's hands before she got herself food poisoning.

"The hell was that?" she asked.

"I'm protecting you from the kitchen," I replied. "You want honesty? I'll give it to you. One, the soup is the only thing on this menu that won't use your stomach for target practice. Two, I need a favor and some goodwill in the law enforcement community and everyone thinks your ex is a walking herpes sore. Taking your case helps me as much as it helps you, so tell me how to make his life worse and ours better."

Colleen picked up her water glass and took a long sip.

"What's the favor?" she asked.

"Doesn't matter until I earn it."

"It always matters."

"Not this time. Not unless you're suddenly in the habit of paying bills before they come due," I replied. "Listen your oldest was what, 14, 15, when we met? She's gotta be nearing college now and unless you plan on burying her in debt, you need that alimony. When the time comes you'll tell me what I want to know or you won't, but it's irrelevant until I do my thing and Nathan signs that check."

Colleen tried her soup now, wincing a little at the saltiness, but seemed satisfied the concoction wouldn't kill her.

"And if I say no when it's all over?" she asked.

"Well, you're still gonna pay me in actual money, right?"

She nodded.

"Then I'll be pissed at you for a few days, I'll write your number on the wall of the boys' bathroom, but otherwise, I'll get over it," I said.

Colleen looked around the room, rubbed her hands together and then stared into the soup steam like she was thinking. The bar across the street, Hanley's, was a known cop and firefighter dive that served the kind of fatty pub meals and mock Irish fare that I actually wanted to eat. Most of those guys wouldn't be caught dead inside of Nori, but given her ex's penchant for underhanded tactics, I respected her caution.

"Nathan's up to the same shit. He's been out on disability from the sheriffs for months after some minor accident during a chase. Moron has been playing the hero card for free drinks in every cop bar from here to Montclair, but I heard he hit a mailbox, had nothing to do with the actual arrest," she said. "Anyway, he's supposed to be sitting home, but a friend told me he's got a security gig in New Brunswick. It's off the books, which means it's not getting factored into the alimony, which means he's stealing from his own daughter because he's a fucking…"

She stopped herself midway. I had no plans to begrudge her fury, but Colleen had stopped taking my offers for beers and venting sessions long before I stopped being a reporter. She didn't like complaining about Nathan, said it gave him power.

"The point is I can't go near him without my divorce attorney having a heart attack and his claiming harassment," she said. "But I need proof he's working this other job."

And she needed me because none of her cop buddies would go anywhere near Nathan. He was a shit officer but a smart person, and rumor was he'd become more than friendly with the duly elected Sheriff of Essex County, a political player named Vincent D'Annunzio who had an eye on a senate seat. No one in cop land could afford that kind of enemy, not if they had any sense of self-preservation.

"So, you need me to walk into a bar, take some photos when he's not looking and sign an affidavit?" I asked. "If I knew it was that easy I'd have returned your calls months ago."

"I never said anything about easy," she replied, smirking. "I didn't tell you where he's working yet."

***

There was a time, maybe five or so years ago, where I'd have dropped in on a show at Court Tavern, New Brunswick's punk rock temple.

The basement bar looked more like the inside of a garage than a music venue: open since 1981, decrepit since 1982, and on the verge of closing at least four times since. Every now and again some now famous act that got its' first whiff of local celebrity there, like the Bouncing Souls or the Smithereens, would hold a benefit show to keep the lights on. But whatever money they raised was never used for renovations. The ceiling tiles above its cramped stage got kicked up whenever anyone crowd surfed, raining dust onto the sweaty music aficionados below.

It made sense that someone like Nathan would wind up working here. New Brunswick was far enough away from Newark that no one would recognize the cop on disability from an hour north standing stage left with his arms crossed, and the work couldn't have been that taxing. I'd heard Nathan could more than handle himself, but you didn't need a black belt to stop an overzealous 22-year-old from throwing one spin kick too many during a breakdown. Court Tavern had enough problems with cash flow, code enforcement and noise complaints, so the owners didn't need some college kid who didn't belong in the room breaking his arm in a pit and attracting ambulances.

The Tavern eliminated some of the usual hurdles to capturing an incriminating photograph. Where most people might have more than a few questions about someone snapping pictures at their job, Nathan could easily mistake me for a band photographer, fan or local music blogger.

The photos weren't the problem. It was the speed with which they would put me in Colleen's good graces. If I simply gave her proof of her husband's disability fraud, she'd still need to use that as evidence in court to validate his additional income and beef up his alimony payments.

I needed him signing checks and making her smile faster than that. I needed unconditional surrender. Because I needed to decide if taking on Kevin Mathis' case was worth the potential professional suicide.

If there was any real heat on Henniman's squad, anything worth knowing about the shooting I saw on that cell phone video, Colleen could confirm it.

So I needed something that would really scare the shit out of Nathan, the kind of threat that would make his life hell outside the context of divorce proceedings.

I needed Dina.

I punched my ex-girlfriend's number into my phone from memory, because as a serial drunk texter, I knew better than to keep it saved. My brain had a harder time putting those 10 digits in the right order when it was floating on a river of bourbon.

It rang twice before she picked up.

"*Intelligencer*, Colby," she said, impersonal as possible even though she knew it was me.

"Got a tip for you," I said.

"I'm listening."

"Need to show you in person."

"Russ, it's barely 7 p.m., way too early for you to try the whole let's get a drink and fall back in love routine."

"Hey, I haven't pulled that in at least three months now," I said.

"So, you're keeping score?" she asked.

"First of all, shut up. Secondly, maybe.. Third of all, I got a line on a delicious bit of police misconduct. Might be better if you saw it for yourself."

"Don't you remember what happened the last time you told me how to do my job?" she asked.

"Yeah, you dumped me," I replied. I'd thought about it so many times by now it was simply a fact rather than a painful memory. "Think of this as more of a suggestion. I'll text you the address. We both know you're gonna say yes."

She didn't. For about 10 seconds, making me wait just because she could.

"Fine," she said. "But this better not be about anything but work."

Of course it wasn't, but all those rules about being honest with her went out the window when she broke my heart. Or was it when I broke hers? Didn't matter. I was more about results than truth these days anyway.

48

CHAPTER 4

A piece of friendly advice: If you ever date a woman as gorgeous as Dina, as smart as Dina, and then decide to act like a massive heel and get yourself dumped, follow up those acts by moving to Guam.

Because if you stay in the same city, the same state, you will see her again. And every time you do, you'll spend the next 48 hours thinking about time travel and the satisfaction that would come with using your past self as a punching bag.

I was sitting at the upstairs bar when she walked in, bobbing my head to the ska outfit that was doing a weak Catch-22 impression downstairs. She was wearing black wedge boots and slightly ripped jeans under a tight grey sweater. The band launched into a shitty rendition of "Dear Sergio" played a half-step too slow, but I pretended it was the real thing and let myself move to it. Dina's hair was down, the light brown swinging slightly across her chestnut skin, and I decided she wore it that way because she knew I liked it.

Maybe pretending wasn't so bad.

Dina was eyeing the leather jacket and fishnet crowd nervously as she moved along the bar, probably already wondering if whatever I'd called her down here for was worth wading through a crush of suburban punks.

"This is that place you always told me about from college, isn't it?"

she asked.

"Yeah, it is."

"But you never took me here?"

"Because you've been here for five seconds and you're already looking for the exits," I replied.

"I listen to rock sometimes, Russ," she said, rolling her eyes.

"Matchbox 20 and The Lumineers are not rock," I replied.

I slid her a rum and Coke and raised the Corona I'd been sipping. It wasn't my drink, but the Court Tavern wasn't going to class itself up by serving craft brews.

"Thanks for coming," I said.

"You said you had a story," she replied.

Dina had a long-standing restraining order against compromise. She saw the world in two colors, and if you got painted black or white, you had better get comfortable in that shade. Dina didn't allow ex-boyfriends to turn into friends, but she occasionally stayed in touch with me if I could be useful as a source. Every now and again I thought about lecturing her on the ethical quagmire of taking information from someone you used to date, but then I'd remember that I got most of my checks from sideways cops needing favors, and that I liked hearing her voice.

"There's a guy downstairs doing security. He's a Sheriff's deputy, got hurt in a chase a few weeks back. Supposed to be out on disability, but he's tossing idiots out of the mosh pit here at least two nights a week," I said. "Sounds like fraud to me."

"Why do you care?" she asked.

"Ex-wife's a client."

"Fair enough," she said. "Why do I care?"

"Corrupt cop caught red-handed," I said, fanning my hands out to show the imaginary headline. "Shouldn't that get you enough page views to keep your editors happy for a few weeks, maybe give you enough time to do some real work?"

Her eyes narrowed. I took a big swallow of my beer, knew I'd gone too far, and prepared for the hurricane.

"Red-handed? You gonna go on the record? No, of course not. Which means I need your pictures, then I need to pull court records, call the Civil Service Commission, the Sheriff's department, his lawyer, run the whole thing past our lawyers, then probably wait for someone to start an internal investigation, then confirm that, all before I can write anything. That sound like red-handed to you Russ?" she asked. "They'll never give me enough time to put all that together."

She was thinking six moves ahead, as always. Most men, myself included, had a bad habit of focusing on Dina's looks whenever she walked in a room. They were far from her best asset.

It took me more than a few seconds to strike back, and I had to stop making eye contact to get my thoughts into something approximating English.

"Then make the time," I replied. "Or fight for the time. We both know you hate the way they do things now, running from crime scene to crime scene, spitting out four paragraphs on six stories each day. This is a chance to do things the way they're supposed to be done. The way..."

I tried to stop myself, but no one had ever accused me of knowing when to shut the fuck up.

"-- the way I used to do them," I said.

She pushed her drink away, splashing a brown mix of convenience store rum and flat fountain soda onto the bar top, a waste of perfectly mediocre alcohol.

"What way is that Russ?" she asked, her voice rising, me slumping back, now fully aware I'd not only kicked open the flood gates but pissed into the torrent for good measure. "Fighting editors at every turn? Bitching about the business until you washed out of it? Fixing problems for the same kind of cops you used to take down?"

I finished my beer, then looked at her half-wasted rum like I hadn't seen a drink in weeks.

"Ouch," I muttered.

"Truth hurts," she growled.

I looked at the empty space on her ring finger, the place where the jewelry I'd bought a year ago should have been.

"Yeah, it does," I whispered.

We stood there like that for a minute. The ska band downstairs stopped ruining my high school soundtrack and received a lukewarm round of applause. Next band up was some New York outfit called Kids Carry Germs. It sounded vaguely obnoxious and punk enough to mean there'd be a pit, which might force Nathan to do something worth photographing. I needed to get downstairs and into position.

"I'm sorry," I said, not sure if I meant it or I just needed peace to get the job done. "Shouldn't have said all that."

She sat back down, not looking at me.

"Me either," she replied.

Our fights never ended this fast when we were together. Of course, there wasn't anything left to fight for now.

"No, you had something resembling a point," I said. "I'm trying to take better cases where I can. Like this one, for instance. This guy is a piece of shit, alright? And his ex needs that money. But it's also cramped down there and if he notices me, or some idiot smashes into me near the pit, there's a chance my camera gets busted. I wanted to make sure I had a second set of eyes, someone I trust, and that list kind of starts and ends with you. I'll snap some pictures. You snap some pictures. Odds are one of us leaves with what we need. Now you can do whatever you want with them, but I need this. Might help me get onto some better work, more meaningful shit."

She picked her drink back up, sipped a little more through the plastic stirrer sitting at the lip.

"You mean like the way you used to do things?" she asked.

***

Nathan Faltz towered over the mix of straw-framed punks tracking sleet and grime across the already shit-caked floor of the Court Tavern's basement. Easily 6'5 with a full head of silvered hair and a face red enough to stop traffic, the guy looked every ounce the Irish heavy, and I'd heard he could back it up.

Sure, Faltz was a nothing cop, probably couldn't solve a homicide if he started with a confession, but I'd heard plenty of stories about him being a street sweeper. The patrol tales on him were comic book lore: Faltz taking out three guys, one armed with a bat, when he'd stopped a robbery in progress. Faltz showing up during a protest turned riot and laying waste to a bunch of looters who were surrounding a couple uniforms inside a pawn shop. Faltz being asked not to enter the charity boxing tournament against the fire department one year because a couple of battalion chiefs got tired of their guys using vacation days to recover from the beat downs.

He was an urban tall tale. Paul Bunyan with bruised knuckles.

It was rare, but not unheard of, for a client to run up on me if they realized I'd done my job and found them doing something they weren't supposed to do. Most would yell, flail, but none of them had the potential to put down a big hurt like Faltz.

I moved camera-first through the four dozen kids milling around the stage as the band finished its sound check and started taking pictures. Still frames of the guitarist tuning, the drummer fiddling with his kick pedal and the singer staring at the microphone like he had something really profound to shriek. I'd happily be confused for a scene rat if it meant Faltz didn't notice me, and the big guy's gaze seemed to be elsewhere.

The camera I carried was an old Nikon, sold to me by a down-

and-out photographer whose buyout from the paper wouldn't keep his head above his mortgage for more than six months. I heard he was working for UPS now, and I prayed he never learned what I'd been using his camera for.

A couple of loud chords brought the crowd to life, and the singer stepped to the mic and announced the band's name and where they were from as if half the people at the foot of the stage weren't friends from home who already knew. An elbow bit into my ribcage and I jolted my right shoulder back on reflex, boxing out my space as the crowd circled up. I took a quick peek back at Dina before the four-piece band launched into its first song, trying to make sure she was upholding her end of the bargain.

On first glance, Dina looked lost in her cell phone, but I noticed the back end of the device was pointed up and toward the stage, trained close enough to Faltz to catch him.

Something hit me while I was mid-admiration, the shove coming with enough force to make the camera strap tug at the back of my neck. I turned to find the pit taking its natural form. A few kids had hopped in the middle for some unspectacular thrashing, but four or five skinny drunks throwing half-assed air kicks wasn't going to make Nathan bat an eye.

A pair of three-minute songs passed without incident, outside of the occasional minor collision and hard stare that seemed like a threat down here but would have prompted laughter in the parts of Newark I'd grown comfortable in. I'd seen enough local shows to know these guys had only three, maybe four, speedballs left before the promoter hooked them for the next act, and the polite punk crowd they'd drawn wasn't going to cause enough trouble to move Nathan.

The pit, if you could call it that, was just kids swiping by one another with barely any contact. The rest of the circle was a protective barrier, arms up to keep those who wanted a front row seat safe from any accidental elbows or knees. Dina was near the edge, wearing the same disinterested stare as she kept her phone ready and waiting for something to happen.

The song transitioned out of a somewhat catchy chorus into a messy breakdown, just enough double kick pedal to launch a few more stragglers into the pit, maybe just enough action to make Nathan move. The circle widened as the bodies in the center doubled and started colliding. I saw Dina get swallowed up by the surge, forced to step forward to avoid being pushed toward a wall. She slid closer to the epicenter as the safety rail of interlocking arms began to collapse, the circle now evaporating into a tangle of limbs that would inevitably connect with someone's head. Nathan took a step or two away from the stage, ready to intervene if someone gave him a reason to.

I trained the camera on him. No one in here was going to require medical attention when it was over, but if the Tavern had hired an actual cop for security I'd imagine they wanted him to be as strict as possible. A kid flew past me toward the stage, tumbling ass over tea kettle after a body check from a fat guy in a Misfits shirt, and that finally served as a starter's gun for the big cop. He unfolded those gorilla arms and used them to clear space, Moses parting a sea that mostly smelt like ass and cigarettes.

The husky dude who sent the kid flying past me was the overeager type you find in every pit, the kind who got bullied in the real world but used his size to act like king of the morlocks down here. He avalanched someone else just as Faltz was closing in. I raised the camera, locked on to my next paycheck, but saw something disconcerting at the edge of the frame.

Dina hadn't just been pulled closer to the pit by the human riptide, she'd been drug all the way in. Persistent as always, she was still trying to aim her phone at Faltz but kept getting jostled by a flying Mohawk or sweat-drenched arm that was mid-windmill. They were glancing blows, not direct hits, and I tried to remind myself she dealt with way worse in Newark. She was tough. She didn't need my help. The implication that she needed my help was how I lost her the first time anyway, and I had Faltz dead-to-rights on the camera.

I put the device into burst mode, got more than a few shots of Faltz wrestling the wannabe pit boss into submission, and lowered the camera just in time to see a combat boot slice within a few centimeters of Dina's face, just close enough to tussle those long locks I'd been fawning over upstairs.

My feet got moving before my brain could stop them. The guy seemed a little bigger than me, but pure size doesn't help much when you catch a blindside shoulder block while off-balance in the dark. He went clear past Dina and into one of the ancient concert posters that covered the brick walls of the Tavern basement. The stragglers at the edge of the circle cleared out after I turned the guy into a human missile, giving Dina and I a clear path out.

"The fuck happened to subtlety?" she asked, trying to shout above the din of a furious ride cymbal.

"Time to go," I hollered back.

"I agree," said someone else.

I turned around just in time to see Faltz wrap one of his bear paws around my shirt.

***

As Faltz tossed me headfirst into the trash-lined alley behind the Court Tavern, I realized things could have been a lot worse.

The camera wasn't broken. I'd gotten some decent shots, and so had Dina. As long as he didn't figure out what I was up to before I got back to my car…

"What are you doing here?" he asked in a voice that sounded more permanently hoarse than it was deadened by the cold.

"Nothing man, just shooting for the band," I replied.

"You're ten years older than everyone down there, including the band, and I've never seen anyone's Dad jump into the fray like that," he replied. "So, let's try this again, with less horseshit."

I looked toward the street, which was lit by one of those rustic looking lamps New Brunswick loved to put up anywhere near Rutgers. It was maybe thirty feet from here to there, but it looked a lot longer when Faltz stepped to the right and filled the lane.

"I'm waiting," he said.

I looked down at the camera, made sure I had clear enough pictures of the big man wearing a shirt that said security as he grappled with the fat kid from the basement, and made my play.

"You're Essex County Sheriff's Deputy Nathan Faltz, correct?" I asked.

His expression changed in a way that made my ribcage prepare to relocate, but I kept talking, because it was all I really knew how to do sometimes.

"You don't have to answer. I know you are. I also know there's an Essex County Sheriff's Deputy Nathan Faltz who's supposed to be home on injury leave because he crashed his patrol car chasing some idiot around Millburn a few weeks ago," I said. "Which makes me really curious why there's all these pictures on my camera here of Essex County Sheriff's Deputy Nathan Faltz performing strenuous physical acts while employed by a rock venue in New Brunswick."

"I have no idea what you're talking about," he said.

"People always say that," I replied. "Like it's going to make everything better."

"I just snatched you up smashing a kid into a wall," he said. "One call to New Brunswick PD and you get arrested for simple assault. Maybe you'll talk less in lock up."

"I wouldn't talk less at a funeral," I replied. "And do you really want a police report written with your name as witness to the arrest of a guy who just so happens to have a camera loaded with pictures of you committing disability fraud?"

Normally, this was the part where the color drained from a guy like Faltz, when he realized he was out of moves, and he made some half-assed insult before negotiating agreeable terms.

But Faltz stepped to me with all the swagger there was in the world, cast a shadow over a frame I wish I'd spent more time honing at the gym, and smiled.

"Already told you I didn't know anything about any fraud," he said, his planet-sized palm swooping toward my lens. "And I don't see any camera either."

"Yeah, but I do," said a voice I knew would be lecturing me in a few minutes.

We both turned to find Dina standing at the back door of the Tavern, cell phone in hand.

"How do I spell your name Deputy? F-A-U... one L? Two Ls? What is Faltz anyway, Dutch?" she asked.

"It's mind your own fucking business," he said, turning to her and seeming to forget about his previous plans to erase me from existence.

She shook her head, let a confident smile loose, but I caught the quiver in her lip. I knew where this was going. It was my kind of move, not hers, but she was playing it right, even if it was making her nervous.

"Well, I guess I'll paraphrase that. Too bad. That would have been a great quote," she said.

"Quote?" he asked, fully locked onto Dina now.

I took a step or two back, waited to see if he noticed. He didn't, so I moved behind him and opened up a clear path out of the alley. Almost worst-case scenario: we could run if we needed too. Worst case scenario: I could hit him in the back and pretend I had a chance for five seconds while Dina ran and he killed me.

"Yeah, for this article I'm going to have to write about you," she said, holding up the phone to show it was recording. "My name's Dina Colby, I'm with the *Signal-Intelligencer*, and I'm pretty sure you just threatened this man because he accused you of committing disability fraud. Speaking of that, care to comment on accusations that you're committing disability fraud?"

He turned back to me now, eyes narrowed, jaw line grinding like he was clenching his teeth just to stop himself from yelling.

"And you are?" he asked.

"Russell Avery. I guess you could call me a private investigator but, really, I just fix things for people," I said. "Wanna hire me?"

"Are you fucking kidding me?" he asked.

"No sir. I wouldn't joke about that. You're in a pretty bad way right now," I said. "Way I see it you're about to be the subject of some disparaging press, maybe an internal investigation, maybe even a criminal one. Seems like you could use my help."

I looked at Dina. She still had the phone out, recorder going. Fucking reporters.

"This part is off-the-record," I said.

If Dina had any plans to write any of what she'd seen tonight, she would have argued with me until one of us didn't have the breath to keep shouting, but I knew she had no intention of wading into the ethical sinkhole I'd created. Still, Faltz didn't need to know that.

She clicked the recorder off.

"Stop fighting Colleen on the alimony, then all the pictures and all the recordings go away, simple as that," I said, waving the camera around. "Soon as she gets the check, this Internal Affairs wet dream goes bye-bye."

"That thing really off?" he asked, pointing back to Dina.

I nodded. He nodded.

Then he snatched my camera with speed a man of his size shouldn't be legally allowed to possess.

"And if I just smash all this shit to a thousand pieces right now, then what happens?"

"Then he needs a new camera, and your name is still in the paper in a day or two," she replied.

"That phone can break easy too," he said.

"Hey, that's an iPhone numb nuts. Ever heard of a Cloud?" I asked. "All the dirt she needs to bury you is already backed up and stored on a server somewhere. You smash her phone and all you're doing is destroying private property."

He turned to her, then to me, then to her, his last four brain cells struggling to keep both balls in the air.

"He serious?" Faltz asked.

"Yep," she said.

"And if I pay the alimony?" he asked.

"We were never here," I said.

Faltz backed away from me, took a long menacing look at Dina, then nodded to both of us. He handed over the camera and stomped back to the basement without another word, the sound of a glass being flung against a wall punctuating his exit.

Dina and I both knew damn well her work phone didn't have Cloud backup. Knowing the cheap fucks at the paper, she was lucky she wasn't carrying a beeper and returning calls via pay phone. Faltz, of course, couldn't know that. Just like poor Tonio didn't know Scannell's friend was bullshitting him about needing to submit Internal Affairs complaints in person.

But lying's plenty fair when everyone does it.

By the time I'd completed my mental victory lap and smiled over the thought of Colleen telling her oldest daughter she wouldn't need to apply for financial aid, Dina had already stomped past me and onto Elm Street.

"Hey, where are you going?" I asked, moving into a half-jog to keep up with her pissed-off quickstep. "C'mon, that was fun."

"That was blackmail," she replied, not turning around, nearly driving her shoulder into one of the scene rats who was smoking on the corner near the bar's entrance.

"It's only blackmail if you profit from it. All we did was force that deadbeat to put his kid through school," I replied. "Way I look at it, that's called problem solving."

She kept going, still not bothering to look at me, cutting into the crosswalk and toward the parking structure where we'd both hidden our cars.

"The way you look at things isn't the way most people look at things, Russ," she replied. "You realize what you just made me a part of, right? If anyone finds out, that's my career."

"No one's gonna find out," I replied. "Trying to go after you only creates more problems for him. This won't hurt you."

Now she stopped just in time to get backlit by one of the overhead lights at the edge of the parking deck. The halogen and shadows caught her face in all the right places. It took a special kind of pretty to make a sneer look beautiful, but Dina pulled it off with ease.

"Oh, you know that for a fact?" she asked. "What happens if he does something else sideways in his career? Or he's part of some big investigation, or any other news I might have to cover. How am I supposed to interview him, or go within one hundred feet of him ever again Russ? You never think. At least not about how what you do might affect the people who aren't you."

I tried to put a hand on her shoulder. Not my best move.

She didn't just push it away like a normal person, she grabbed my wrist and twisted, enough to make me wince before I yanked my arm back. Guess she'd taken one or two of those self-defense classes I'd suggested before she took over the cops beat. Not that she'd admit I'd ever given her good advice.

"How long have you been waiting to do that?" I asked, trying to get the feeling back in my arm.

"Long enough."

"Fair. But would you relax with this? It all worked out," I said. "We helped karma catch up to an asshole. We helped a single mother put her kid through college. And like I said, this might open a door for me. Get me room to do a real investigation. Something necessary. Something you might want a piece of."

"You think you can justify doing bad shit by promising to do better later, Russell? That's not how it works," she said. "And if all your tips are going to pan out like this one did, then do me a favor and keep them to yourself. I can find stories without getting dragged down into your messes."

"You think I like working this way, Dina?" I asked. "I told you this was a step toward doing something better."

She smirked. A normal person might mistake that for friendliness, but I knew better. That was a reporter's smirk. An "I was really hoping you'd say that" smirk.

"Two minutes ago, this was about helping out your friend, whoever it was that made the mistake of marrying that guy. Now it's about you," she said. "Do you remember what you used to say to me, when I was struggling with the top of story. When I was overwriting?"

Of course I did.

"Get out of the way and let the story tell itself," I said.

I was pretty fond of giving advice. Following it, not so much.

***

Two days after I'd dealt with Faltz, Colleen called me to celebrate her receipt of the first of many overdue alimony checks.

It was the kind of call I hadn't received since I left journalism. The "you changed something" phone call. The "you, in the smallest of ways, made the world a slightly better place" phone call.

I was proud of myself. For about twenty minutes. Then Colleen came to my office to satisfy her end of the deal, and I was back to feeling like an asshole.

Dina's words were still sitting with me, the way a heavy meal does long after you should be done digesting. Colleen thought she was coming over to celebrate, but I was just waiting to collect the bill.

It was her day off, marking one of the few times I'd ever seen her out of police blues. Off-duty Colleen was a jeans and sweatshirt girl. She looked like a friend who'd dropped by for a cup of coffee, but I needed to flip her back into source mode.

"God, I wish you could have heard his voice, Russ. I could literally hear his teeth cracking the way he was grumbling," she said, moving her hands around the way she did when she got excited. "I've heard him like that a thousand times. But he couldn't yell. He just had to ask how much and how often and when and … Christ, do you have any idea how good that felt? It's been so long since I had any leverage on that bastard."

I nodded, smiled, laughed, did those things friends do when someone is telling a story they've been dying to let out.

"And Sarah is so excited," she said, invoking their daughter who would benefit most from all this. "Now she can go out of state without drowning in loans. She's been looking at Fordham. They've got a good English program."

"She wants to be a writer?" I asked. "Careful, you've seen how some of us turn out."

"You don't have to fish for compliments, Russell," she said. "My daughter woke up smiling because of you. So did I."

"That means a lot," I replied.

I looked around the room, eyes bouncing from the framed article over my desk to the thrice-bleached glass ashtray next to my laptop. The one I wished I was tapping a cigarette against.

She leaned back in the chair, drummed her hands against her thighs.

"Just ask me already," Colleen said.

"What?"

"Just ask me," she said again. "Your favor. We had a deal. You don't have to be nervous about it."

"Well I was just letting you vent, or whatever."

"Russ, when I need to vent, I'll call the people I vent to. I needed something, now you do. This is business."

For a moment, I decided Colleen was right and Dina was wrong and I had nothing to feel guilty about. But then I remembered Colleen was only smiling because she hadn't looked down at the check yet.

"You guys have any officer-involved shootings lately?" I asked, narrowing my eyes at the ashtray, silently telling it to go fuck itself.

"Define lately."

"Last month or two," I said.

Her eyes wandered up to the ceiling tiles.

"Hmmm … three or four," she said. "Just one fatal, why?"

"I might have some questions about that one."

She drew a long breath, chewed her lip for a second, and leaned forward.

"This was why I asked you what the favor was before I hired you, you know that right?" she asked. "You have to know that. Because you also have to know that any fatal use-of-force that happened in the past few weeks is going to be under review. By the prosecutor's office, and by me."

"Not necessarily, not if it was obviously a clean shoot," I said.

"Those don't exist anymore, Russell. Not with the way things are these days," she said. "And even if they did, this isn't one. So, I'm not sure how much I can tell you, ethically speaking."

"Colleen, I'm not really sure if I should have blackmailed your ex-husband, ethically speaking," I replied. "But I did right by you. All I'm asking is you do the same."

"I didn't ask you to do that," she said.

"And yet you're happy with the results."

Collen opened her mouth to say something but stuffed it back in, the same way Faltz had when I cornered him earlier in the week. Maybe the mutual short fuses brought them together at one point. Maybe it was the same thing that blew them apart.

"Just ask your questions," she said, an edge to her voice now, a rasp that wasn't there when she was celebrating her alimony checks. "I'll answer what I can."

"Who's the dead kid?"

She tapped her finger on the edge of my laptop.

"You forget how to use this? That's public record."

"Humor me."

"Luis Becerra."

"Anything worth knowing about him?"

"He dealt, a little," she said. "Enough that we knew who he was, not enough that anyone cared about him."

"How'd the shoot look?"

"You ever heard the phrase 'lawful, but awful?'"

Of course I had. It was cop speak for 'We fucked up, but in the heat of the moment, we had reason to believe we might not be fucking up.' In more artful terms, it meant the officers involved believed they were acting to end an imminent threat to their lives or the lives of others, even though hindsight showed there wasn't one.

"They thought he was reaching?" I asked.

"They did," she said.

"But you didn't find a gun?" I asked.

"We did not," she said.

Of course, I knew all this already. I'd seen the video. This wasn't about finding out what actually happened. This was about seeing if the officers involved in the shooting lied. They hadn't. So if they weren't trying to cover tracks, why would the cops shoot Kevin Mathis like his father so wanted to believe they had?

"Anything else?" she asked.

Just one more question. The one that would move her from moderately aggravated to full on pissed.

"I need the name of the officer who shot him," I said.

"And I needed a husband who wasn't fucking our neighbor while I drove our daughter to soccer practice."

"I thought you said we had a deal."

"Well then I guess I'm going to have to owe you a different favor Russell, because I can't go that far," she said. "There's a reason we don't put that information out there. I'm not endangering a man's life just because you asked me too."

"So it's a male officer then?" I asked.

"Not funny Russ."

I stood up and moved to her side of the desk, leaning against the edge, peering over her. It was one of those things people think gives you a psychological advantage in these kinds of situations. Hell, maybe it was a move Colleen taught me, because she was up and meeting me nose-to-chin before I'd even gotten comfortable.

"I'm not a reporter anymore, Colleen," I said. "This isn't about putting information out in the open. The shooting just links to a case I'm working on, that's all."

"I already said no, Russ."

She had, but only to the "you owe me" and the "trust me" approaches. There was a third tact, the kind Dina had yelled at me for two nights earlier.

"I'm gonna go ahead and assume the department is thankful there isn't a ton of media attention around this case," I said.

66

"Please tell me you're not trying to threaten me," she said.

"No, I'm not. I'm just talking. But I'm assuming the director and mayor don't want to see any additional news attention around an officer-involved shooting of an unarmed minority, right? I asked. "Not with … how did you put it before? The way things are these days."

"That still sounds like a threat."

"I don't threaten my friends, Colleen. But if I was, I'd probably say something about how I might call one of my old friends at the paper about this," I said. "If I was, I wouldn't warn you that the reason I'm looking into this is because my client has a video of the shooting."

Colleen closed her eyes and let out a long, slow exhale. She wasn't thinking about me now. She was thinking about how twenty seconds of cell-phone video had turned so many other cases around the country into media circuses. How there was never a right answer once the snippet went viral. Decide the shooting was fucked, and your cops hate you, accuse you of bowing to public pressure. Find the shooting was clean and the demonstrator types decide you're just another white woman blind to endemic racism.

"You know I need to see that," she said.

"And maybe I can help with that in the future," I replied. "But I need a name first."

"And if I don't give it to you that video goes public?" she asked.

"Colleen, for the third and hopefully final time, I am not threatening you. I don't even have the video," I said. "But the client is … um… emotional. And the client does have the video. So, if I don't get them some answers soon…"

She took a step back from me, jammed her hands in the pouch of the sweatshirt and chewed the lip again. Her eyes were moving in circles, like the icon on a computer screen when something is loading. She was doing the math. But she knew it was better to have me firing out of her tent than in.

"If this video winds up on YouTube..." she said.

"It won't."

"And if this name gets out."

"It won't," I said again.

She looked away from me.

"Mike Lowell," she said.

The name didn't mean anything.

"Where does he work out of?" I asked.

"Wait, you seriously don't know this guy? With everything you've been up in to the past year?" she asked. "He's in Major Crimes Russell. He works for Henniman."

CHAPTER 5

All the info I'd gathered about Kevin Mathis could add up one of two ways, depending which screw I twisted.

On the one hand, one of Henniman's guys got caught on tape killing an unarmed suspect in protest-inducing fashion, then the owner of said tape wound up dead, and I found Henniman at the crime scene long after he had any valid investigative reason to be there.

My suddenly flush bank account was mostly filled by bailing out troubled officers under Henniman's command. The neighborhood kids had told me Mathis wasn't beefing with anyone and had carte blanche to sell in an otherwise Bloods-controlled part of Newark, meaning Austin's belief that his son hadn't died behind some drug bullshit still held water.

Simple math says a squad that's always in trouble benefits from dropping the witness to a questionable officer-involved shooting involving one of their own. It says they're smart enough to make it look like a drug thing because no one would look twice at a black kid killed over heroin or coke in Newark at two in the morning.

On the other hand, Henniman's involvement was as much of a reason to retreat as it was to push on. Looking harder at this meant running up against the Major Crimes lieutenant, and that meant setting

69

fire to my private investigator's license. Bill was not the understanding type.

Also, the fact that Mathis wasn't beefing with anyone over drugs didn't exactly excuse the simpler fact that he was a drug dealer. Maybe he didn't get dropped by a banger, but any number of thieves, dissatisfied customers or garden-variety assholes might have reason to kill someone slinging in the West Ward. There were plenty of other reasons he could have been dead that might have had nothing to do with the video.

Simple math there said nothing ventured, nothing lost.

I had no concrete evidence to show why Mathis was dead, but I had plenty of evidence that my life was about to do a triple lundy into a pool of shit if I took a run at any of Henniman's people.

Simple math said keep looking into it, there might be something to find, but there might be a steep price to pay for finding it.

But truth told, I'd felt less like shit in the two days I'd spent looking for a reason to take or drop Austin Mathis as a client then I had in a year of simply cashing checks from the waylaid cops who'd asked me to do simpler work with far less downside.

And there was that look Dina gave me in New Brunswick. The hard stare that said "what have you become" and hinted that maybe, just maybe, she was right to kick my ass to the curb and drive away with the tires squealing.

Maybe doing something like this would cause her to think twice about her hapless ex-boyfriend.

Maybe it would at least prove her wrong.

I wasn't convinced enough to call Key, at least not yet. Formally taking on Austin Mathis as a client would put me squarely on the wrong side of Henniman and I was better at winning fights when the other guy didn't know he was in one.

There was plenty to do before I put my fists up.

Like pull all the public records I could find on Kevin Mathis, the dead kid in the video, and the officer who shot him. Like fill my front seat with those records and drive to West Side Park for a meeting with a guy named Hard Head who might want to hurt me but might be able to tell me more about what Mathis was into.

That's a lot of work for a case I kept telling myself I wasn't gonna take.

The phone rang. It was Key, again. The 19th or 20th or forty-fucking-seventh of her calls that I wasn't answering. I didn't want to talk to her until I was sure, and the court dockets in front of me had raised a few more questions.

Mathis' rap sheet told a story that was almost tragically interchangeable with that of any other corner boy working off South Orange Avenue or near the Meeker Homes. Possession of heroin, possession of marijuana, loitering, a public intox here, a receiving stolen property there. But nothing violent.

He'd been picked up with oxy twice, which stuck out a bit. Brick City addicts didn't have the money to snag the kinds of opioids that came with prescription numbers. They usually went straight to horse because it was about twenty dollars cheaper per hit. The training wheel painkillers were for the suburban kids who crossed just far enough out of Montclair or Bloomfield, who crept just a bit outside the Seton Hall campus, to get their fix. The white kids who made the opioid boom front page news in the 2010s even though black and brown folks started dying with needles in their arms long before that.

Mathis' probation reports, which were public since he'd had a recent open case, made me a little more curious. He'd been given the court-ordered drug rehab all non-violent first time narcotics offenders get in New Jersey. Pre-Trial Intervention, or P.T.I. It was rehab for the ten percent of folks who wanted to get straight and find Jesus, and the equivalent of a get out of jail free card for people like Mathis.

71

The first time he screwed up after that was the stolen property case, but he did less than six months at Essex County Correctional for it. The next two serious charges he saw, the oxy cases, were both pled out no contest. Suspended sentences and three years' probation each time, in spite of the probation officer's written screed suggesting Mathis was more likely to cure cancer while being struck by lightning than he was to satisfy the terms of his release.

City Councilmen had become state senators and local prosecutors had moved up to the attorney general's office by promising to battle the scourge of opioids in New Jersey, so the idea that anyone with anything to gain would be light on Mathis on pill-dealing charges didn't wash.

Otherwise, the court records matched up with what his father said. He'd never been caught with a gun, never faced a gang enhancement on any of his cases, meaning the cops couldn't prove he'd actually committed on a crime on behalf of a specific set. If he was affiliated, his probation officer either didn't mention it in the report or didn't know, but that seemed unlikely, and his known associates didn't ring any bells. The kid didn't seem like a banger.

But if I wanted to be sure, and if Key ever wanted a callback then I needed to be sure, then I needed to talk to Hard Head.

Except I really, really did not want to do that.

Hard Head, real name Trey Mills, didn't like me very much, or at least that's what I'd heard. He was supposedly annoyed by some things I'd written three or four years ago. He allegedly had a temper. Oh, and he was definitely an O.G. with the Sex, Money, Murder set of the Bloods street gang, otherwise known as the crew that controlled most of Newark's drug trade.

I was sipping tea in the front seat of the Cutlass, because it was supposed to calm your nerves and a fourth cup of coffee would have sent me into an epileptic fit that morning. But I nearly jumped out of my seat when I heard the wrap of someone's knuckles against my window.

The offending party was Reek, the guy who'd set up the meet. He flashed his fanged grin and motioned for me to unlock the door, and I returned his smile with a nervous scowl.

He swatted some of the files off the passenger seat as he slid in, gave me the once over, and laughed.

"Are you sweating?" he asked.

"I had the heat on in here."

"Motherfucker, it's 20 degrees out and we both know the heat barely work in this shit box," he replied. "If you're so worried about this then why'd you ask me to put in a word for you?"

"I have to ask the man some questions," I said. "That doesn't preclude me from being nervous."

"Well if you could try and like, not shit yourself in the process, that'd be great," he said. "I don't need this blowing back wrong on me."

"Have I ever fucked you over before, Reek?" I asked.

"Nah. And that's the only reason we here."

Reek had been a good friend of Deon Whims, the subject of the article framed over my desk, the Bloods banger who died one way when the police told it another. Reek's name never appeared next to any quotes in the story, but he'd helped me land interviews with Whims' loved ones, find the quotes that tied the tale together. We'd stayed in touch after it was over, formed something of a friendship, or as much of a friendship as an ex-journalist and an ex-gangbanger can have.

Yeah, I said "ex." It's difficult, but not impossible, to walk away without paying the cost in bullet wounds. Reek had been a Blood since I was in kindergarten, but he'd also come up with Hard Head. When he asked to be out, he wasn't facing a charge, and he'd never done the set wrong. The way Reek told it, Hard Head made clear that Reek had carte blanche to walk away untouched, and that anyone who defied that edict would feel pain three times worse than whatever they felt the

73

need to deliver to Reek.

"Listen man," Reek said, his hand wrapping around my wrist to stop me from rattling my fingers against the shifter. "If he had a real problem with you, Hard Head wouldn't be agreeing to no sit down. Like the namesake, he ain't exactly known for calm. He's gonna give you some shit, he's gonna rattle you a bit, he's gonna laugh at you, and then you talk, alright? Just go along with it and everyone's gonna leave happy."

I nodded. He got out of the car. I didn't follow right away. Reek stared at me for a second then decided to dispense with patience, marching around to my side of the Cutlass and opening the driver's side door.

"You need me to hold your hand or some shit?" he asked.

"Maybe," I said, reaching out for his, causing him to recoil.

"Man, what did I tell you about making jokes like that?" he asked. "And don't try none of that cute shit with him, 'less you want an actual reason to worry."

Reek started moving toward the park, toward some shapes I could barely make out in the snow. Not wanting to be too far away from the only person who liked me in the neighborhood, I finally gave up the relative safety of the car and trudged after him. The November wind bit at my face, triggering the little shaving cuts on my cheeks, so I pulled up the hood from under my jacket collar to block it.

Reek stopped moving when he reached a set of wooden bleachers at the other end of what I guessed might be a football field hiding under the snow. Three men were sitting there. The one at the center with the broad, bald dome sticking out of a down jacket had to be Hard Head. His skull looked like it was trying to escape from under his skin, jutting up almost to a point, like it was a weapon. He wore a black down jacket, thick grey gloves and dark jeans that flowed over a pair of construction boots. Hard Head ran his tongue across his teeth as I came up.

"This your boy?" he asked Reek, now moving on to a full laugh. "With the fucking hood wrapped around his head like his momma sent him out on the first day of school. This is your hard ass private eye?"

I considered making a joke about how it was his mom who helped me get dressed that morning, but thought better of it as my brain flashed forward to the line in my obituary about how I got shot to death for making a "yo momma" joke to a gang lord.

"So you the one who wrote that story about Deon?" he asked.

I nodded.

"Meaning you was the one who thought it was alright to tell the whole word he was a snitch?"

"It was the truth," I replied. "And considering how the cops forced him into it, it seemed wrong to let them tell his story their way. So I wrote it."

"So you a righteous man?" he asked.

"I didn't say that."

"So you saying I'm wrong?"

"I didn't say that either."

Hard Head's eyes widened, stretched up in feigned surprise, creating enough space that each one looked like a saucer of milk with one green Cheerio iris floating in the center.

"So then what are you saying?" he asked.

I looked to Reek for help, but he was clowning with the other two guys on the bleachers, barely even paying attention.

"I asked you a question," Hard Head said, stepping into my field of vision, cutting me off from my less than interested support. "You thought it was alright to put Deon's business in the street like that?"

Any answer I gave seemed like it'd be wrong, so I went with honesty and hoped that played.

"I thought Deon did right by me in the time I knew him, and I thought he'd rest better if I did right by him when I wrote about him," I said. "People out here knew he'd flipped long before I did. That's what got him killed. Didn't seem to make much difference what I wrote, other than throwing a little dirt on the feds for putting him in that position. Otherwise he would have gone down as another dead drug dealer on the West Side, and at the end of it, that's not who he was."

Hard Head nodded, ran his tongue against the inside of his upper lip, made a sucking sound and winced his eyes like he was thinking.

"You know they never caught no one for that murder, right?" he asked.

I nodded. I knew. I also knew where he was going with this and felt my stomach drop down to my ankles.

"Meaning you asked to meet with me, not really sure if I gave the order or not?"

I nodded again. My stomach left my ankles and burrowed into the snow for safe keeping.

"That ain't a concern for you? Like you didn't think maybe I wanted to take a piece out of you for putting all that information in the air? Maybe that story caused me a headache or two from the cops, and you gotta pay a price for that? You didn't think maybe we arranged this meeting so I could arrange a meeting between you and Deon?"

I shook my head no. My stomach was on a plane to a non-extradition country but it had left a note for my bowels to behave in its absence.

"You forget how to speak English?" he asked.

I had not, and it seemed silence had carried me as far as it would.

"I'm here to talk about now, not then. If you wanted to do something to me over what I wrote about Deon, I figure you would have done it already," I said. "If I'm wrong, and you want to do something about it now, then I figure there's nothing I can say to stop you."

"Well, least we agree on one thing," he replied.

Hard Head stepped back, raised his hoodie just a little bit from his waist. I closed my eyes, like a little kid afraid of the monster in the closet, hoping that would somehow make the gun that had to be there disappear. When I opened them, I saw nothing but Hard Head's belly button, which was an outie for those keeping score, and Reek laughing in the background.

"Man, I told you he was alright," Reek said.

Hard Head was eyeing me up and down again. He looked disgusted and amused.

"Really? This white bread motherfucker right here, and he just stands tall?" he asked. "No flinch, no beg, nothing?"

He turned to Reek, pulled out a wad of bills from his pocket, peeled off a few and sat down, shaking his head but still trying to fight off a smile.

"The hell was that?" I asked.

"Man, I had to have a little fun with you, can't make it too easy," he said, fishing what looked like a black and mild out from another pocket and lighting it. "But let's get on with this."

I narrowed my eyes at Reek, who looked way too proud of himself as he counted his winnings.

"Why you wanna know about Kevin?" Hard Head asked.

"Because someone's paying me to find out how he died," I said.

"He got shot. The end. That was in the paper," Hard Head replied.

"Yeah, but my client wants to know who shot him. And why."

Hard Head took a long drag, the brown paper curling into ash that blended in with the dirty snow.

"Since when does anyone care about black boys getting shot in Woodland Cemetery? Ain't that just part of the plan to your people?" he asked.

"It's not part of the plan to his family," I said.

Hard Head took another long drag, let the smoke out slow in a concentrated stream. Maybe the invocation of Kevin Mathis' grieving loved ones was enough to make him curb his attitude for a second.

"You're working for his people? I can respect that," he said. "Don't know how much help I can be, not like I seen it go down, and from what little talk there's been about it, no one else did either."

"Then maybe you can help me with the why, not the who," I replied, stepping into his smoke cloud, hoping the mini-fix would chase off my latest craving. "I've been told Kevin was allowed to deal in this neighborhood but didn't claim your set. Freelancers don't last in this city, but judging by Kevin's rap sheet, he had a long and prosperous career before last week. I'm guessing if he was allowed to operate around here without trouble, he had your blessing."

Hard Head nodded, his face flashing slight annoyance that I knew as much as I did.

"Man, I thought you wanted to talk about Kevin? Now you wanna ask about my business? That's not what we agreed on."

"This is about Kevin, not your business."

"And you're assuming the answer to your question don't make them one and the same," he said. "I don't know you like that, and from what Reek tells me, you spend a decent amount of time talking with cops so..."

He stopped himself mid-sentence, pursed his lips, raised the black and mild like he was gonna take another pull but then stopped again, flicking the ash to punctuate whatever was bouncing around his battering ram of a skull.

"Actually, you got good relationships with the NPD then, right? Like friends and shit, people who might do you favors?" he asked.

"That's not exactly how that works."

"But it's kinda how it works?" he asked.

I didn't answer, but I guess that was all he needed to hear.

"Meaning you might be a good person to know if I ever need any favors," he said. "Alright then, that'll work. I'll tell you what you wanna know, and let's just say you owe me one."

Trading in unnamed favors was fine, when I was on the receiving end of the task to be requested later. I didn't like the idea of owing someone, especially a dude like Hard Head, but given he was Reek's old boss and Reek was my only friend in the middle of the frozen park where we were standing, I liked the idea of trying to negotiate even less.

"Fine," I said, wanting to move past that point as soon as possible.

Hard Head rubbed his gloves together and clapped, the sound getting muffled in the wind, before standing up and putting an arm around me, leading me further away from Reek than I felt comfortable being.

"So, if you read Kevin's rap sheet, then you learned he was moving more than the usual around here right?" he asked.

"The pills?"

"Yep. You seen how the police get about that oxy shit. They could give two fucks about brothers dying behind the needle, but when little Johnny starts breaking into houses in Montclair to feed his pill habit, then they calling press conferences and shit," he said. "Still, there's money to be made in that, provided you got the right amount of distance from it. So yeah, Kevin moved a little H here and there, but for the most part, he was running scripts to the scholarship crowd. He bought his shit from us, through a third party, so we got a cut. Wouldn't make no sense for one of my guys to have bumped him off then. Now I'm guessing if his people sent you out here asking questions, they don't think he got dead over the usual shit right?"

"Right," I said.

"Yeah, well I don't either. I wouldn't have put just anybody in a spot like this. He was smart, reliable. Didn't use his own shit, got popped a few times but didn't make no deals that hurt me," Hard Head said. "But

79

then I started hearing things…"

I thought back to the court files. The two no-contest pleas. If Kevin had turned snitch he wouldn't have been long for this world, just like Deon.

"You think he became a C.I.?" I asked.

"Didn't believe it, but the rumor was bouncing around. And if that was out there, well it wouldn't have mattered much if it was true."

"Any idea where the rumor came from?" I asked.

"Yeah, one of my crew who supplies him. Name's Levon," Hard Head said. "You got a pen? I'll let you know where to find him."

I pulled out a notepad and a black onyx with the cap half chewed off.

"Thought you wasn't a reporter anymore?" he asked.

"Old habits die hard," I replied.

He took another drag off the black and mild, let out a dry cough and frowned.

"You telling me," he said, jotting down an address and a time.

With that Hard Head pointed back to Reek, signaling that he was done with me.

"Don't forget our little arrangement," he said. "I need to cash in that favor, you best make yourself available."

"Doesn't sound like I've got much of a choice."

He clapped his hand down on my shoulder and squeezed, causing me to wince, letting me know he could do a lot worse if he felt like it.

"You learn quick. Smart man," he said. "Then again, Deon was a smart man too. Just don't go and get too clever now."

Reek pounded it out with the two men on the bleachers and half-jogged toward me, exchanging a nod with Hard Head as he walked away.

I waited until we got close enough to my car to ask the question that had been stuck in the back of my throat for the past ten minutes.

"Yo man," I said, almost stammering, more afraid of the answer than I was of Hard Head. "What happened to Deon ... did he…"

Reek put a hand up, cut me off.

"Listen, I know how you are, but some things just ain't worth knowing, you understand?"

I was starting to.

***

The phone would not stop ringing.

The number of consecutive calls I'd sidestepped from Keyonna Jackson had to number in the triple-digits by now. I knew she was gonna yell at me whenever I picked up, but her cigarette-withered rasp seemed preferable to hearing Apple's signature chorus one more goddamn time.

I reached for the iPhone while approaching an intersection, fumbled the snap, and stopped rooting around on the passenger side mat just in time to see brake lights ahead of me.

My reflexes were better than expected and the Cutlass slid to a stop well before I rear-ended the Buick in front of me. My decision to avoid disaster caused a series of similar sudden stops, and then came the car horns.

I turned around to see a line of vehicles that needed the same amount of cosmetic upkeep as the Cutlass. There was a town car back there that looked decidedly less shitty than the vehicles belonging to everyone else who was mad at me, but I just decided that guy was lost.

I exhaled, slow rolled forward when the light changed, and called Key back, switching her to speaker so I could use the GPS during the impending tongue-lashing. I wasn't sure where I was going or what I needed to do, but I had some time to kill before taking Hard Head's advice and tracking down Mathis' supplier at night.

"Key!" I shouted with as much mock enthusiasm as I could muster. "Haven't heard from you in days! How the hell are you?"

81

"I know you're not getting smart with me after ducking all my calls," she replied. "I know you're not stupid enough to be doing that Russell."

"Just been a little busy is all. Thought you could take a hint, show some patience."

"Patience is for people who don't get shit done," she replied.

I found myself rolling to another stop, about a block from Woodland Cemetery, where Mathis had died. Whoever designed Newark's grid must have had an affinity for labyrinths because none of the side streets cut from one main artery to the next. If you needed to get out of a neighborhood, you'd end up on the same seven or eight main roads, and you'd end up seeing a lot of the same places.

"You decide whether or not you're gonna do the right thing here?" she asked as the light changed again and I cruised past the mylar memorial to Kevin Mathis' life.

"There's a right thing here?" I asked. "It's a little more complicated than that."

"A man's son is dead. Cops shot another man's son with no cause," she replied. "Seems pretty simple to me. There are questions to be asked."

"And I've been running around asking them. But I need to ask a few more before I sit down with Mr. Mathis again, so you're gonna have to ask the man to wait."

"Wait? His boy got killed. How long would you wait?"

"This isn't about me," I shot back.

"You're the one gumming up the process Russell, so maybe it is."

I took a right on Martin Luther King Jr. Boulevard as I got near the courthouse, not wanting to get funneled into the parking lot of Broad and Market. If I cut back out toward the highway I could get away from the traffic and near a pretty good Chinese spot. I hadn't eaten all day, maybe some MSG would help me figure out my next step.

82

Something odd flashed in my mirror as I made the move right. The out-of-place Town Car from back when I almost rear-ended the guy on Springfield. I tried to slow down but Key's voice broke my concentration.

"If you were just gonna keep ignoring me Russell you didn't have to pick up the phone," she said. "Mr. Mathis needs an answer. Or else he's going to have to start considering other options."

That didn't sound good. That sounded like a really vague threat. Really vague threats were my shtick, not Key's.

"What other options?" I asked, knowing the answer.

"People need to see that video, and the story behind who took it and what happened to him is really compelling," she said. "Kind of thing you would have written on back when you were at the paper."

"Don't start that shit Key. We don't know enough to put that out in the air yet. All you're gonna do is start fires," I said. "Not to mention if Austin's even halfway right about the cops being involved in his son's death, it's gonna be a lot harder for me to look into with a mob of TV cameras around."

"More eyes on this city the better. Makes it harder for things like this to get swept under the rug," she replied.

"It also makes it harder for me to do my job."

"Well that sounded a little bit selfish," she said. "I told you this was about you."

I checked the mirror again, noticing a small fleet of cars inching up behind me. I'd let my foot off the gas too much while going back and forth with Key. I merged left again, trying to get out of the way and avoid another chorus of honks, when I caught sight of the town car a third time.

Maybe I was just paranoid from the meeting with Hard Head or the pressure from Key or the glare Henniman had given me the other day. Maybe I just had a feeling that the charter members of the "Fuck

You Russell" club had held a meeting and unanimously approved a proposal to conspire against me.

Or maybe, I'd picked up a tail.

I needed to get Key off the phone and figure out if I was paranoid or observant. But she was also pissing me off.

"You're gonna come at me about selfish?" I asked. "Like it doesn't benefit you to up the city's protest game a little? Your weekly rallies haven't exactly been well-attended lately."

"You know me better than that, Russell," she said.

"You're right, and you know me well enough to trust me to handle something like this. I've got a line on something that might knock a few pieces into place, but it isn't going down until tonight. Can you give me to the morning?"

"I can give you that much," she replied. "But if you don't deliver something soon, I might start to agree with Austin about turning that video loose."

"Deal."

"And Russell?" she asked.

Whatever came next, I was glad I was out of slapping range.

"Yes dear?" I replied.

"You ever imply I'm manipulating a grieving father for personal gain again, and they'll be fishing your teeth out of the Passaic, you understand?"

I did, but I hung up without saying so.

With Key off my ass, I picked up speed and let my eyes drift back to the mirror, searching for the town car to no avail. I saw Spruce Street coming up on my left, a nowhere block that cut through two rows of run-down apartments and took the turn hard before slowing down on the empty street. Best case scenario, I'd lose the tail or confirm I was hallucinating. Worst case, I'd gain the momentary relief of confirming I had a tail before riding a panic wave as I tried to figure out what the fuck to do about it.

Spruce wasn't exactly the best place to slow roll. There were a few kids on the stoops as I went by, smoking while shivering, mean-mugging anyone who came through. Moving slow on a block like this made the local predators wonder if you were a cop or a customer, and I didn't want to be confused for either.

I checked the rear-view again and noticed the nose of the town car trying to inch across MLK and turn left.

Well, at least I wasn't crazy. Nope, now I was just a completely sane, normal guy, with a tail, who had just left a meeting with one of Newark's most dangerous gang bangers and was dipping his big toe into an investigation that might piss off one of Newark's most powerful cops.

I thought about gunning it, before remembering I wasn't in a movie. There was no way I was outrunning anyone in a Cutlass whose odometer was in the six figures. I took the left on University and weighed my options. Whoever was following me wasn't being terribly discrete about it. Maybe they just wanted to scare me, and if so, message received.

A little square on the dashboard turned orange and ominous. Low fuel. Another dozen or so scenarios popped into my head, none of them good.

I needed to get rid of whoever was following me, and not in a "World's Wildest Police Chases" sort of way.

Another light turned red at University and I caught sight of a familiar liquor store where I used to buy cigarettes, nervously slipping ten dollar bills through a plexiglass slot while homeless people eye-fucked my wallet.

By chance or instinct, I'd driven back to a place where I might be able to lose my newest fans.

The light turned green and I cut through the intersection and under the cement overhang where I'd smoked way too many cigarettes on graveyard shifts, slipping past a box truck emblazoned with the two words that were part of my identity for longer than anything else, and pulled to a stop outside *the Signal-Intelligencer.*

CHAPTER 6

In the five years I'd worked there, the *Intelligencer* newsroom felt more like home than any of the mediocre apartments I'd rented around Essex County. Hell, I'd probably spent more time at the paper than at home anyway, and that was just fine with me. You're not a workaholic when your job doesn't feel like a job, and I had better conversations at crime scenes than I ever did with the rotating cast of whoevers I'd been shacking up with.

The walk up the ramp from University to the newsroom lobby was the last part of a routine I'd established five days a week for five years. I'd park across the street, light up my second cigarette of the morning, and spike it by the time I got to the food truck run by the tiny Brazilian woman who stretched her vowels out like rubber bands. I'd slip her two dollars every morning, one for the burnt coffee she served and the other for a tip, then slip up the ramp and greet the ex-Newark cop who worked as a guard most days and never complained when he had to open the elevator because I'd lost my security badge, again.

But after dumping the Cutlass on the sidewalk and watching the tail car glide past, as if it wasn't going to circle back in ten seconds, I realized my walk up the ramp was going to feel more like an invasion than a homecoming. The food truck was gone, probably parked outside a different office building that hadn't laid off 20 percent of its staff.

87

A bright white "no smoking" sign hung on the brick wall where the truck used to be parked, a crude paper printout with an arrow taped underneath, directing the smokers away from the building.

As I stepped into the lobby, I noticed another split between reality and my pleasant memories of the place. The trophy case that used to face the doorway and display the awards won by the editorial and advertising staffs was gone, replaced by a clean coat of green paint. Four white letters, G.S.M.G., sat where the trophy case used to be, each one outlined in a fluoride blue stripe. It looked like the after-effects of a sneeze while brushing your teeth. The acronym stood for Garden State Media Group. I guess it sounded more Silicon Valley, or made the place seem more marketable.

"Little different than you remember?"

The voice was kind, familiar. I turned left to find the best part of my old morning routine was still seated behind the bulletproof glass that separated the reception desk from the lobby.

Wearing glasses dwarfed by his silver bushy eyebrows and the same puckered smile that always seemed set to burst into a laugh, Nate waved me away from the nauseating present and back into the past. The old security guard had retired from Newark PD a decade ago, and he'd started his gig at the paper almost immediately after that. I'd thought we made fast friends because he liked talking shop with the cops' reporter. But it didn't take long to realize Nate could talk to anyone about anything. The man was conversational catnip, and I'd left him my number after my ignoble exit from the newsroom, promising we'd get drinks sometime.

We never had, and I couldn't remember whose fault that was. If it was mine, Nate sure wasn't acting like it.

"You still recognize me old man?" I asked, grinning like I hadn't in a while as I tapped on the glass. "Thought you'd be in one of them homes by now."

"I could still bounce your ass from this building if I wanted too kid, I got some moves left," he said, flashing the same wide grin back as he shadowboxed with the microphone in front of him.

Nate reached down under his desk, flicking the switch to unlock the door between us. I stepped inside, into a long hallway that led to a different part of the building, one that stretched a couple hundred feet past Nate's security station. As happy as I was to see him, our accidental reunion had nothing to do with my decision to stop at the *Intelligencer*. The building was old, cavernous, and there were at least a dozen ways out that led to three different side streets. Barring some extreme bad luck, I'd be able to slip out a different door than I'd come in from and leave whoever was following me to stare at my parked car until nightfall.

I probably should have just sprinted down the hallway and out one of the fire doors toward Court or Washington, jogged down side streets and disappeared into the mix of daytime vendors and pedestrians crowding the area around City Hall.

But Nate was Nate. I'd spent a lot of time in Newark chronicling the lives of people who didn't seem interested in living, and not nearly enough with the ones who wanted something better for a city too long associated with death and disrepair.

"So how the hell you been son?" he asked, popping out of his chair and giving me a handshake that easily flowed into a hug. "Been a year since you jumped off this ship, right?"

"I didn't exactly jump," I replied. "Kinda got thrown overboard."

"See I was trying to be polite here. I'm not that old, not like I'm forgetting things yet," he said. "I remember that day. Greene came down here with his face all red like he'd got hit."

"He's lucky I didn't hit him."

"You are too," Nate said, swinging his handcuffs from his belt, twirling them and sliding them back. He always did that when we

89

talked, liked reminding me that…

"We're friends, but I'll still arrest your ass," he said on cue, dropping in laughs at every pause like he couldn't help himself. Probably because he couldn't. Nate thought every conversation was a stand-up routine.

"Oh c'mon, like you ever had to use those here?" I asked.

"Nah, but it's come close. Especially during the last round of layoffs a few months back," he said. "Most people just left in tears, but some got it in their minds to start throwing things on their way out the door."

"Can you blame them? Hard to stay calm when your career gets stolen out from under you," I said.

"Didn't say I blamed them. But I had to keep them moving. I got a job to do," he said.

I thought another one of his regularly scheduled punchlines was coming, but Nate just looked away from me and sighed.

"Least for a few more days," he said.

"Oh, fuck no," I replied. "You too?"

"Yep. Guess I'm not cost-effective," he said. "Not as many people working here, so they don't need as many guards on rotation. I probably make more than the younger cats so… I'm out next Tuesday."

"That is bullshit."

"Just reality," he said. "Least I'll have a little more time for my kids. When they visit from Atlanta."

I could stay up for thirty-six hours straight bitching about the endless flow of journalists being marched off a plank at newsrooms across the country, but at least we were being mourned. Nobody ever thought about the collateral damage of those cutbacks. The guards and the janitors and the support staff that get swept away when there's no one left to secure or clean up after.

"Damnit Nate. I'm sorry."

"Don't be. It happens. And at least I got to catch up with you," he said. "Couldn't have done that if I wanted to keep this job."

Nate pointed a slightly bent finger to the wall above the window, where a row of black-and-white printouts waved from the gentle gust of a ceiling fan. Each one contained a grainy mugshot that I recognized as an employee photo printed out from a machine that must have been desperately low on ink. I remembered this wall of infamy from my regular visits to Nate's security station back in the day, the faces of those who had been banned from the building. I shouldn't have been surprised to see my own dead-eyed headshot among the *Intelligencer*'s least favorite ex-employees. But I was more than a little pissed about being lined up with the IT guy who jammed tennis balls into all the toilets in the 2nd floor women's room.

"They banned me? They banned me!" I shouted. "Jesus, I fucking yelled at the guy. I didn't kill anyone."

"Well now, you're just a portrait of restraint," Nate replied.

"I yelled!"

"Yelling is what you're doing now," he said. "That day I think you went a step or two past yelling. I believe you called your boss, and forgive me I may be paraphrasing a bit here, a limp-dicked fuck weasel?"

My memories of my last stand at the paper were a little hazy, probably because my last days there led to my last days with Dina and my brain had limited storage when it came to misery. But I know it came down to a verbal brawl with one of the paper's top editors, Elliot Greene.

My exit came a few months after the paper decided to adopt a ridiculous quota system, where reporters would earn a certain percentage of their pay by way of incentive bonuses. Kind of like how football players get extra cash for certain yardage benchmarks, except they were playing a game and we were, you know, doing something that mattered. I'd done well enough to juggle my journalistic responsibilities against the paper's slavish devotion to page views for a few weeks. Crime, after all, wasn't exactly a hard sell to the readership. But I'd started slipping in the month before I got fired.

I had dug in deep on an investigation involving the police chief in Irvington, the next town over from Newark, the bite size version of the Brick City that was home to the same daily fiascoes.

With my numbers sagging, Greene had asked me to put together a list of Newark's most wanted criminals. A glorified photo gallery. The kind of thing most reporters derisively referred to as a "listicle." I politely declined. But Greene kept pushing and pushing and pushing. Smashing me over the head with the usual corporate doublespeak about "being a team player" and "thinking beyond myself" and "focusing on what really matters" for the paper.

That last line, for whatever reason, burst open a dam for me. Was writing 20 inches of clickbait copy really a hill worth dying on? Considering what I'd been doing since the last time I'd walked into the newsroom, maybe not. But something in what Greene said or the way he said it, like he could really justify me focusing on what was best for business over what was best for our readers, told me the newspaper I wanted to grow old at had died prematurely.

So, I tore into Greene, part of me not caring about the consequences, the other part just arrogant enough to think I was talented enough to verbally flash fry a top editor and walk away unscathed. Cue "limp dicked fuck weasel" insult. Cue me collecting unemployment checks for a few weeks. Cue Henniman helping me get the P.I. license, and me learning there are a few things worse than mortgaging your journalistic integrity, like mortgaging your actual integrity.

"So, considering how you left," Nate said, twirling the handcuffs. "You wanna tell me why you're back?"

"Just visiting some old friends," I said.

"Mhmmm," he replied. "Except if I remember, most of those old friends went out the door with you. You sure it's got nothing to do with that unmarked that pulled up right before you came in?"

I followed Nate's bent finger again, this time to the security camera feeds. He was looking right at the follow car that drove me back to the building.

"You sure those are cops?" I asked.

"Yes sir. Recognize that plate. It's an older design. The state logo's a little smaller on the ones they made before 2005," he said. "Worked motor pool for a little bit, tend to notice these kind of things when you're bored out your damn mind all day. So why are the cops chasing you?"

"I didn't do anything."

"You know how many times I heard that?" he asked.

"Probably more than enough to know when someone's lying about it," I replied.

Nate didn't say anything. His smile had retreated for the moment.

"I'm just trying to slip them for a minute, and you know this place has enough exits to make that happen," I said. "You know me man. You know I wouldn't come anywhere near you or this place if I was actually caught up in anything."

He scratched his salt and pepper beard and took a step back, easing into his uncomfortable chair again, turning his back to me before flipping the switch that opened the elevator door.

"Guess you forgot your security badge again," he said, not facing me but letting just enough of that smile loose to signal we were OK.

I grabbed a pen and wrote my cell number down on a pad.

"You should call me after your last day, old man. Maybe we can celebrate your retirement," I said.

"We ain't celebrating shit," he replied. "But you can sure as hell buy."

I stepped back out into the lobby, fist bumping the glass like we used to, him returning the favor.

"You should probably go out one of the Washington Street exits," he said through the microphone. "There's a stairwell on the third floor that will take you there."

Third floor? Shit.

The newsroom was on the third floor.

***

I drummed my fingers against my hip as the *Intelligencer*'s long out-of-date elevator cage rocked its way toward the newsroom. It was the same nerve-driven tic I'd had before my meeting with Hard Head, and I felt stupid for equating the two situations.

I knew what would happen if I ran into Greene because I'd been practicing some form of the confrontation in my head for a year. Every time I drank, every time I got in a foul mood, hell, even when I just couldn't sleep, I was getting in reps for the rematch with my former boss, mentor and friend.

There was a time when I called him Elliot. He'd been my sensei in the newsroom, fighting for me to get hired in the first place and then pushing to give me the police beat ahead of more veteran reporters when the job opened up. He was a good guy, but he was also a survivor. If he ever took my side in a newsroom fight, it was only because it was a fight Greene knew he could win. The man was close to the top of the paper's food chain, but he wasn't the building's apex predator. If I'd crossed anyone above him, he'd have crossed me off.

When the paper got all web-savvy, I should have seen the change coming. Should have known he'd push the parent company's agenda because he had a house in Short Hills with a mortgage that made my student loan debt look like the cost of a middling first date.

I gritted my teeth, exhaled, tried to remind myself that there was no gain in confronting Greene. All I needed to do was get out of the building and away from the tail car.

Confident in my very complicated escape plan, that being to keep my mouth shut and my head low and avoid eye contact with any of my former editors, I stepped into the hall and immediately made eye contact with one of my former editors.

Elliot Greene was standing in the doorway of the conference room that was off to the side of the elevator. He peered from behind black rimmed glasses, the wrinkles on his face seeming to crease a little more at the sight of me, like his antennae had been raised. A few other editors formed a small circle around him, some I recognized and others I didn't. I looked up at a clock and figured the bosses were having their afternoon planning meeting, deciding what stories would go on the front page of tomorrow's paper, or more likely, what stories needed to be placed at the top of their god forsaken website.

Greene was locked onto me, not paying attention to the editor who was chirping in his ear. I took a few steps out of the elevator, waited to see what he'd do, and thought about making a run for it.

"Russell? Russell Avery?" he asked, louder than he needed too. "What are you doing here?"

All the heads turned. The editors I recognized looked surprised, maybe intrigued. They were mostly in their 50s, allegedly mature, but most people can't resist that schoolyard urge to watch a fight unfold.

Normally, I would have obliged. But I'd made enough enemies for one day.

"Hey Mr. Greene," I said, choosing formality over fury. "Just passing through really quick. Dina has some of my old files and I need them for a case. Can't stick around."

"Well Dina's out on an assignment right now, so you'll have to stick around for a bit," he replied, turning toward the editors flanking him. "We're just about done here anyway. Why don't we catch up for a bit?"

Probably because neither of us wants to go down for felony assault today?

"That's OK," I said. "I'll just get what I need from her desk."

"Well, we don't let ex-employees rummage through our current employees' personal property," he said. "Besides, we should talk anyway."

He stepped back and held the conference room door open. I really should have just run. Wasn't like Nate was going to come after me if they called. But if I did that, they'd take it out on Dina, and she didn't need any more reasons to hate me right now.

I followed him into the conference room and plopped into one of the plush recliners that lined the sides of the marble desk at the center of the room. Front page designs dotted the wall, printouts of the more recent ones and then framed versions of layouts from years earlier. My byline was on more than a few of them.

"Why are you really here?" Greene asked, closing the door.

The pretense of friendliness he'd put on in front of the other editors was gone from his voice, replaced by the same pent up aggravation I'd been carrying. Guess he'd been waiting for this too.

"I told you…"

"No, I mean what are you doing here, specifically? In the newsroom?" he asked. "You're not even supposed to be allowed in the building."

He moved toward a chair across from me, placing a hand on the headrest, choosing to leer over me instead of sitting down.

"I bribed the guard. Or maybe I stole someone's key card. Why does it matter?" I asked. "You don't want to talk to me. I don't want to talk to you. I'm here, I'm not going to piss in a coffee cup or start a fight or curse you out again. So why don't I just get up and walk out, and this time we don't involve security?"

"You're still mad about that?" he asked.

"You had me taken out of here like a crazy person," I replied.

"You were acting like a crazy person."

"All I did was call you out on your hypocrisy."

"Using enough profanity to make George Carlin blush," he said.

"One, George Carlin would never blush," I replied. "Two, I really didn't come here for this."

"Then why are you here? Did Dina really call you? She knows she'd get in a lot of trouble for bringing you anywhere near this place."

"No, she's not that stupid. She actually has no idea I'm here," I said. "To be completely honest, I just want to walk out of this room and exit the building through the distribution garage, and I'd like to do that without talking to you for any more time than is absolutely necessary."

"This have anything to do with your new job?" he asked, the slightest hint of a laugh creeping into his otherwise stern tone. "I heard you're an umm ... detective now, or something?"

I had started toward the door. But that snicker froze me. I wasn't letting him run me out of my newsroom a second time.

"Oh, that's funny to you?" I asked, turning back.

"No, it's just strange," he replied. "I mean with the lecture you gave me, that whole sermon on the mount about accountability journalism, I figured you'd be in the city or L.A. or at one of the other national papers by now. You did make it clear that you were above our new business model."

I needed to let it go. Needed to get out. I had bigger problems involving police misconduct and mysterious cars tailing me and my pending meeting with a drug dealer.

But fuck him.

"You really wanna do this, Elliot?" I asked.

"I don't want to do anything. I just want to know how you went from judging me to snapping photos of cheating spouses at motels," he said. "Or is it helping cops? I've heard so many rumors."

I cut back across the room and pulled away the chair he was leaning on, stepped close enough that I could see the caffeine stains that put light hints of yellow in his teeth.

97

"I know it's hard for you to grasp this, being that you sit in a glass office all day, but life's difficult for the rank-and-file out there. You've never been within fifteen feet of a layoff, but the rest of us, we spent our days hiding in tall grass while you assholes walk around with machetes," I said. "I tried to get back in the game after you got rid of me. And for your information, I got offers. Even had an interview with the *Times*, but some editors got concerned when the references at my last job wouldn't call back. You have anything to do with that Elliot? Don't answer, because we both know you did. So yeah, I'm doing something I don't want to be doing right now. To survive. You wouldn't know anything about that either."

I figured that rant would be enough to cut him down. Elliot wasn't used to arguing with people he couldn't fire.

"I know plenty about that, Russell. You think I like what's happened here? I don't. But if I don't get in line with the company, then they fire me and find someone else who does," he said. "It's a balancing act, and at least with me here, we might actually get some work done now and then. Like the industry would stop changing if we just asked it nicely. And you know what? We still cover this city pretty well."

He didn't move. Fine. I wasn't done anyway.

"Cover it well? Please. You have no idea what the hell is going on out there," I said. "You know why I'm here? Because I'm looking into something that pissed someone off enough that I'm being followed. That's what we're supposed to do, Elliot. Make people uncomfortable. Ask about shit with ugly answers. And you know what the worst part is? You guys actually covered what I'm looking at, for all of five seconds, in one of your stupid quick hit posts. But you were too busy running past the story to actually see it."

I gave Elliot one last look as I moved for the door, hoping to find his face twisted up in anger or regret or some other kind of sign that I'd won that round. But he was just scratching his beard, thinking.

And that was when I knew I'd fucked up.

Whatever I thought of Elliot now, the Elliot I knew back then wasn't your typical editor. He'd been a reporter for a while. He had that sense of pride that came with owning a story.

I had just implied that I knew something he didn't. That there was something he had missed. And if any of the old Elliot was still in there, he wasn't going to rest until he figured out what that was.

CHAPTER 7

Hours later, I was leaning against a street light along Littleton Avenue, trying to get comfortable against the metal ridges, wondering who I was going to make my next enemy.

I was on a West Ward drug corner, just late enough that standing in the area wasn't the best idea. I had to talk to Levon, the dealer who had apparently told people Kevin Mathis was a snitch. Hard Head may have told me where to find him, but he sure as hell didn't go as far as making any introductions.

Sure, I was a half-bright P.I., not a cop, but Hard Head probably didn't want his people thinking he gave up their locations all that easy. I was going to have to approach Levon blind, and once I started asking pointed questions about his now dead former colleague, he was probably going to run, hit me, or both.

There wasn't much I could do to prevent a confrontation once I started pushing him for info, but there were a few ways to improve the situation, maybe at least delay the running and punching. The people driving and walking up to the stoop where he'd set up shop were overwhelmingly white. It wasn't too hard to see that after Mathis died, Hard Head had placed Levon in control of the ever-profitable pill enterprise.

That thought marinated in my head for a bit, and it didn't take too long to wonder if Levon knew that might happen, that he'd benefit from Mathis going down hard. Leaking information about a fellow drug dealer being a snitch is an easy way to kill someone without actually doing the killing yourself.

I'd have to add those to the list of difficult questions I needed to ask, but either way, Levon's white college age client base meant I could at least shuffle up as a customer, start the conversation off from a place where he felt like he was in control.

Except I had no idea how to act like a junkie.

I ran a few scenarios in my head, trying to figure out how I'd ask Levon for pills, how I'd talk my way past the other two guys that were roaming the corner with him. But for all the time I'd spent writing about drugs, I'd never actually taken any. Outside weed, which pretty much stopped counting by the early 2000s. Pretending to be a fiend was beyond my already limited acting range.

This wasn't how I approached a confrontational interview as a reporter. I was more patient then and patience was the great equalizer. If you wanted to start a conversation with someone who had no reason to talk to you, and you had the luxury of being somewhere that the TV cameras weren't, you waited to get them alone. Separated them from their backup, from the people who might block you off, from the people they might not want to be candid in front of. Everyone had basic needs, from a drug dealer to a grieving relative to a politician. If Levon was gonna stand out here and sling all night, he'd need food and a bathroom.

I walked down Littleton until I hit South Orange and found myself bathing in the neon glow of an all-night deli, the only place open in the immediate vicinity. If I knew my ancient corner stores, then I knew a regular might get bathroom privileges. If this was Levon's corner, he had to be on the preferred customer list.

A street of soaked cardboard boxes squished under foot as I

entered the store, the owner's sad attempt to keep customers from tracking slush inside. I nodded to the cashier, an older Middle Eastern man with wisp-thin black hair covering a bare scalp. He responded with a practiced smile, one of his hands noticeably hidden beneath the register. It didn't matter if he actually had a gun there, as long as he at least made visitors think there might be one. The store must have been struggling, because there was no plexiglass shield keeping him separated from the entrance way and aisles.

I milled around a bit, snatching up a magazine I had no plan on reading, and a pack of Reese's Sticks, because Reese's Sticks are awesome. The store was empty, giving me enough time to putter around and get the lay of the place. There were four aisles, all with shoulder-high shelves, bracketed by two rows of refrigerators lined with mostly beer, and a deli stand with meat I wouldn't consume even if I was starving. The register was by the door, near the entrance to the cardboard highway that seemed to lead into a darkened area past the moldy cold cuts. Best guess, the bathroom was that way. Given the store's lack of hiding places, it looked like I was going to have to wait until Levon needed to piss to get a word in.

"That's it?" the clerk asked as I walked up and placed my items near the register.

"Almost," I replied. "Any chance a loyal customer could take a piss back there?"

"Sorry, employees only."

"Oh c'mon man," I whined. "Please?"

"There's plenty of trees outside," he said, not even looking at me. "That'll be $7.50"

I shot him a dirty look before paying up, pulling my hood over my head, and stumbling outside. Waiting for Levon could take a while, but I needed to be close enough to make a move without loitering in the store and irking the unfriendly cashier. If you want people to avoid eye contact with you, looking homeless is a pretty safe bet.

Wearing my long overdue for a wash hoodie pulled up around my head, ripped jeans and the oldest pair of cross trainers in existence, I plopped down on the sidewalk and took to huddling and appearing miserable. A few minutes passed, maybe ten or twelve in total. I asked a couple passers-by for change just to try out the role. No one obliged, because if you were out on the west side after midnight, you probably needed that dollar I was asking you to spare.

The foot traffic slowed and I ran out of people to bother. The minutes started blurring together as I thumbed the gossip magazine's pages, unable to focus. I should have grabbed a copy of the *Intelligencer*, but I couldn't look at that thing without getting angry, and I didn't need to get angry, because I knew what was coming next. Another smoke jones, one of the worst I'd had in my five weeks without a cigarette. Stakeouts were the ultimate chain smoking trigger. It was easier to measure time in drags than seconds.

Another twenty or so minutes ticked away, long enough for me to get cold and start rocking back and forth to keep warm. I must have looked pretty jumpy, because someone actually handed me a dollar without my having to even ask.

More Reese's Sticks for me.

Just as I started to wonder if I had a future in panhandling, I saw a young black kid entering the deli. He was short and stocky, with little dreads peeking out from under a wool hat with the ABA New Jersey Nets logo. Levon.

I waited for him to disappear through the door, then stood up and followed.

I moved into the candy aisle as I watched Levon banter with the cashier. He appeared to be ordering food, then nudged his head toward the back. The cashier nodded, then turned around to start making Levon's late night snack. I watched to make sure he was fully engrossed in meal prep, then cut across the store to get behind Levon.

The trail of cardboard boxes lining the aisle dumped out into a shadowy artery at the back of the store. Levon was moving toward what appeared to be a one-seater bathroom with a drawstring lightbulb overhead. There was a metal screen door that led outside next to it.

As Levon swatted the bathroom door aside, I stepped behind him and tried to come up with a clever icebreaker.

"Yo," I said, because I'm not all that clever.

Levon half-turned, his hands perilously close to his waist, peeking over his left shoulder at me. His eyes were green and a little bloodshot.

"I'm on break," he said.

Guess he gave me the once over, clearly assuming I was a customer.

"Not here for that man," I replied. "Just wanna talk."

"I'm not a big talker, and I'm trying to take a piss. So why don't you just go ahead and fuck off?"

It occurred to me that my plan of waiting for Levon to separate from his muscle and pretending to be a homeless guy to get in close didn't account for what would happen if he didn't feel talkative.

In the reporter days, a no comment was a no comment. I could take no for an answer. That wasn't really an option here.

"Can't really wait man," I said, inching closer.

Levon spun around and drove a forearm into my chest, pressing me up against the wall.

"Do I look like someone it's a good idea to fuck with?" he asked.

I winced, whimpered, made all the string bean junkie stereotype sounds he probably wanted to hear. But I also looked down, saw his sweatshirt pull up around his waist, noticed what wasn't tucked there.

He wasn't carrying. Of course he wasn't. That's what the muscle outside was for. He was already risking prison time by moving weight, why chance the gun enhancement?

So, to answer his question, he did look like someone it was a good idea to fuck with.

"Like I said, Levon," I started.

That was all he had to hear. I was an unknown who knew his first name, and that meant I was a problem. His eyes widened, and he balled up his free fist.

"I don't know which one of my regulars thought it was a good idea to send your suburban ass here unannounced, but they fucked up," he said. "That ain't how it works. Sorry to say, now I gotta send you back all messed up to make that fact clear."

"What's going on back there?" the cashier shouted.

"This isn't how I normally talk to people," I whispered in Levon's ear. "You wanna take a chance of him calling the cops when he sees two guys fighting in his store, or you wanna answer a few questions and get rid of me in under five minutes?"

Levon's eyes screamed murder, but they hid a brain that was probably listing all the problems he could avoid by not fighting back.

"Man, you got too much shit laying around back here. I tripped into the door," he shouted.

The cashier didn't answer, apparently satisfied by that. Levon turned back to me.

"You a cop?" he asked.

"Nope."

"Then you gotta realize it ain't that smart to come at me like this. If you know my name, then you know who I'm hooked up with. Be a lot less hazardous to your health if you just walked away."

I'd known some decent guys involved in the life. Reek, for example. But what pissed me off about most gang bangers was their need to wave their affiliation around like it was some magic cloak. Levon's name didn't mean what Reek's once did. He was just a foot soldier, a punk, and I'd taken enough shit for one day.

"You think you're the only one with friends? How do you think I

105

found you?" I asked. "I didn't come here to fight and I sure as shit didn't come here for a dick-measuring contest. I got some questions you can answer, and the sooner you answer them, the sooner you can take a piss and get back to making money. Sound fair?"

He rolled his eyes, one last play at defiance, then nodded.

"Whatever man," he said. "What you want?"

"You knew Kevin Mathis right?" I asked. "I'm trying to find out why he died."

Levon pursed his lips, twisted up his face like he was all upset.

Then he turned and ran for the back door.

Levon hit the metal screen like a linebacker bearing down on a defenseless receiver, rattling the damn thing so hard that the crash could probably be heard in the apartments above. I ran after him, increasingly worried that the armed cashier would follow.

The door led out into a small courtyard and another few fences that lined the backs of homes along Littleton Avenue. Levon was halfway to the first one, scrambling into the next yard. He was slow though, out of shape, struggling to get a foothold. Six months earlier, the cigarettes might have made this a closer race. Instead, I closed the gap before he was even halfway over the fence.

I grabbed at his foot but he kicked out, spastic and without much force, barely putting any pressure on my shoulder. I grabbed again, but my grip slipped from his ankle in the cold. I grabbed again, but he'd gotten a little higher now, and the next kick down caught my nose.

Hand pressed to my face, I stumbled back. Coughed. Tasted blood. I looked up at Levon's ass struggling to scale the top of the fence and let the adrenaline take hold again.

I grew up playing pick-up ball in Brooklyn, and that meant finding ways up and around all kinds of fences to get access to courts in public schools. Compared to Levon, I might as well have been Spider-Man.

My sneakers slipped into the diamond shaped footholds on the fence just like the old days, and it only a took a few seconds for me to get up and over the foothill that had conquered Levon like Everest. He was hauling ass to the next fence, huffing and puffing as he got to the base. I was only a few steps behind when he got there, and he was already slowing down. It would have been easy enough to just grab hold of him. But it also would have been easier if he'd chosen to have a conversation without making me taste my own blood.

I dipped my shoulder as I bore down, driving Levon face first into the second fence he'd planned to embarrass himself climbing over. He hit it hard and bounced back, rebounding toward me like a wrestler running off the ring ropes. I caught him around the waist and drove him into the dirt. He smacked into the frozen ground and let out a long groan when he landed, ending his wounded whine with a simple "fuck."

I placed a forearm across his chest and held him there as he writhed, breathing heavy as I licked some blood off my upper lip. It took a few seconds for the frenzy in me to subside. I didn't need to hit him. But the asshole didn't need to run. Maybe he deserved it.

A good number of excessive force lawsuits I'd written about flashed in my head. Part of me suddenly sympathized with the cops who went that one step past what the rules allowed, understood the cold clarity of aggression.

Part of me wondered what the fuck was wrong with the other part.

"Why'd you tell people Kevin was a snitch, Levon?" I asked, louder than I meant too, realizing all the noise might attract his friends. "You want him out of the way, think it might increase your little pill profits?"

"Nah man, it ain't like that."

"Sure as shit looks like that."

"You don't understand," he replied, still groaning from the impact or the weight of my body on his chest.

I noticed him wincing, struggling a bit to breathe, and backed off.

107

This had already gone further than I'd wanted it too.

"Then make me understand," I said.

"Why do you…" he trailed off, still searching for air. "Why do you care man?"

"Cause someone asked me to. Someone who doesn't think he died in a drug beef like the cops are saying."

He closed his eyes, grabbed the back of his neck and exhaled.

"Look man, I don't know who did it or why or anything like that," he said.

"Then tell me what you do know. Like why you went around telling people he was working with the police."

"Cause someone told me he was about a week or so ago," he replied.

"And you just believed it and put that out there, knowing how that might end up?"

Levon shook his head.

"I didn't want him to get killed alright. Cut off, out of business, maybe out the city? Sure," he said. "But dead? Nah. He was a pain in the ass, but that was all."

"Was he actually snitching or not?"

"That's what I was told," Levon replied.

"What you were told?" I asked. "So you didn't know for sure? You just heard a rumor that could get a man killed and you went with it."

"Wasn't no rumor. That shit came from a reliable source," Levon said. "Guy who told me about Mathis was a cop."

CHAPTER 8

I couldn't understand why a cop would out a snitch.

Well, scratch that. I could understand why, but the logic didn't sit well. Being confronted by the idea that a cop might have committed murder for the second time in a week tends to fray the nerves when you work with cops and occasionally for cops, and you're about to meet up with a cop.

I wrapped my hands against the decades-old marble table-top of a booth inside the Tick-Tock Diner, slurping coffee number two of the day. I hadn't slept much after my dance with Levon, waking up intermittently to stare at the text message I'd sent to an old source.

"Need to meet. Urgent. I know it's been a while, but it's worth it."

That was all I sent to Frank Russomano, the retired Newark detective who'd been my best source in Major Crimes when I was still with the paper. He was close to Henniman, but he didn't share his monastic devotion to the badge. Shit bird behavior is shit bird behavior, he'd once told me. Didn't matter if the person wore blue.

I'd noticed the ellipses in the text window the fourth time I'd woken up in the middle of the night. His only response was "Tick Tock. Noon." I hadn't seen Frank in a while, and he was probably just as confused to receive a text from me as I was to send it. But I knew he had a thing for the burgers here: mushroom, swiss, grilled onions every time.

You're not supposed to become friends with your sources. It's sound advice, kind of an unwritten rule, and something I was completely incapable of doing on the cops' beat.

Half the problem came from the nature of what I used to write about. Life, death, tragedy, corruption, blood … it all provoked a visceral reaction. Frank helped me do what I once believed was the most important job in the world. More often than not, the stories I wrote were the last that would ever be told about a person. Frank's intel helped me get them right, and in some cases, helped ensure they got told at all.

He seemed to believe in the same things I did, and he was a conversational ninja during those "just one more round" kind of nights back when we used to connect at bars on a regular basis. It was hard to keep him at arm's length.

And then there was the part I didn't like admitting. That cops like Frank made me forget about cops like Henniman. That when the job was done right, the boys in blue could still be what I thought they were when I was a kid: superheroes, just like the ones I watched on TV every Saturday morning. It's an unpopular stance these days, but it's one that stuck with me even when I wrote story after story about officers who were less inclined to serve and protect and more interested in serving their own needs, from the overtime thieves to the ones who just wanted a license to hit people.

Still, we both knew it was a transactional relationship. He'd retired from the department around the same time I'd been unceremoniously tossed out of the newsroom. When he went into private security and I went into being Henniman's lackey, we quickly ran low on things to talk about. After our last pained interaction, when we'd gotten together under the guise of catching up and mostly just stared at a college basketball game in silence, we'd both kept our distance.

My eyes wandered to the door when I saw what had to be the tallest man in the diner fill the vestibule and scan the room for me. Frank came from the cigar-chomping, conditioning-averse cop generation, but he didn't look it. Around 6'4 with well-defined but far from bulging arms, the ex-Rutgers University nose tackle still looked every bit the ass-kicker he'd been when he was knocking down doors and throwing hands with suspects in the South Ward.

He found me with little challenge, since his field of vision was basically the entire room.

"Wait, you own jeans?" I asked.

On the job, Frank wore one of four suits nearly every day, and I swore three of them were carbon copies of the same charcoal blazer and slacks.

"You're really giving me shit about fashion choices?" he shot back. "Aren't you the same guy who used to tell me that if I ever saw you in a suit…"

"It meant I was covering a funeral," I replied.

He smiled as a waitress came by, ordered a cup of coffee and sat down.

"What was so urgent?" he asked.

"What? No small talk? No catch-up? Don't we have to bullshit for a few minutes and pretend we care about one another?" I asked back.

"I miss you. I talk about you all the time. My wife's getting jealous," he replied.

"Asshole."

"You texted me in the middle of the night saying something was urgent Russ, so forgive me if I didn't ask you about the weather," he said.

"All I'm saying is it usually took a little flirting before you'd help me back in the day."

"I wasn't bored then," he replied, scratching his beard. "You know what retirement looks like for a gang cop? I run private security at an

111

event hall in Livingston. I keep drunk mistresses of wealthy men from contacting their wives and making them less wealthy. I stop kids from getting in slap fights and politely ask the one or two teens who need to smoke pot to cure their anxiety to keep it off the grounds. It's a long way from dragging heroin dealers and killers out of high-rises."

The waitress came by again. He ordered his burger, medium rare. I went with the same thing, out of nostalgia or a desire to punish my stomach further beyond the waterfall of coffee.

"Hey, being out to pasture's no peach for me either," I said.

"Yeah, how's your neck?" he asked. "Figure Henniman has that leash on you real tight."

Frank thought he was hilarious. He wasn't. But I laughed politely, because that's how you work sources. It was like an arcade game. Drop a quarter's worth of dignity into the machine and hope the claw grabs the big prize.

"You wanna be an asshole or you wanna find out what was so urgent?" I asked.

"I can multi-task."

"I can ask someone else for advice."

"Only if you want shitty advice," he replied. "Shoot."

I sipped my coffee, thought about this for a minute. Frank was trustworthy, and he'd been more than happy to leak me information on fuckery within Major Crimes when he was on the job. Excessive force complaints, dodgy tactics. Didn't hurt that, in exchange, I was also more than happy to pay extra attention to the hero stories that Frank played a role in. The heroin shipments intercepted and gun busts and gang sweeps that, if I'm being honest, didn't need the obsessive level of detail I painted them with. Cops doing their jobs was just as typical as the kind of West Ward drug murder I'd often grant two paragraphs of ink.

But the corruption stories were worth it, and Frank wasn't against

112

rooting people out of the unit who might one day embarrass the department.

He was also close to Henniman, closer than he'd ever been to me. They may have disagreed about policing, but they still loved the department that raised them. I wasn't sure how much to tell.

"I'm looking into a case," I said.

"For Henniman?"

"No."

"The plot thickens," he said.

"It might if you let me tell the damn story," I replied.

He raised his hands in mock surrender.

"Kid's dead. He was slinging, but unaffiliated. Considering where he fell, and how, it seemed like a drug thing. Family doesn't agree," I said. "Asked me to dig."

"You know better than that."

"I do. But I wanted a breather from all Henniman's bullshit," I replied. "So I start looking into the kid. Nothing too interesting. But I came across a bizarre street rumor in the process."

"How many times did you come to me with some intel you got from a crack baby or a Black Panther and I had to knock it down?" he asked.

I cringed at the phrasing. If my source was wrong, he had to be black.

"Plenty," I replied. "But there's something off here."

The waitress had the unfortunate timing of showing up with the burgers before I could finish my thought. She seemed to notice our conversation had frozen at an inopportune time and set the plates down before scuttling off without a word.

"And that is?" he asked.

I took a bite. Mulling how to phrase it.

"Why would a cop dime out a C.I.?" I asked.

"He wouldn't," Frank replied, laughing as he placed a hand on the bun. "Unless he was trying to get that C.I. killed."

Frank took a bite. I didn't say anything.

"Oh c'mon," Frank said, his words slightly muffled as he chewed. "You stopped writing the news and now you're watching it too much? Drunk on all this anti-cop hype?"

"Just humor me Frank," I said. "Short of murder…"

"You're seriously asking me this question?"

"You said you were bored."

"Not this bored," he replied.

Frank took another bite, a big, mauling, predatory one.

"Alright. Eliminating the very likely possibility that your source has no idea what the fuck he or she is talking about," he said. "There's a threat I would use sometimes. Never on a C.I., but on someone who wouldn't flip. Just a tactic for real hard cases. Tell them you're gonna put it in the air that they're informing, even if they aren't. Some of these guys, the all the way in types, they'd rather cough up someone they don't like then see their rep take a hit once I spread that kind of rumor. Sometimes they'd just get spooked by the real, lethal risk, that people believe they've gone informant. When it doesn't work, sometimes they bitch about it, talk about how they stood tall. My best guess? Maybe someone tried that on your dead kid, he complained about it, and here we are."

"And if you're wrong?" I asked.

"How many times did you have to run a correction on something I gave you?"

"Almost never," I replied.

"Almost?"

"You told me the wrong set once when two gang members got hooked up for a double murder," I said. "You said they were Hoover Five-Deuce. They were Grape Street."

114

"Grape Street's Los Angeles. How was I supposed to know there were two West Coast idiots lost in our fair city," he replied. "And if that's the worst I ever did..."

Frank had a point. His hunches weren't gospel, but they weren't too far off.

I started eating again. Frank hadn't been as helpful as I'd hoped. If he knew what was going on, if he'd heard something from Henniman or was inclined to help here, he'd have let that slip by now.

"So that's all you asked me here for, advice?" he asked.

"Mostly," I said.

"What else?"

"How bored are you at this new job?" I asked. "Like, you need to hit the bar after work more often bored? Or mid-life crisis let's do some crazy shit bored?"

"Don't ask me to help you with this," he said.

"I'd very much like it if you helped me with this."

"Don't do polite. It's weird on you," he said. "Also, no."

That was quick.

"What happened to the Frank who helped me root out shit cops? Who was about the right thing, no matter who got dinged up in the process?"

"He got a pension," Frank replied. "And you got a new job."

"We are who we are," I said. "You're gonna honestly sit here and tell me I didn't make you curious?"

"Of course, you made me curious. I'm retired. I'm not dead," he said. "But aside from the fact that you've got nothing more than a rumor and a brain that's susceptible to conspiracy theory, you're not looking at the big picture here."

"Something shitty may have happened. I wanna know more," I said. "That's all that's it ever used to take."

"Yeah, back before the world changed. What you're hinting at, that doesn't happen in a vacuum. I remember all the street activists you were tight with. You raise this with the wrong person, start the wrong rumor, and this city becomes CNN headquarters. YouTube videos and marches. I have no desire to see car fires on Broad Street," he replied. "Not to mention, the job's changed. You can't make war on the department one week and hope to still have friends there the next. Everyone's tribal now. They don't see critics, they see barbarians at the gate. You run a P.I. business that mostly caters to cops. Unless you plan on becoming independently wealthy sometime soon, that's a problem. And do I need to state the obvious?"

I stayed quiet, letting him know that he did.

"On the slim chance you're right, and some cop did publicly burn a C.I., that means they were OK with someone getting killed to keep something quiet. What do you think they're gonna do once they find out you're looking to dig up what they want to keep buried?"

The thought had crossed my mind, but it felt different hearing someone else say it. Sad part was, I was a little excited about the idea that I might matter enough again for someone in Newark to want me dead.

"I don't know Frank," I said. "We've both been in some pretty dangerous situations. You way more than me. Never stopped us before."

Frank shook his head and looked up at the ceiling, like maybe he'd find some way to communicate it better up there.

"Listen Russ, I get it. You miss the old days, so do I. But I had a department behind me then. You had the paper. We had certain protections. You know what we have now? A lot to lose and a little to gain. We're citizens. We're out," he said. "It's someone else's job to give a shit."

***

The hardest part of cracking a story isn't learning something you're not supposed to know, it's figuring out when you can share that something.

Journalists are notoriously terrible at keeping secrets. It's why no one can even think about sleeping with a fellow reporter without an entire newsroom knowing all your kinks. There's some primal desire to be the town crier buried deep in our genetic code. I broke my first story when I was eight. Overheard my mother say the assistant coach of our third-grade basketball team had died. My whole class knew before the bell rang the next day. My teachers were not pleased.

I've had a hard time keeping my mouth shut since.

The piece of information Levon had given me after I went all enhanced interrogation on him could have been huge, or it could have been useless. But I wanted to tell someone nonetheless. Someone besides Frank. Someone who believed it meant something. I could feel it running around under my skin, begging for release.

If a cop had really told a Bloods gang member that Kevin Mathis was a snitch, it made his father's story a lot more plausible. At the very least, it pushed "drug beef" down the list of potential motives for the kid's death. If he was actually talking to the cops, that made his death a witness murder. If he wasn't, but a police officer wanted people to think he was, that meant someone in the department wanted Mathis dead.

Either way, Levon's tip and the meeting with Frank were the bad doses I needed.

Austin Mathis was officially my client. Now I just needed to tell him that before Key shot it all to hell.

I was sitting inside Jackie's Bakery, the Spanish equivalent of a greasy spoon along the stretch of Broad Street that spilled into Route 21. Key and Austin were on their way, demanding an update on my investigation, and I'd ordered enough food to make sure I had a safety valve in case I started talking too much. I wasn't hungry, especially after the burgers with Frank, but the plate of pork empanadas in front of me was more of an "in case of emergency" thing.

I was bad at keeping secrets. Key was straight up allergic to it. If she knew what Levon had told me, if she got even the smallest, ill-fitting, puzzle piece to a police conspiracy, she'd be outside City Hall with a megaphone the next day. This situation did not need that kind of light, not yet anyway, because you can't kill a giant when it's looking right at you.

If I was going to dig into Kevin's murder as a potential police misconduct thing, stealth was going to be critical. The minute anything like this went public, information would freeze up. It might prompt a prosecutor's office review. At the very least, it would make people think three or four or five times before talking to me.

Oh, and there was Henniman, who would try and grind me into paste if he thought I was coming after his unit.

There was also the possibility that Levon was lying. Or that the person who talked to him was lying about being a cop. Or that the whole "Kevin is a snitch" thing was the same kind of nonsense rumor that had sent plenty of men to their graves in Newark before, the kind of wrong-headed info Frank had protected me from in the past. All I had was a tip, a whisper. Something I needed time to confirm, time Key wouldn't afford me if I filled her in.

She'd already threatened to let Austin go public once, and that cell phone video his son took could have easily turned Newark into a tinderbox.

The city's residents and police had been operating under an uneasy truce since 1967, when a race riot blew the Bricks apart and left 26 people dead and countless more injured. The city caught fire after two white cops arrested and beat a black cab driver in public before dragging him inside the 4th Precinct, the one that patrolled the West Ward. A rumor spread that the cab driver had died. He hadn't. But at that point the truth gave way to years of repressed anger in the neighborhood, and things got real ugly, real fast.

They called in the National Guard. They had rifles. The residents didn't.

Plenty had changed since then, and plenty hadn't. The police force was more diverse now, and the rank-and-file looked like the community it policed, with minority officers making up the majority of the roster. But things still went wrong. Force was used when it shouldn't have. People still felt like they were unfairly targeted even when the people doing the targeting looked familiar. The stats agreed with the community, with the percentage of black males getting stopped and searched far ahead of their census representation. The ACLU had filed lawsuit after lawsuit and drafted a petition asking the Department of Justice to investigate the NPD. The feds being the feds, were taking their sweet time deciding what to do.

With all that kindling piling up, I was looking into the death of a black kid, possibly at the hands of the cops, in the same neighborhood where the match was lit 50 years before.

If this story was going to end with history repeating itself, I needed to make sure that story was accurate.

Key and Austin Mathis stepped through the door, both pausing to shake the cold out of their bones before cutting across the room to my table. Key was rocking her usual whatever wasn't in the hamper fashion, with an oversized blue coat covering a black sweatshirt and faded straight line jeans. Austin was one big bruise, black cap and shoes sandwiching an all navy pants and shirt ensemble, and it took me a second to realize it was his NJ Transit uniform. Poor man was either coming in from a shift or heading out on one, using what little free time he had to discuss his son's death with me.

"So, what'd you find out?" he asked, beating Key to the table.

Her face twisted up somewhere between amusement and annoyance. She wasn't used to being the passenger in a conversation.

"Some stuff, not enough yet. I'll get there in a minute," I replied,

119

doing my best to look friendly for him before hardening my gaze and turning toward Key. "First we gotta talk about something."

Key met my pissed off stare with equal menace.

"We didn't come here for a lecture," she said.

"But you're gonna get one anyway," I replied, keeping an edge to my voice before turning back to Austin. "Listen, I know you're hurting. I know you want answers. But it's going to be a lot harder for me to get them if there's a million eyes watching. Now Key told me you were thinking about going public with that video on Kevin's phone. I understand why you may think that's a good idea, but I'm hoping you'll let me explain to you why it's not."

Key's eyes were wide, tongue pushing at her bottom lip like it wanted to leap out, but Austin just nodded and said "OK."

"I've already pissed off a few people asking about this. I'm nowhere close to knowing what happened to your son, but I'm pretty close to agreeing with you that it wasn't a simple drug murder," I said. "But if I'm going to play this out, I'm going to need to work with some of the cops, maybe against some others. I'm going to be talking to people involved in the part of your son's life you weren't exactly proud of. That's hard enough on its own, it gets a lot tougher if there are TV cameras around and official inquiries and what have you. When that happens, case files get sealed and people stop talking, and then you're waiting months instead of days to find out why your son is dead, if you ever find out at all. Neither of us wants that. Do you understand where I'm coming from?"

"I do," he replied, his voice sounding like it was too tired to make sounds. "But you need to understand where I'm coming from as well."

"Fair enough," I said.

"I've been taking double shifts since this happened, half to keep from going crazy sitting around, the other half to scrape together enough money to bury my boy properly," he said. "The funeral's in a few days, and I have family coming in from Detroit. When they get here, they're gonna ask why we're burying family. And I have to tell them something, a story that makes sense. Cause if I don't, well, they'll know what it means. I cannot have my family thinking my son died that way, looking at me like I failed, like I let him get into a life he couldn't get out of. I can't have them remembering him like that. I saw what they wrote up in the paper, or what they barely wrote. Like it was nothing. Like it was supposed to happen that way, so it wasn't news. I can't …"

He trailed off, eyes welling up.

"I won't let that be his story," he continued. "You do what you have to. I know you're trying, and I appreciate that, but sooner or later, I may do what I have to do as well."

I looked to Key, waiting for some kind of follow-up, but she had her eyes down in her phone. She was texting somebody, thumbs moving like pistons.

I didn't like what he was saying, but I respected it. A counter-argument started forming on my tongue, so I jammed an empanada in my mouth so it couldn't do anything stupid.

We sat there like that for a minute or two: Austin taking big nasal breaths and blinking away the tears I imagined had been with him for days, me chewing on grease and wondering how much to tell him and how much to withhold.

I waited for Key to kick start the conversation, but she was still in her phone, which was making me uncomfortable. I'd been caught in the eye of her mass text hurricanes before, but she'd never wandered down a cellular rabbit hole when we were meeting face-to-face.

"So," I said, tapping two fingers against her edge of the table to get her attention. "Let me tell you where we are."

Austin folded his hands under his chin and sat straight up, attentive. Key locked eyes with me but kept glancing back down at the phone.

121

"Kevin was dealing. You know that," I said. "But I asked around and it seems like he had some kind of arrangement with a local player, guy who runs the neighborhood where…"

I stopped. I still felt uncomfortable stating the fact, like that would make it less true.

"Where he died," Austin said, somehow handling this better than me.

"Right," I continued. "What I'm saying is that if Kevin had carte blanche to do business there, it's unlikely someone from a rival set would have come in and done this. If they had, that crew would have hit back, and as far as I know, that hasn't happened. So that part of your story, I buy. As far as that video you have, I did ask some cop friends about it. Seems Internal Affairs didn't know it existed. Now that doesn't totally discount your theory Austin, but I obviously would have a hard time believing that a cop killed your son over a video they didn't know he had. I need to find out more about that. I need time."

I paused, waiting to see if he had any reaction, giving myself a minute to figure out what to say next. He didn't need to know about the shooter being part of Henniman's squad, or Henniman being at his son's murder scene long after he had any reason to be. Those facts were troubling, but I didn't know what they meant yet. Without context, that information was a time bomb.

"There was also a rumor going around about Kevin in the neighborhood where he worked," I said. "I just need to ask … do you have any idea if your son ever cut any deals with police or prosecutors?"

"Deals?" he asked.

"You know what I'm saying, Austin. He'd been arrested. I pulled his rap sheet. His prison stints were always curiously short," I said. "Do you know if he ever gave up any information on other dealers, about other crimes?"

"How the hell would I know that?" he asked. "Things he did …

wasn't like he came home and talked about work."

"Alright, well … some people seem to think he was snitching. And I don't need to tell you how easy a rumor like that could have led to all this," I said. "I need to find out if there's any truth to it. I'm going to assume you have a number for your son's lawyer."

"Which one?" Austin asked. "Every time he got in trouble, the public defender's office would just send someone else down."

Of course. Austin Mathis didn't have the money to pay for a private attorney, and as swamped as the public defender's office was, they had probably rotated in a different lawyer every time Kevin got arrested.

"Alright, I'll look back through the records and find out whoever repped your son on the last case. I'll also see what else I can find out about the shooting on that cell phone video," I said. "But again, that's going to take a little time. So just to be clear, nothing public, at least until we talk again, OK?"

Austin nodded. Key was still in her goddamn phone.

"Key who the hell are you talking too?" I asked. "You spent four days calling me nonstop and now you don't say a word?"

"Not a whole lot to say," she replied, not even looking up. "He's the client, not me. You two play it how you want. But you know where I stand. Something terrible happened in that video, and it might have something to do with something else terrible that happened to his son. These are the kind of things people need to know, so they stop pretending it's just one incident in one city every now and again. This happened here. Where we live. Where we sleep. People should be out there talking about it, raising their voices. But you want it kept quiet so it makes your job easier."

"And you want it on a front page so people start coming out to your weekly rallies again," I spat back, immediately regretting it.

Her eyes widened like they always did when she got angry, like she'd been hit with a caffeine jolt. At least she'd finally put the phone down.

"I don't want people in the streets so I can be some kind of local celebrity, Russell. I want them out there because there's things happening in this city every day, things like what's on that video, that people need to stand up and speak on," she said. "Don't lecture me about what you don't understand. This doesn't happen to your neighbors, your relatives."

Austin touched Key's wrist in a weak effort to calm her down, but it seemed to be enough.

"We'll call you in a couple of days," he said.

He started to get up to leave but Key was still fuming, still locked onto me, clenching her teeth as if to hold in more venom. We were both holding something back.

I looked down at the cell phone. She snatched it away, but not before I noticed the text messages she had been furiously typing, an exchange of big block paragraphs with a contact whose name wasn't saved.

All I saw was a phone number. It was all I needed to see.

I'd committed Dina's digits to memory a long time ago.

***

The shriek of car horns forced me to stop punching Dina's number into my phone as I drove away from Broad Street. Apparently, I'd run a red light and the truck driver who was kind enough not to broadside me was not happy about it.

"If you're calling to apologize don't waste your time," she said.

"I already apologized for what happened at Court Tavern," I replied, deciding to actually obey the next traffic signal.

"Not really, and that's not what I'm talking about."

"I haven't even seen you since then!"

"And yet, you're still causing me headaches," she replied. "This is why I have that rule about not staying friends with exes."

I'd pissed a lot of people off in the past few days, or even hours, but I was having a hard time recalling a second sin committed against Dina.

"Why'd you visit the office?" she asked.

Oh, right. That.

"It's a long story," I said.

"Next time you need to sneak back into the place you got fired from, don't use my name to do it."

"Look, I'm genuinely sorry about that, but that's not the reason I called," I said. "Why are you talking to Keyonna Jackson?"

"That's none of your business."

The light changed, and I weaved into the bus lane and around the crush of traffic where Market split from Springfield. I had another lead to chase down, and if Dina was in touch with Key, I needed to do it quickly.

"Dina, I don't know what you're doing, but I'm involved in something that you don't…"

"That's none of my business either, Russ," she said. "And please tell me you're not about to lecture me on how my actions might affect you. You didn't seem to care so much when the roles were reversed a few nights ago."

"You don't need to convince me I was an asshole the other night Dina," I said. "I was an asshole. And I was an asshole for using your name when I went back by the newsroom too. I'm guilty as charged on all asshole counts. But I'm looking into a thing with Key that is extremely sensitive and if it ends up in the paper…"

"Another lecture on the job now," she said. "You ever get tired of repeating yourself?"

"Why did you call her, Dina?"

"I didn't, actually," she replied. "Not that I care about alleviating your paranoia, but she called me. To talk about a story that I already ran. A story Greene was suddenly interested in after your visit. She had some follow-up information. That's all."

"What story?"

"Buy the paper, Russell," she replied. "And the next time you call me, it had better be to give info, not get some. That's how this whole source-reporter thing works."

She hung up just as I pulled into the parking lot of the Essex County Veteran's Courthouse.

I didn't know what Dina had published, but if she was talking to Key, and Key was itching to go public with the video from Kevin Mathis' phone, I knew what she would eventually publish. The only way to stop that was to find something that would convince Key and Austin I was moving in the right direction, that I was their best shot at figuring out why Kevin was dead.

I had two leads, neither terribly promising, but it was better than nothing.

I needed to get something useful out of Mathis' lawyer, or the cop who opened fire in the video on his phone. The former seemed like the path of least resistance, and I'd had enough resistance for one week, so the courthouse was my next stop.

After skimming Kevin's court records again, I realized his father wasn't as knowledgeable about his son's legal situation as he thought he was. While most of Kevin's cases saw him ride the public defender carousel, the same attorney had represented him on his last three runs through the criminal justice system, including the two oxy cases where he miraculously managed to avoid jail time. The attorney's name was Eddie Lazio.

The public defender's office didn't take requests, so there had to be a reason Lazio and Mathis were paired up that many times in a row. Maybe it had something to do with Kevin's rumored snitching. Maybe it was another puzzle piece I couldn't see.

I half-walked, half-jogged out of the parking lot toward the tall glass doors that led to the security checkpoint at the entrance to the courthouse. The line wasn't bad that morning, so I breezed past the metal detectors and dipped left toward the elevator bay, careful to keep my head down. I'd been a regular in the building for years and didn't love the idea of Henniman or any of his friends in the prosecutor's office bumping into me and wondering why I'd chosen the aftermath of Kevin's death for a return visit. NPD's major case unit worked closely with the prosecutor's V.I.P.E.R. squad, a gang and drug interdiction task force that was a nexus for powerful police in Essex County. It was a prestige assignment. People who went into that unit didn't leave often, and most of them knew my face.

Lazio was on the docket three times, representing defendants accused of a diverse spread of stupidity. He had an arraignment for a domestic violence defendant on the third floor, a motion hearing for a drug suspect an hour later two floors above that, and a status conference for a sad sack lewd conduct case to finish the day.

Arraignment court is an actual circle of hell, since no one ever gets called on time and the docket rarely follows any sort of alphabetical or logical order. I had plenty of time to grab a copy of the *Intelligencer* and figure out what Dina had written to spark Key's interest.

I didn't have to search for too long.

While a Trenton story led the paper, Dina's byline was tucked neatly beneath the fold, atop a piece on Newark's surging yearly homicide count. I'd lost track of the city's murder stats because I couldn't tolerate the paper most days, but apparently Newark was on pace to see its annual homicide total surge into the triple digits. It would be the first time in at least five years that homicides climbed above the century mark, and Newark's popular mayor, who everyone expected would run forSenator soon, had declined comment for the story, probably because he was too busy strangling the police director to pick up the phone.

Dina's piece placed the blame on an increase in drug-related killings, driven by an influx of guns into the state from Pennsylvania and Ohio, a stock excuse that could have applied to any year at any time. The article also highlighted a recent string of shootings on the West and South sides, about ten in the span of two weeks.

Kevin Mathis' shooting was mentioned, the last in a "wave of senseless drug-motivated violence," according to Lt. Bill Henniman of the Newark Police Department's Major Crimes Unit.

"Shit," I said out loud, earning a few bemused stares as I entered the courtroom where Lazio was scheduled to make his first appearance of the day.

Now Dina and Key's contact was even more troubling. The old activist must have seen Henniman's version of events and started sharing her own. Dina wouldn't be able to print on Key's word alone, and when she pushed Key for more, Key would turn over the video and the city would go to hell on a skateboard.

The sound of a gavel forced me to put down the paper and stop panicking as the court was called to order. At least things were getting started. Hopefully Lazio would show up soon, and I could do something to stop the approaching storm.

The first case the judge called involved a Stephen Banks, and I recognized the name from the court docket. It was Lazio's client. Maybe things were turning around.

"And I assume Mr. Lazio won't be joining us today," the judge said as soon as I finished forming that happy thought.

Someone else, a younger woman who couldn't have been more than two years out of law school, stood up and announced that she would be standing in for Lazio. Maybe he was just running late? Either way, I had less than no reason to suffer through a nothing court proceeding if Lazio wasn't going to be in the room. I snatched up the paper and headed to the fifth floor, where he was supposed to be representing a drug defendant in less than an hour.

But the same scenario played out. The judge called the defendant's name and then simply acknowledged Lazio was missing in action, like his absence was normal.

I headed back downstairs for the lewd conduct case to wait for Lazio's last scheduled appearance of the day, fully expecting to hear strike three called. I only had to wait two hours for the judge there to confirm my shit luck. I'd burned half my day for nothing. Sure, I could find Lazio's home address or go to the public defender's office and ask to speak with him, but those were low percentage shots and I was short on time.

I stood up to leave after Lazio's replacement began to speak and noticed someone else had moved in the gallery at the exact same time.

"Colleen?" I asked as the head of the Newark Police Department's Internal Affairs unit tried to move past me.

She didn't even look at me, but I didn't take well to being ignored.

"Colleen?" I asked again. "What are you doing here?"

That came out louder than expected, probably because I was talking in an otherwise silent courtroom. I turned around to notice the judge was less than thrilled with my outburst, hitting me with a death stare for injecting some life into her otherwise droll proceedings. I turned back to find Colleen giving me the same look, but at least now she was paying attention to me.

"Aren't reporters supposed to be discreet?" she asked as we stepped out into the hallway.

"I'm not a reporter anymore."

"What are you doing here?" she asked.

"I asked first."

"I hate you."

"I'm getting that a lot these days," I said. "So, what are you doing here?"

"Nothing of interest to you, and nothing I can talk about anyway," she said.

"That, in and of itself, is interesting."

"Goodbye Russell," she said.

Colleen started walking away, past a trio of detectives I thought I recognized from the gang unit. She ducked their gaze the same way she ducked mine, so I decided to press.

"It's just a coincidence that you got up to leave the same time I did?" I asked, louder than I needed too. "Just when we both figured out a certain someone wasn't in court."

She spun on her heel, a perfect academy-approved about face, and charged right back toward me.

"Do you have an off switch?" she asked.

"Nope."

"Are you going to keep causing a scene every time I try to ignore you?"

"Yep."

"What do you want, Russell?"

"To talk to this Eddie Lazio guy," I replied. "Seems like you do too. Mind telling me why?"

"Yes, I mind, but it doesn't matter anyway," she said. "As you might have noticed, he's not around."

"Sounds like we need to find him then."

"I need to find him," she said. "You need to stop giving me a migraine."

"Well, then maybe we can help each other," I said.

Colleen ran a hand through her hair with enough force that she almost broke her pony tail loose.

"We already did that Russell, remember? And that ended with you pushing me for information I really should not have given you. I appreciated the favor, but now you're making me regret it."

Whatever goodwill I'd earned by taking care of her ex had clearly been spent. I needed to trade her something.

"What if I go first this time," I said.

"What?"

"I'll tell you why I'm looking for Lazio, maybe you help me with something else in return?"

"Are you not listening? The last time we traded in unnamed favors, it ended in you threatening me."

"It wasn't a threat. And it's still a real problem that I'm trying to head off, but if I don't make some real progress, that video is going to make it out into the air," I said. "Neither of us want that."

"And that still sounds like a threat," she said.

"Just hear me out, Colleen. If you're sitting in arraignment court hoping Lazio pops up, I'm guessing that means you haven't been able to find him through the normal means? Like his house, other properties, checking for credit card use."

"That's not a bad guess."

"You need a different way in."

"You could say that," she said.

"And if I told you I've been in contact with one of his former clients …"

"Then I'd say it's your turn to give me a name," she said.

"I can't do that."

"Then what the hell are you wasting my time for?"

"They're not exactly trusting of law enforcement right now. If I send you their way, they're going to wall us both off and then we'll be back here with our dicks in our hands."

She narrowed her eyes at me.

"Well you know what I mean … it would sound weird if I said…"

"You write better than you talk," she said.

"All I'm saying is, the longer I stay on this client, the better chance I run into this Lazio character. If I find him, I have no problem telling you where and when."

"And in exchange for you maybe giving me something useful down the line, you want?" she asked.

"To talk to Mike Lowell," I said.

"Let me get this straight … you give me nothing, and in return I help you get in contact with the officer involved in a shooting I'm investigating? The same officer whose name I wasn't supposed to give you in the first place?"

"I'm aware of how shitty that sounds, but it doesn't look like either of us has a better option. You need to find this Lazio guy. You also need this video to stay off the 11 o'clock news, and I can't keep that from happening without fresh intel. Lazio and Lowell are my only leads. If I go back to these people empty handed, both of our lives get worse."

She looked up and down the hallway, then took my arm, pulling me toward a payphone bank near the restrooms that nobody used.

"If you find Lazio, you do not go near him. You call me immediately, you understand? If you screw that up, or that video goes public, do not expect any more favors from me," she said.

I nodded.

"You should go by Hanley's tonight. Lowell plays in a darts tournament there every week, like clockwork. You know Hanley's, right?"

It was Newark's largest cop bar. Frank used to go there all the time.

Henniman and his boys still did.

CHAPTER 9

Few cop bars are as blatant about it as Hanley's.

The place occupied a piece of prime real-estate on the corner of Central Avenue but seemed to work actively to keep the Rutgers-Newark and NJIT kids from spending their parent's money inside. Giant replicas of Newark police shields and fire department crests stained the front windows. Inside, the old, splintering redwood bar and barely operational lighting made it seem like the perfect place for a detective to drink his sorrows away in the second act of a bad novel. It wasn't exclusively populated by cops, but it wasn't a great place to voice your opinions on Black Lives Matter or criminal justice reform either. Unless you had a vendetta against your own teeth.

Hanley's was the rank-and-file watering hole. Most of the command staff drank in the plastic-wrapped wannabe gastropubs around the Prudential Center, or one of the pricier tapas spots in the Ironbound. Or, just like anyone else who had money in the city, they got the fuck out of Newark at 5 o'clock and held their evenings somewhere that made it hard to see the poverty line. Millburn, Short Hills, Morris County, wherever.

I'd only been inside of Hanley's a few times, with Frank. He was just about the only cop I knew who was well-liked enough to get away with bringing a reporter inside.

133

Son and grandson of Newark police, Frank was basically raised by the agency. He went to high school in the city, played college football at Rutgers, then came home because the pro scouts don't care about second-string nose tackles from the Big East.

But the guy with an almost jingoistic Jersey pride fit right in doing his father's work. He wasn't a test-taker, but it wasn't for lack of intelligence. While he'd made his name slamming down doors as part of a narcotics task force, he wasn't the kind of cop who saw community policing as an academic buzzword meant to destroy law enforcement either. He built rapports with the victims of the crimes he investigated, he'd let people walk on small stuff, put the fear of god in them once instead of effecting an arrest that might ensure they'd meet like that again.

His fists made him popular with a decent share of cops, but it was Frank's brain that won over people like me.

Not that those fists didn't get him into trouble. An excessive force beef here and there, one that sparked a lawsuit. But the guy who filed on him was a Megan's Law offender, someone whose face I didn't mind seeing turned to hamburger.

Maybe it helped that he was willing to trade me information on a bigger scandal as well, a corruption probe into another member of Henniman's crew. The kind of guy whose problems I fixed for Henniman now.

Frank wasn't perfect, but he was closer to what I hoped a cop could be than the wrong-headed lawmen I sometimes crossed. I wasn't going to fix the whole agency from a newsroom, and at least Frank helped me laze targets that mattered.

It was funny. Back when Frank was helping me earn a reputation as a thorn in the department's side, I needed him as a shield to even enter Hanley's. Now, I was hoping the opposite rep I'd earned as a fixer for Henniman's boys would keep anyone from getting too concerned with my presence.

At least I until I started talking to Lowell.

I still wasn't all that sure what I was even supposed to ask. Pointed questions weren't exactly practical given the venue. But I was out of leads. Hopefully I'd at least be able to get a sense of the guy, who he hung out with, whether or not he was a devout member of Henniman's flock.

I walked in, headed straight to the bar and ordered an amber ale. Figured it'd best to go easy. The TVs behind the bar were broadcasting a Knicks game, and a few guys were yelling at the screens. I nodded at the bartender, a long-haired amicable guy with a neck tattoo who went by B-Man, and he handed me a flight of darts after a brief "hey, how are ya" exchange.

I took my beer and headed to the second floor, where all the pool tables and dartboards were. The tournament or league or whatever it was started at 8 p.m., and I'd arrived an hour early, hoping Lowell was the type to prepare.

When I turned the corner from the staircase, I found a guy with short cropped black hair and a slightly noticeable scar on his right cheek towing the line near one of the boards, flicking missile after missile into the black triangle under the number 20. He was in a black tee-shirt with the bar's name across the back and slightly faded blue jeans. After the courthouse, I'd spent a couple minutes searching through the Newark FOP's Facebook page, long enough to get an idea of what Detective Mike Lowell looked like.

I sunk against a wall behind him, placing my beer on a corner table far enough away from any of the other small groups floating around, and watched Lowell for a bit. He was good, efficient, grouping his shots tightly in each of the areas you'd need to hit to win a Cricket matchup. Three darts into the 20. Another three into 19. He finally missed twice when he started in on the 18s but caught a triple ring on his third throw and erased the prior errors.

The three darts I'd brought up from downstairs rolled back and forth in my palm. It had been a while since I'd thrown, but I quickly realized that might help. Hey, if women could pretend they didn't know how to shoot pool to reel a guy in, why couldn't I do the same thing with a dartboard? Source development was just flirtation anyway.

I stepped to the line next to his board, watched his form, then tried to do the exact opposite. My first shot hit the chalkboard meant for scorekeeping, and I tried to convince myself that was simply part of the act. A few sets of eyes turned my way as I fired a second shot. This one at least hit the board.

He didn't seem bothered by my spastic attempts. Hell, he didn't even seem to notice. The guy was all focus, like he was preparing to throw in Game 7 of the World Series, not a Newark cop bar dart tournament. I watched his form again, the effortless wrist flick, the almost annoyingly controlled breathing. In response, I started to bounce a little bit before my next shot, dipped my knees like I was taking a free throw. I unleashed an arcing toss that actually fell neatly into the corner of the 20, just above the green bullseye ring. Maybe I was getting better by osmosis.

"Nice grouping," I said as I watched Lowell bury another trio of darts into the same part of the board.

He grumbled a "thanks" as he plucked the darts out and walked back to the line.

"I gotta learn your form," I said, deciding to talk my way through his obvious disinterest. "I feel like I start out OK but then..."

I let another looping shot loose, watching it sail like a paper airplane and dive into the black at the bottom of the board for a whopping zero points.

"You're moving too much," he said, still only scanning me on the peripheral, letting off another series of deadeye attempts.

"What do you mean?" I asked, bending my knees for another shot.

Out of either genuine politeness or a desire to stop me from committing further dart-related crimes, Lowell mercifully tapped me on the shoulder and froze my throwing motion.

"Watch," he said, stepping back to his spot. "Line it up before you throw."

He took his stance, one foot on the line, the other a full step behind and to the left.

"You're not shooting a basketball. It's a straight shot, no dip. Breathe and…"

He flicked his wrist, keeping the rest of his body rigid, the dart embedding itself into the fat part of the 20 section. He nodded, and I watched as he moved another dart in his hand and did the same thing to the 19.

"Damn man, you're like the Terminator with those," I said.

"Just play a lot."

"Well, I'm sure all that time at the range doesn't hurt."

He stopped mid-motion.

"This is a cop bar right? Oh, and I saw the gun," I said, pointing to the bulge on his hip. "Sorry, I'm not really from here and I'm kind of observant and my cousin warned me that I talk too damn much."

He dipped out of his throwing stance and stepped to me, sized me up and then let a little smile creep to the corner of his mouth.

"Guess that shot's not the only thing about you that's jumpy," he said.

I met him with a nervous laugh. It was part of the act, I swear.

"My name's Russ," I said extending a hand.

He eyed me like I was something strange.

"Mike," he said.

Well, we'd made it to first-name basis without anyone handing me my ass, so I was counting that as a win. I looked around for a reason to extend our newfound friendship and noticed an empty beer glass at the table near the spot where he'd been carving up the dartboard.

"You uh, need a refill? I was gonna head down anyway, Knicks are on."

"So you like misery too?"

Self-deprecation? Definitely a Knicks fan. I thanked the source-building gods for common ground.

"Ha, yeah. Mom gave me the curse," I said. "She had a thing for Dave DeBusschere and I grew up during the Ewing years."

"Uncle did the same thing to me," he said. "But it was that Allan Houston shot in 1999, against the Heat. Nearly tore down his apartment in Nutley."

"Nutley?" I asked. "Shouldn't you be a Nets fan?"

"You've seen the Nets play, right?"

He snatched up his empty glass and we headed back to the bar, finding two seats just to the left of the taps. I ordered up another beer but he called for a bourbon on the rocks. Either he had a lot on his mind or he was just the kind of asshole who only ordered hard liquor on other people's rounds.

We fell into an easy conversation about hoop as the Knicks struggled to stay within 10 points of the visiting Oklahoma City Thunder. The usual sports fan complaining ensued: he didn't like how "no one played real defense" anymore. We both lamented draft picks traded away and misspent. I suggested that if someone were to drag the Knicks owner, James Dolan, out of his office and bang his head off every hot dog cart in Manhattan, no jury in the five boroughs would reasonably convict.

It went on like that for a while. The game moved to halftime, with the Knicks down by 12 thanks in part to an aversion to defense, and then the TV jump cut to a breaking news item.

Someone had been shot in Louisiana. Black man, done in by a white cop. Sgt. Whoever, spokesman for the Baton Rouge Police

Department, told the local media that the suspect had a gun, but several cable networks had obtained cell phone footage that seemed to suggest otherwise. The raw video was as ugly as it was unclear.

It was a mad-lib of every controversial shooting that had come before in the past two years, the same sad set of facts listed in a different order. I was starting to have trouble telling them apart, and that seemed to signal a problem in and of itself.

A collective groan went through the room, and I turned to see what had to be a platoon of off-duty cops all beginning to make the case for why the dead man definitely had a gun. One of them was particularly portly, wearing the kind of forced tough guy sneer that looked like it had been practiced in a mirror.

It was Scannell, the half-bright and fully corrupt cop I'd helped out of an Internal Affairs beef a few days earlier. Of course, he'd assume the cop couldn't be wrong.

Not that there was much in-depth analysis happening on the other side of the aisle either. Somewhere in Louisiana, people were taking to the streets convinced of the gospel fact that there was no way this man they had never met or heard of had a weapon. The cops had to be lying, because that's what they do.

Nobody actually knew a damn thing, but facts are no match for tribalism.

Lowell swallowed the rest of his bourbon and seemed ready for another.

"How do you deal with it?" I asked.

"Deal with what?"

"That," I said, pointing to the TV, which was showing stock footage of other protests in other cities caused by the same thing happening too damn often.

"Bourbon helps," he said, flashing a quick sad smile. "But for the most part I just ignore it. People got opinions. They can express them.

139

I still have a job to do."

Well that was … level-headed? I had expected Lowell to be like everyone else in the bar, meeting the idea of criticism with a reflexive eye roll.

"Yeah but this can't make it any easier. I mean you're putting your life on the line every day and these guys don't show any appreciation for it," I replied, both disturbed and impressed at my ability to sound like Henniman.

"Listen, I'm not about to get out there in the streets with them. And the ones out there shouting "pig," shouting about bringing down the whole system, yeah, I could live without that," he said. "But they're out there because someone's dead, and even if that shoot is righteous, it doesn't mean I raise a drink and celebrate when it's over. Right and wrong don't mean much when the day ends in a funeral."

The bartender drowned the ice in Lowell's glass with three fingers of bourbon, then looked at me funny when he saw my second beer was still nearly full. I waived him off and tried to figure out who I was talking to.

"Yeah, but you guys still gotta go home at the end of the day, right?" I asked.

He took another sip, placed the glass down slow and rocked his head back and forth, a quiet nod that seemed to signal yes. Then he went somewhere, staring off at nothing.

"Yeah, we do," he said. "And we gotta deal with how we got home. And what it might take to get home again."

This guy didn't pray at the same church as Henniman, which made me wonder how he'd lasted in Major Crimes so long in the first place. The Lieutenant only surrounded himself with true believers, cop's cops, thin blue line and all that. Lowell seemed particularly bothered by the idea that he'd shot someone, and suddenly, I questioned the part of my brain that thought he wouldn't be.

Lowell checked his watch then patted his jeans' pocket, revealing a pack of what looked like Camel Golds. Bourbon and smokes were how I'd marked most nights in this bar with Frank, and Lowell was making me yearn for those days again.

"Gonna sneak one before the tourney starts," he said.

"Mind if I follow?"

"Same bad habit?" he asked.

"Nah, not anymore," I replied. "But I still like the smell of it."

"I know all Knicks fans are masochists, but you're taking it a little far," he said, motioning for me to follow.

I did miss the smell. But I also needed to keep this conversation going.

Lowell lit up barely a step-and-a-half out the door, like the cigarette would somehow fly away if he didn't take a drag as soon as possible.

He turned to face me and took drag number two but said nothing. Guess he was waiting on me to resume the conversation. I probably should have left at that point. I'd heard enough out of Lowell to at least shift my antennae toward Henniman and the missing lawyer for the time being, and I really couldn't ask anything else that wouldn't make him suspicious of this all-too inquisitive barfly.

Lowell took drag number three, and this time the smoke hit me right on the nostrils and woke up all the parts of my brain that liked to kick the shit out of my inhibitions. I really wanted a cigarette. I really wanted to ask him more questions. Neither one would be good for my health.

"You ever have to do it?" I asked.

Lowell cocked his head to the side.

"Do what?" he asked.

"Shoot someone."

The expression on his face made me wish I'd just taken the damn smoke instead.

141

He flicked the cigarette toward the street, catching the side of an NJ Transit bus, causing the cherry to split into a little orange rainbow above the asphalt.

"You weren't kidding. You really do ask a lot of questions," he said.

"I'm just talking, friend," I replied, backing away.

"Who are you?" he asked.

"Dude, it was just a question."

"Are you a reporter?" he asked. "You know I can't talk to you."

"I'm not a reporter."

"Did Henniman send you?"

"Why would Henniman send…"

His face changed. If I knew who Henniman was, Lowell knew I had to be more than a curious barfly.

"I don't know if Henniman trusts this piece of shit anymore, but I wouldn't talk to him either way."

The booming voice came from the entrance to Hanley's. I turned to see Scannell. He'd followed us outside. Maybe he recognized me when I recognized him.

"What are you talking about, Anthony?" Lowell asked.

"C'mon you really don't remember this guy?" Scannell asked. "This is Russell Avery. Used to be some hot shot cop reporter for the *Intelligencer*. Now he just does odd jobs for Henniman to keep a roof over his head. Or at least he's supposed too. Kid got hired to help me out with something a few days ago, but it went wrong."

"You're still employed right?" I asked Scannell.

"And light a few grand," he said.

"That's not my problem."

"It's about to be," the fat man said.

I was standing halfway between Scannell and Lowell. There was plenty of street to run down. But I didn't want to give Scannell the satisfaction, and I still had questions. Why would Lowell think

142

Henniman sent me after him? Hell, why would Henniman be sending anyone after him?

"Looks like you two have your own issues to work out, and I've got a match upstairs," Lowell said, stepping past me and toward the door.

"Now hang on," I replied, jabbing a finger toward Lowell, which was a marvelously bad idea.

He snatched my wrist out of the air and applied just enough pressure to let me know he could apply a lot more if he wanted too.

"You, stay away from me," he said, letting go and turning to Scannell. "And you, tell your master to stay away from me too."

"The man needs to talk to you, Mike," Scannell said.

"The man doesn't need shit, and I don't need shit from him."

Lowell disappeared back into his less complicated world of darts and bourbon. Scannell turned back to me.

"Think we're alone now," he said, the sneer becoming a sadist's smile.

"You're not my type," I replied. "I'm into guys who don't need a search party to find their dick."

Scannell closed the gap between us in two big, laboring steps. There was beer on his breath, enough to let me know he was drunk enough to get violent.

"You really think it's a good idea to talk to me like that? You don't have anything over me now, and we're on my home turf," he said.

"Well then I guess you're gonna beat on me no matter what, so I might as well get my money's worth, you fat fuck," I said. "I mean seriously, who did you bribe to pass the department physical? They probably measured your mile time in days."

He swung, doubling me over with a soup bone fist to the stomach. I backpedaled from the force of the blow, lucky to stumble out of the way of a follow-up uppercut.

This wouldn't end well. I could handle myself in a fight, but that was mainly because I picked fights with people who couldn't.

Scannell lumbered toward me again, and he was already breathing heavy. His lack of cardio and my month-long lack of cigarettes were my only advantages. I squared up, then realized I'd be punching walls of cheeseburgers, so I stepped to the side and launched a kick into his right thigh.

The big guy pulled up for a second, either stunned by the kick or my decision to actually throw a kick in a street fight. Sure, leg strikes look flashy, but they're only useful when they're employed by people who know what they're doing.

Scannell brushed off the kick before trying to grab me by the neck. I got out of the way again, but not by much.

"You trying to dance or fight?" Scannell asked.

"Neither," I said. "Just hoping you have a heart attack before you hit me."

"Little shit," he said, charging again. I moved left, but he changed course, the weight of his shoulder crashing into my chest. I spilled to the asphalt and rolled, creating just enough distance that he couldn't pin me to the ground. I scrambled to my feet, but the blow had knocked me off-balance, and I tumbled toward him instead of away, running into a right hook that sent me down again.

He pounced before I could dodge a third time, straddling me and raining blows. The first split my lip. The second made an ugly sound when it hit my nose. I tried to turtle up, but the punches and elbows kept coming, and the metal taste of blood started trickling down my throat and washing over my tongue. A fifth or sixth shot caught me straight on the dome, and I wondered if this was what a concussion felt like.

Scannell kept cursing at me, but the punches started to slow. The dude was in truly terrible shape, losing his breath even while sitting down and using me for target practice. But he'd hit me enough times to render me useless, and I couldn't have moved his giant ass even if I hadn't been beaten and bloodied.

He reared back for another strike, one that might actually turn the lights off, but his arm snapped to a stop. It looked like his shoulder simply gave up. Scannell turned to see what was keeping him from ruining me, but his face twisted into an expression of absolute pain within seconds.

Something got hold of his arm and turned it in a direction it wasn't meant to go, dragging the big man off me and introducing his face to the sidewalk. I scurried backwards, wiping the blood off my face as someone continued to apply pressure to Scannell's arm, pinning a knee in the groove between his shoulder meat and spine. The big man's confident baritone collapsed into a desperate whine, and he let out a couple more shrieks of pain before my unidentified savior punched him in the back of the head. Scannell rolled over once his arm was released, eyes glazed and chest heaving in search of breath.

The figure that I definitely owed a beer flexed his shoulders and dusted off the arms of what looked like a charcoal suit. Then he turned to me, extending a hand and a smile framed by a goatee that I'd recognize anywhere.

"I thought you only came here with me," said Frank Russomano.

***

"How do you not have any hydrogen peroxide in your house?" Frank asked as he tore apart my medicine cabinet.

"Why would I ever need hydrogen peroxide?" I replied.

"To clean cuts, in the event you get the shit kicked out of you," he said.

I was sitting on the rim of the toilet with my head tilted back to keep my nose from leaking all over the place, swallowing hot metallic globs of blood and wishing the damn thing would clot already.

"I don't make a habit of this, Frank," I said.

"And yet, here we are."

This was ridiculous, and embarrassing, and more importantly, ridiculous. I'd spent years writing about Frank Russomano. We were equals then, two important forces in the city working with and against each other depending on the day. Now he was patching me up after a beating like a Mom preening over her son after a hopeless playground brawl with the school bully.

Not that I didn't need the help. Scannell had opened several new holes in my face and battered my rib cage. A cough worked its way up from my bruised midsection, causing me to choke when it collided with the blood flow coming down from my nose. I felt like I was going to vomit. Considering the amount of blood I'd chugged, I probably needed to.

The retired detective disappeared through the door, stepping over the blazer he'd shrugged off when we decided to turn my bathroom into a field hospital. He came back with his sleeves pinned to his elbows, a roll of paper towels tucked under his arm, a bottle of lemon juice in one hand and my last two beers in the other.

"You have lemon juice but no peroxide?" he asked.

"That's old. I made fish once. It didn't go well," I replied.

He moved over to the sink, placing the items raided from my kitchen in a line. He started carefully dabbing the citrus onto a torn paper towel, then pressed it against a slash under my left eye. I winced and pulled away, then took hold of it and clasped it against my face when he shot me a stern look. Frank went back to the sink and twisted open one of the beers as I held out my hand eagerly. Then he took a swig and placed the other beer out of reach, unopened.

"This is all you've got left. I'd say you owe me more than one drink," he said.

That was Frank. Controlling the room, regardless of whether or not it was his room to begin with. I dabbed at my face with the paper

146

towel, letting the citric acid burn at the cut. He'd stepped away with the beer, and with my head pointed skyward I could barely see him out of the corner of my eye.

It was the same obscure view I had when he showed up to save me from being hospitalized by Scannell. A blur at the edge of my field of view, popping up seemingly out of nowhere. I was glad to see him, but I also had to wonder why I was seeing him.

"Frank?" I said. "Not that I'm not appreciative and all, but why were you at Hanley's tonight?"

"It's a cop bar in Newark. I used to be a cop in Newark," he shot back. "Mystery solved."

"This has nothing to do with what we talked about the other day?" I asked.

"Scannell beating your ass have anything to do with what we talked about the other day?" he shot right back.

"No. Well, maybe? I'm not sure."

"Well, maybe I can help you figure that out," he said.

"Thought you said you weren't that bored."

"I'm not. But I told you that it sounded like you were poking at something dangerous, and now I'm wiping blood off your face," he said. "I know you. You're not gonna drop this. And I'm not a big fan of seeing you get your head caved in."

He still hadn't told me why he was at Hanley's at that time, in that exact moment when my ass needed rescue, but it was the first good news I'd received all day. Maybe it was just time to take it.

"Guess I need to catch you up then," I said.

He tilted the beer bottle back again but found nothing inside, shook his head.

"Yeah, you do. Just let me get rid of this," he said, leaving the room to find the recycling.

I slapped at my pocket for my phone, realizing I hadn't checked my messages since Scannell put the hurt on me. It was tough to fish the device out blind, and when I finally got a look at the screen I wished I'd left it tucked away.

In the other room, I heard the TV buzz to life.

"Oh fuck," Frank said.

I looked down at the phone. Three missed calls from Key. Two calls and a text from Colleen, in all capital letters reading "WHAT THE FUCK DID YOU DO?"

The drone of a cable news anchor filled my apartment. I walked out of the bathroom, dispensing with the tissues because I had a feeling that blood stains on my floor or clothes were about to fall very far down my list of problems.

An anchor from News 12, Jersey's main cable station, was talking so fast he was tripping over words. But phrases like "controversial shooting" tend to stick out these days. I knew what was coming next, tilted my head back more so I could avoid looking than to stop the blood flow.

But it was impossible to ignore the video from Kevin Mathis' cell phone as it splashed across my TV screen.

CHAPTER 10

The city had been waiting for this.

In the video that had made its way from News 12 New Jersey to YouTube to CNN, they didn't see Luis Becerra being shot down while unarmed by a Newark police officer.

They saw that cousin who claimed he got roughed up during a stop-and-frisk while walking home along Nye Avenue. They saw their neighbor who swore a city cop planted drugs on him while he hung out on a corner in the West Ward. They saw everything they'd read about when the ACLU called for a federal takeover of the police department.

Fact and fiction were irrelevant at this point. It was about a visceral reaction. A raw, in the blood, feeling that Newark's police were guilty of some kind of injustice. The film was proof that, if this shooting wasn't wrong, some other one carried out by the NPD had been. It gave credulity to otherwise unprovable claims, shined a light on the nasty shit that was known only to those who used force and those whom force was used against. It took the high stakes of those whispers of what might have been and beamed it into the living room.

I'd stayed home the first day, wondering how much of the blame for what would come would fall on me. It didn't take long for Frank to connect the video on the nightly news to the bits and pieces he knew of the case I was working on, and it took him even less time to walk out of my apartment after that.

The first night was light on chaos, simply because of the time the story broke. Key got a healthy crowd into the streets, but it was mostly made up of the contingent who'd followed her during the anti-violence demonstration days from when we first met. They were loud, they gave blistering quotes to the local television cameras as well as the national affiliates that had descended from New York, but they had no desire to turn Broad Street into Newark's version of Florissant down in Ferguson. There were a few arrests, but not for anything more serious than failure to disperse. For all her sometimes radical talk, Key could have made money in public relations if she wanted too. At the end of night one, a video of a white cop shooting an unarmed black man was now buttressed by images of police in riot gear handcuffing non-violent black protesters.

By night two, the ranks of the aggrieved had grown, and they had grown beyond Key's control. The teens and the twenty-somethings poured out of the neighborhoods that had been on the receiving end of Newark's past sins, the people who lived next door to Kevin or Luis. They huddled with her for a bit, joined her chants, nodded when she called for action, but got fed up when she didn't deliver anything past a march. One group broke off and stomped along the McCarter Highway and onto Route 21, snarling traffic and drawing the attention of the State Police.

News choppers captured footage of cops trying to chase them off, sparking a dangerous cat-and-mouse game. The protests splintered from there, with smaller groups bent more toward payback than progress mixing it up with the police. One report emerged of an off-duty cop getting pistol whipped. The police union president tweeted something about how officers will do what they need to defend themselves.

There were no storefront fires. Bedlam hadn't hit the city yet, but it one or two wrong moves away, and I couldn't help but feel it was partially my fault.

Had I done enough to keep Austin Mathis and Key from turning the case into a media circus? Was it even wrong that the city now had a thousand eyes on it? Becerra and Kevin Mathis weren't likely to be mourned without being part of this style of controversy, their deaths a blip on the local news cycle and invisible on the national one.

Now their names were both suddenly part of a larger, bloodier, lexicon.

I wasn't sure if that was fair. Then again, I wasn't a part of the aggrieved community either, so maybe it wasn't my place to make that determination. After years spent knee-deep in cop land I'd seen my share of heroism and hypocrisy. I could see the ways Becerra's death might have been justified. Becerra turned, and from Lowell's point-of-view, the officer could have feared the kid had a weapon. The officer had a right to defend himself.

All the same, Becerra had a right not to be executed for what was in all likelihood a minor drug crime.

I needed to get out of my house. I needed to find out more about why Kevin Mathis was dead. I needed to find Eddie Lazio, the lawyer who might be able to fill in some of the blanks in the narrative. I needed to talk to Lowell again, fill in the gaps that the video of Becerra's death didn't show.

My head swam as I stood up from the couch. Scannell's fists had left their mark on my face in the form of a long horizontal cut across the bridge of my nose, but there was also a fog hanging over my head. I snatched the remote off the coffee table, deciding to mute the constant feed of protests and pundits that had been using Newark as a backdrop since the night before, but the sound was replaced by a knock on my door.

No one had been here since Frank. When I got to the peephole, I found a cop, but not the one I wanted to see.

"You've got some fucking explaining to do," Lt. Bill Henniman hissed as soon as I opened the door.

He was in a dark suit that looked a little wrinkled, almost like he'd been sleeping in it, though the bags under his eyes made it clear he probably hadn't slept at all. His shoulders slumped, and his normally straight-razor clean face was now home to some dirty snow stubble. Given what the TV was showing, I wasn't surprised that Henniman had been too busy to groom or rest, but I was immediately troubled that he had somehow made time to give me hell.

"Shouldn't you be busy?" I asked.

"Patrol can handle that," he replied, stepping unnecessarily close to me. "I'm trying to figure out why they're in the street in the first place."

"And you think I had something to do with it?"

"I heard about your dust-up with Scannell. He's not the only one of my guys who wants to put dents in your face, by the way," he said. "Also heard you were pushing Mike Lowell about his shooting not long before you got your ass beat. Then not two hours later that video winds up on TV and my city turns on its head."

"Why would I leak a video to the press?"

"I don't understand why you do a lot of things, Avery," he replied. "I don't know why you were skulking around a drug dealer's murder scene a few days ago."

He pulled something out from his jacket, a manila envelope. He spilled its contents out across my coffee table, displaying a series of grainy photographs.

"I don't understand why you were meeting up with a drug lord in that same neighborhood not long after that," he said.

The pictures were of me talking to Hard Head, the meet Reek had setup, the one that sent me after Levon. At least now I knew who put the tail on me, like there was ever any doubt to begin with.

"You're having me followed?" I asked.

"You're poking into some sensitive shit. I wanted to make sure you didn't do something characteristically stupid, but I guess I was too late," he said, pointing at the TV.

"I didn't put that video out there. I don't even have a copy," I said.

Maybe it was the beating, or Henniman's surprise appearance, but I was off my game, answering questions he hadn't asked.

"But you'd already seen it," he said.

"The hell difference does that make?" I asked.

"I'm just trying to figure out what angle you're working, understand how much of a problem you want to make of yourself."

I felt my head get a little light again. I'd been on the wrong end of Henniman's ire plenty of times while I was a reporter, and his red-faced screaming was certainly enough to leave a person violently uncomfortable. But I'd never been in a position where he could actually threaten me.

"There's people in the streets accusing your police department of murder twice over. You've got national voices suddenly backing a local call for the feds to take over," I said. "How in the hell do I even qualify for your list of problems?"

He went back to the coffee table and moved the photos out of the way, revealing the morning copy of the paper.

"I need to know if you caused this, or if you can stop it," he said.

Dina's byline was there again, atop the story Key had been threatening to help her write. It talked about the video of Becerra's death and how the shooting was one of several questionable uses of force involving Newark's police in the past couple of years. It referenced the threats of a federal "pattern or practice" investigation and calls from the ACLU and other activists for the DOJ to step up its timeline for investigating "systemic, historic and institutional mistreatment of

African-Americans at the hands of city police officers."

That last quote was attributed to Keyonna Jackson, a local social justice advocate. It left out her other title: constant pain in Russell Avery's ass.

The icing on my shit sundae was the quotes from Austin Mathis, who had provided a copy of the video to the *Intelligencer*, out of fear that his son had been killed for possessing it.

I didn't know exactly what made Key and Austin turn to the press, but I had my suspicions. Dina's past story dismissing Kevin's killing as a drug murder. The incident in Louisiana that had been dominating national headlines a few hours after that. Maybe it all pushed the grieving father to action.

"You're saying you didn't do this," Henniman said. "But I'm looking at a front-page story written by your ex-girlfriend, the same ex-girlfriend who published the video that turned everything upside down, featuring quotes from the local activist I know you work with from time to time. She's shoulder-to-shoulder with the Mathis' kid's dad in half these pictures, so I'm guessing you took him on as a client?"

"Figure all that out by yourself?" I asked.

He nodded.

"Good. I'm proud of you," I said. "Now get the fuck out of my apartment."

Henniman picked up the paper, held it right in front of my face.

"This shit is wrong, and it's being pushed by people I can't break bread with, Russell. Now I think you're an asshole, but I also know you care about this city as much as I do," he said. "You want to see it burn up over a half-truth? Because I came over here to drive home the full story. No police, not in my unit, not anyone carrying the same shield as me, had anything to do with this Mathis kid getting killed."

"And I'm just supposed to believe that? Knowing that he died holding a video of one of your officers involved in an ugly shoot?" I

asked.

"So that's your theory? We killed someone in order to quash that little YouTube clip?" he asked, dropping the paper. "Lowell's shoot was legitimate. The kid turned, hands near the waistband. That'll hold up in any court, clear as day, no matter how many chants or marches they have. And besides, if I was to entertain your little conspiracy theory, why would we kill the kid and not take the phone after doing it?"

"Maybe he didn't have his phone on him at the time," I said.

"Have you met a 20-year-old who can disconnect from his iPhone?" he asked. "Use your head. This isn't what you think it is."

"Then tell me what it really is," I replied.

"Something you don't want a part of," he said.

"You're not giving me any reason to back off here, Lieutenant," I replied. "I work on facts, logic. Not cryptic promises from a guy who showed up at my house trying to blackmail me."

"Then maybe you should focus on that last part," he said, pointing toward the photos. "You need to get your ex, your professional protester friend and this crackpot Dad in line. They're spinning a story that doesn't make sense, and the streets are only going to get uglier until they stop. Just keep them quiet until I get the facts. Then I can get rid of those pictures."

"Those pictures don't prove shit. Sometimes it's my job to talk to assholes," I said. "Present company included."

"They don't need to prove anything. What they need to do is go into a file, making you a known associate of Trey Mills, a.k.a. Hard Head, a.k.a. one of the most dangerous bangers to walk Newark in the past 10 years. That means anytime he or his people do anything sideways, you might get questioned," he said. "You might end up in a gang database. Hell, maybe I can even hit you with one of those fancy gang injunctions, make it so there's parts of the city you can't go to without getting a contempt charge. That's not the kind of thing any of your future clients would like, and it damn sure wouldn't look good if anyone sent it up to the State Police. Might make renewing your license hard. Hell, it might get it revoked if I call in the right favor."

I thought about screaming at Henniman, but I had a better idea. He was fuming, looking like cartoon smoke might come out of his nose. Emotional people talk too much.

"So you'd never seen that video before?" I asked.

"I already told you that."

"You didn't even know Mathis had it?"

"No."

"But you guys knew Mathis? Had dealings with him?"

He paused, only for a second. A blink and you'd miss it kind of mistake. But he'd made it all the same.

"No," he said, weaker than before.

If this wasn't about the video...

"What do you know about a guy named Eddie Lazio?" I asked.

Henniman ran a hand over the ridges on his bald head.

"I don't know who that is," he said. "Do what I asked Russell, before you lose another job."

He turned and went out the door. I kicked it shut behind him, the bang louder than I'd expected, adding to my headache. Fuck him. I didn't even like this job.

If Henniman was on me, he'd push to make me persona non grata with as many officers as he could, probably close up most of my info pipelines within the department. He wouldn't have any pull with Colleen, but she wasn't talking to me anyway. Austin, Key and Dina were too busy in the streets to give me any time, and they were avoiding me too. I'd already blown my best shot at Lowell.

But Lazio...

I picked up the paper, scanned the article, searching for anything that Dina had missed. That's when I noticed the one voice that was jarringly absent from the story.

I went back to my office, pulled the court documents I'd been sifting through when hunting for my missing public defender. Lazio's client list was long, but Kevin Mathis wasn't the only nobody defendant he'd represented in recent months whose name suddenly held much more weight.

A few pages in, I found the name that was suddenly famous in Newark. The dead kid on the video that put the Brick City on the national stage.

Luis Becerra.

I turned from my desk quickly, half-jogging back to the living room to grab my keys, and my head got light again. I'd been in more fights in the past week than I had in the past year, and it was starting to seem like things would only get nastier the deeper I dug. I turned to the sink, saw the empty beer bottles left behind from my visitor the night before, the wadded up bloodstained paper towels lining the top of my trash can.

Henniman had the department to use against me. Dina had the paper. Key had the streets.

It was time to call in some reinforcements of my own.

CHAPTER 11

I hated when they called reporters vultures, but given how often we circled the dead, I had a hard time arguing against the comparison.

The swarm outside of Luis Becerra's home was entirely too familiar. TV trucks parked illegally up and down the block. A line of shoulder-held cameras pointed at the house like a firing squad. A crush of TV anchors nearby, microphones at the ready in case anyone came outside. The newspaper reporters milled around at the edges, trying to act like they were above it all just because they stood a few feet from the herd.

I'd been one of them more times than I could count, silently cursing the arrogance required to even stand there and hope that, if we waited long enough, our sheer presence would somehow motivate those mourning the victim of a high-profile homicide to come out and tell their tale.

In truth, none of us wanted to be there. Even the TV reporters, whom I otherwise despised, had enough decency to know that forming a press camp on a grieving mother's front lawn was inherently monstrous. But working in media means, in some respects, submitting to a hive mind. Unless everyone reached an impossible accord and agreed to leave together, you had to stay.

No matter how many times a relative asked you to go. No matter how many times someone threw something at you and you knew you deserved it.

Or, in this case, no matter how many times you watched a little girl peek sheepishly through the blinds of the Becerra home, probably just hoping to see if it was OK to go out and play, only to find a mob of strangers that reminded her nothing would be OK for a long, long time.

I was leaning against a fence on the other side of the street. There were no editors to appease anymore, so I had no reason to box out a prime position and rush the next Becerra relative to walk in or out of the home. Besides, the conversation I needed to have with them had to take place somewhere a camera or microphone couldn't pick up.

I needed a way inside. That would have been hard enough given the crush of media out front and the fact that the Becerra family had no reason to talk to me.

Frank Russomano's black SUV had circled the block three times, and he honked louder at the reporters pacing the street with each pass. He probably didn't have to hunt for parking much back when he had a badge. After a few minutes, he must have given up and dumped the car on a side street, because I saw him walking towards me with his hands jammed in his pockets, his normally easy smile replaced by a slight sneer.

"Thanks for coming," I said.

He looked over at the throng of reporters. The front door opened a crack, and they all surged forward, like a concert crowd as soon as the band made its first appearance. Someone's hand was creeping out through the door, reaching into the tiny black mail hatch affixed to the side of the entrance. The nothing moment might have been the most excitement they'd get all day.

"The hell are we doing here? You miss the worst parts of your old job?" he asked

"I miss all the parts of my old job," I replied. "And so do you. That's

159

why we're here."

"Russell, I'm a retired cop who was at football practice when you were in AP Lit," he said. "Speak English."

"You wanted to know why you wound up patching me up the other night, why I was really at Hanley's?" I asked.

"That uninteresting, unrelated case you were working?" he replied.

"Yeah. It was this one," I said, pointing toward the Becerra home.

"How many anti-cop cases are you working right now?"

"Huh?" I asked.

Frank shook his head and chewed his lip, then looked away from me.

"I thought reporters didn't believe in coincidence," he said. "You think it was magic that I just happened to be at Hanley's when Scannell was trying to put your face through the pavement?"

"You said you got curious after our meeting."

"I did. But then I got a phone call," he replied.

"Explain," I said.

"You weren't exactly forthcoming when we met up at the diner the other day, but you got my attention. Frankly, got me a little worried about you. I asked some friends on the job to keep their eyes open, let me know if you popped up anywhere odd. Then you went to a cop bar you never went to without me. You kinda stuck out."

"You really expect me to believe you went looking for me out of some long-held concern?" I asked. "You've always been a nice guy Frank, but never that nice."

"Well, it was half that," he said. "And half because Henniman asked me to check in on you."

Fuck.

"Nice seeing you Frank," I said, turning to leave.

"Can I explain?" he asked.

"Quickly."

160

"Jesus. You're a lot jumpier than you used to be."

"And you're a lot more of an untrustworthy pile of shit than you used to be."

"Henniman wasn't kidding when he said you two were having problems," Frank said. "Listen, I worked with Bill for a long time. He knows we had a good relationship when you were at the paper and I was on the job. He didn't give me a lot of specifics, just said you were digging into something sensitive and hoped I could impress upon you that you were endangering an investigation. That was it. Considering I spent a night wiping blood off you and today you're freaking out in every direction, I'm guessing there's a bit more to the story."

"There's a lot more," I replied, leaning back to the fence as if I needed it to help prop me up. "But I'm not sure I can tell it to a guy who is running errands for Henniman."

"That would have been an accurate way to describe you about a week ago, wouldn't it?"

"Fuck you," I said.

Frank crossed his arms and craned his neck, letting out some steam breath before staring back at me.

"You're the one who wanted to bring me into whatever this is, remember? I'm the one who saved you from a trip to the ER. I don't know where you get off not trusting me," he said. "What I do know, is that you called me and claimed someone who wears the same shield I once did got someone else killed. Then Henniman called me worried you were poking at something ugly for the department. You know me. You know where I stand on sideways cops. It seems like you need my help, but I can't help you if you don't tell me what's going on."

"You can't help me if you're working for Henniman either," I said.

"I don't work for Henniman. And even when I did, how many times did I leak you shit about one of his guys going off book? How many stories did I give you that turned Bill's face red?" he asked. "He told me to back you off. That doesn't mean I'm going to do it. But you need to give me a reason why."

Frank had a point. He had several. And I was short on allies at the moment.

"So you're gonna help me?" I asked.

"I'm going to give you the chance to convince me to help you."

I looked back at the Becerra home, at the horde. I wasn't getting through that door without an edge they didn't have. When I was still part of their tribe, that edge was usually Frank.

"That video. One that caused all this. I'd seen it before," I said. "I'm looking into the death of the kid who filmed it."

"Kevin Mathis," he said.

"Mathis ate a bullet on the west side not long after filming it. Hennniman put it out in the press that the murder was over a drug beef, but his family seems to think otherwise," I said. "And after nudging a few people, I'm starting to think the same."

Frank didn't say anything, so I kept talking.

"Our dead kid was definitely dealing, wasn't affiliated with any set, but he had the blessing of a local shot caller to work the corners he did. Drug thing doesn't wash," I said. "The officer who did the shooting that was caught on tape was one of Henniman's guys, and as you clearly know, Henniman is not happy I'm looking into the murder of our cameraman."

"So you think Henniman, a decorated and respected police officer … what? He just up and shot a kid? Just to dodge some bad press?"

"I'm not sure if Henniman did it, or if he's somehow responsible for it being done, or if he had nothing to do with it. I don't know enough. But Henniman certainly had a reason to want the Mathis kid gone," I said.

"And where does that rumor fit into all of this?" he asked. "What you told me the other day about a cop putting it out there that Mathis was a C.I.?"

"I don't know yet."

"Well who did you hear it from?" he asked.

"You know better than to ask me that question," I replied.

"Russell. You gonna trust me or not?"

"Trusting you and coughing up the name of a source are two different things," I said. "Maybe Mathis was a C.I. Maybe he wasn't. That's why we need to get in that house."

"You want to talk to his dead friend's family?" Frank asked. "The hell is that gonna accomplish? If he was snitching, I doubt his deceased running buddy's family knows about it."

"Not what I want from them," I replied. "But they both had the same attorney, so if he was cutting deals..."

"The lawyer would know," Frank said. "But first, you need me to get you in there."

I nodded.

"Gently," I said. "They just lost someone."

"You think I don't have enough juice left to talk my way past a couple of uniforms?" he asked. "And once we get in the door, the good people of the what's his name family won't know the difference either. Then you ask your questions."

"Not exactly ethical," I said.

"According to who?" he asked. "It's like you said, I'm not a cop anymore and you're not a reporter. You're talking about investigating a murder with no resources, no help, no nothing. You wanna play nice, or you wanna get shit done?"

I thought about what Dina said, when she warned me that doing bad things now in the name of good things later wouldn't balance out in the long run.

But Dina wasn't around. Frank was.

***

163

I wasn't thrilled about how Frank got us into the Becerra home, but now that the family was lined up in front of me, I was even more upset that it actually worked.

Luis' mother, brother and younger sister were huddled together on one side of the living room. His uncle, who stared daggers as he ignored my offer of a handshake, was standing off to the right, looking past me and sizing up Frank.

He was trying to figure out if we were trouble he could handle. I was. Frank might not be, but I didn't want to test that theory.

The bald uncle with the gray and black bushy moustache and long-sleeve dress shirt had met us at the door, muttering something about how the family had already refused to speak with police.

Frank, who was on a roll after he'd already lied to the patrol cop at the gate and claimed Henniman sent us, told him this was different. That we were with Internal Affairs, and that we were investigating the shooting. As the big man's hand reared back for the door, the woman I assumed was Luis' mother stepped forward, said something to the giant in either Spanish or Portuguese, like I knew the difference, and waved us in.

The Becerra living room would have held a somber atmosphere even if it wasn't home to a family that had just lost one of its own. The lights were off, leaving only the winter sun beams that snuck through the blinds to fill the room. The walls were mostly eggshell white, blankness only interrupted by the occasional crucifix. Some pictures of the kids hung on each wall. The tallest boy framed in each must have been Luis. The scrawny kid's smile seemed to shrink as the years went on. A toothy high-beam from what appeared to be a middle-school basketball photo was drawn into a vacant half-scowl by the time he reached an age closer to the mugshot I'd downloaded.

Luis wasn't the only family member time had taken a hammer to. His mother looked gorgeous in all the family photos, all round lips

164

perched atop an athletic cut and soft eyes that seemed inviting. But in the present day the wrinkles were doing their work, likely exacerbated by exhaustion and the recent trauma. The bags under her eyes looked like they'd been set in motion long before all the crying and missing sleep that had undoubtedly visited in the past few weeks.

I studied the photos for a father and found none. The woman bore the same worn out stare as Austin Mathis, and I wondered if Kevin and Luis might have turned out better if their marooned parents had crossed paths years ago.

Now they were only linked by their son's funerals and my need to uncover the reason for their grief.

"I'm sorry for your loss," I said, facing them, leaning awkwardly against an arm chair unsure if I should sit or stand.

"Sure you are," the uncle scoffed.

"Umberto!" the mother growled, glaring at him. She turned to me. "I'm sorry. We're all having a very hard time right now, as you might imagine."

"I understand," I said.

"If you do, then please make this quick," she replied. "Talking about this only makes it worse, and now I can't even step outside my front door without being reminded of it."

I nodded again and reached into my jacket for the photo that would hopefully keep the conversation brief and point me in the right direction.

"Then I'll just get straight to it," I said, unfolding the photo taken from the New Jersey BAR Association website. "Do any of you recognize this man?"

Mom took the picture of Eddie Lazio and studied the image of the plump white man with the runaway hairline. His gut hung left in the picture, pressing hard against his unfortunate choice of a too tight black dress shirt. What little hair he had left was in scattershot silver patches along his chin, a beard by committee of unkempt spots. Lazio was a remarkably unattractive man, and I hoped that made him recognizable.

It occurred to me that I hadn't asked Luis's mother her name as she handed the photo around. The youngest sister gave it the same studious glance before passing it down. Luis' younger brother stared at Lazio's droopy mug for five seconds, looked at me, then handed it off and kept staring. I didn't bother to see what Uncle Furious did with the picture, I already had a line.

"I don't recognize this man," the woman said. "What does he have to do with my son?"

"He represented him in court a few times. His name is Eddie Lazio," I said. "Are you sure you don't recognize him from any of the trials?"

"There were never any trials," the woman replied. "Luis wasn't shy about how he made his money. He never fought the charges. He just took whatever was offered and then went right back to his business, no matter how many times I tried to stop him."

Was Lazio getting plea deals for Luis too? I hadn't noticed that in Becerra's court file, but admittedly, I had spent more time looking at Mathis' record.

"What does this lawyer have to do with the police murdering my son?" she asked.

Possibly nothing. But once I told her that she was probably going to have her brother bounce us from the house.

"Listen miss… I didn't get a chance to introduce myself before." I asked. "I'm Russell."

"Teresita," she said.

"The truth is, I'm not exactly sure. But your son's death may be connected to another shooting. Did Luis have a friend named Kevin Mathis?"

She drew a long, frustrated breath.

"So that's why you're here?" she asked, her voice beginning to tremble. "The same reason those people are outside my house? Nobody cared about my boy being dead before, and nobody really cares now, unless it has to do with what's all over the news."

The uncle stepped toward me. Any second now we would be told to leave.

"There's no reason for you to believe me, but I do care. Your son isn't the first person whose death I've seen go unrecognized in this city, and we both know it won't be the last. That's Newark, sadly. I wish I could tell you what I'm asking about will help with what you're going through, but I can't promise that. You know who killed your son. You know why. We can sit here and debate the right and wrong of it, but that doesn't change anything," I said. "What I can tell you, is that look on your face right now, that hopelessness, it's the same look I saw on Kevin's father's face a few days ago. Your son's friend. His family doesn't know who killed him, or why. But this lawyer might. Maybe it's connected to your son's death, maybe it opens up a door about that. Maybe it doesn't. All I can tell you is I'm trying to do the right thing here, Miss Becerra."

I looked from Luis' mother to his younger brother. The kid was maybe 15, with hair that dangled just above his eyebrow. He was locked onto me. Mom looked around the room, scanned the crosses, and I wondered if she was thinking about helping me because it was the Christian thing to do.

"I appreciate your honesty," she said. "Now please leave."

I figured that was coming. My pleas for information to the hearts of grieving relatives were well-practiced, but mothers always saw through them.

"Thank you for your time," I said, keeping one eye on the younger brother who'd paused when handed Lazio's picture. "Do you mind if I use your restroom before I go?"

167

She turned her head to the side, looking toward Uncle Furious as if seeking his approval, then met me with a frustrated nod.

The hallway that led to the toilet went past two bedrooms. The one on the left appeared to belong to Mom, while the one on the right was home to a pair of beds that used to be stacked in a bunk. One of them was never going to be occupied again.

I went through the motions in the bathroom. Raised the seat loud enough that the porcelain on porcelain collision would echo out, flipped the light switch, ran some water. But I didn't flush until I heard footsteps moving into the hallway. Unless Uncle Furious had come to check on me, I assumed my window was open.

Luis' brother was in the bedroom when I headed back, holding something small in his hands. He was staring straight ahead at the Kyrie Irving poster on the wall. The image was a sign of a hopeful future for the Nets, who had wised up and fled Newark. The Becerra family was probably wishing they'd done the same.

"Your brother play point?" I asked, remembering the images of Luis in a basketball jersey from the living room.

"My Mom doesn't want you here, so drop the small talk," he said, turning to me. "You believe what the TV is saying? That Kevin might have got killed because he took that video of my brother?"

"I don't know about believe, but I'm trying to find out one way or another."

"And if you do … what happens to the cop who killed Luis?"

"I don't know. The shootings might be connected, they might not be," I said.

"And if they are … then what happens?"

"I'd imagine some people would be going to jail. But we're a long way away from that."

He let out a short, sad, laugh.

"You know, every time Luis got arrested, it seemed like he was

168

in cuffs, then in court, then in jail, then back out again in like two months," he said. "You ever wonder why things only move fast when certain people get in trouble?"

Luis' brother moved closer to me, revealing the item in his hands to be a flip phone.

"I always begged him to stop dealing. I knew he wasn't afraid of dying, so I came at him about how he wouldn't last long in prison. Told him he was too skinny," he said. "He usually ignored me, but one day, when I got really upset, acted like I was gonna cry, he pulled me aside and said 'Gulliermo, I ain't never gonna do real time.' Told me he had his hooks into some hot-shot lawyer. I'm guessing that's the man in that picture."

He handed me the phone.

"If Luis had the man's number, it's in here," he said.

"Thank you," I replied.

I was about to leave, but the distant look in the kid's eyes made me stop. I felt like I had to say something reassuring, as if anything could fill the hole his brother left.

"We'll get to the truth on this," I added.

"Truth," he said, a bitter laugh in his voice. "Truth is my brother's dead and he doesn't have to be. He didn't need to be dealing. The cops didn't need to be shooting him. The truth isn't going to make my Mom feel any better or put Luis back in this house. Nothing is. But you say maybe by helping you, some cops go to jail. I know what happens to cops in jail. Truth doesn't help me. Maybe payback does."

CHAPTER 12

It didn't take long for me to wonder if partnering with Frank was such a good idea.

We were sitting inside Hobby's, Newark's famous Jewish delicatessen and home to the kind of pastrami that could make a vegan forget about their scruples, and Frank was barely touching a sandwich I'd seen him tear apart countless times before. The #5, a pile of corned beef and pastrami drowned in a river of Russian dressing, was not meant to be lazily stared at.

I'd spent the drive over from the Becerra home playing with the cell phone given to me by Luis' brother. Any hopes I'd had about finding Eddie Lazio's phone number evaporated as soon as I turned it on and realized drug dealers generally don't list their clients' names and addresses in burner phones. Short of calling every number Luis had dialed in the past month, I'd need more information to track down the missing public defender. But at least I had something. Based on Luis' brother's comments about Lazio being a get out of jail free card, I had a reason to believe the lawyer was someone worth talking to about this whole mess.

It was a minor victory. Yet Frank was pouting over his sandwich like we'd come up empty handed.

"You gonna eat that?" I asked, gnawing through the crusted end of the first half of my meal.

"I'll get to it."

"I mean I can eat it if you're not hungry."

"I'm plenty hungry," he said, eyes locked onto the unbothered meal.

"Then why are you looking at your lunch like someone pissed on it?" I asked.

Frank nodded his head to the television with the grainy feed that hung near the register. Usually the old Magnasonic with the liquor brown trim was relegated to broadcasting Devils and Nets game, but the owner must have made an exception with Newark in the national eye.

The Becerra video was on a near constant loop, interspersed with shots of protesters marching down Broad Street and talking heads from criminal justice schools in Manhattan trying to make sense of the unrest that was happening a half-mile from my favorite lunch spot.

"We're trying to stop that," I said.

"By digging in on other cops?" he asked.

"By digging into the truth," I replied.

"You sure that's what you want here, Russell?" he asked. "I know that's what you said. But then I saw how understanding you were with that family while they hemmed and hawed about how the police took their son and the police ended his life and made it seem like if not for the police their drug dealing, felon, son wouldn't be dead right now. And it made me wonder."

I reached for the other half of my sandwich, savored the idea of biting in, then realized I couldn't stuff my face and yell at Frank at the same time.

"We needed information from them, so I tried to relate. You know, the same shit you did when you were a detective. And excuse me for showing some sympathy to the family that just lost their goddamn son, brother, and nephew," I said. "Whether or not the shoot was justified, and I'm not saying it was or it wasn't, that doesn't mean anyone should be fine with that kid being dead."

Frank shook his head.

"Play stupid games, win stupid prizes," he grumbled, finally starting to eat.

"You honestly believe that? The kid was a drug dealer, so who gives a shit if he's dead?"

He let his food fall back to the plate, allowing some slaw to escape the bread and skitter off to the floor. I wasn't sure if I was more angered by his sandwich abuse or what he was saying.

"I didn't say that. But I sure as hell don't understand why there's people marching in the streets asking why a cop shot this drug dealer in self-defense, instead of asking why he was out there dealing in the first place. Or why he ran? When are we going to talk about cause-and-effect Russell? When is the question going to stop being 'why did the cop shoot' and start being 'why did someone do something to make the cop shoot?'"

"Because both questions are important," I shot back. "You ever stop to think that every time this happens, no one is 100 percent right? I lived on both sides of this for how many years? Doing ride-alongs, buddying up to cops, then spending how many hours profiling activists, talking to suspects, befriending gang members. This isn't cops and robbers. There's some truth to your anger and some truth to theirs."

"Yet the TV is focused on them, and the narrative is clear. We're the bad guys," he said. "We used to be heroes. Now … I mean, how can you ask someone to get up for work every morning when their every move is subject to criticism?"

"Like I don't know how that feels?" I asked. "Ever heard the term 'fake news'?"

"You're not putting your life on the line every day."

"No. I'm not," I said. "But I don't have the authority to take lives either. Great power, great responsibility."

He reached for the sandwich, but froze, looked at me in a way that the word incredulous wouldn't begin to describe.

"Did you just ... Spider-Man? In a conversation like this, you quote Spider-Man?"

"Uncle Ben says that. Not Spider-Man. That's why he becomes Spider-Man," I replied. "And tell me I'm wrong."

Whether it was hunger or surrender, the sandwich finally won out over Frank's desire to fight with me.

"Listen man. You want to stop what's going on out there, and so do I. It's only a matter of time before somebody, on one side or the other, crosses a line at one of these protests and things get worse," I said. "The only thing that stops that is more information. They're not just out there over the shooting video. They're out there because they think Kevin Mathis got killed for filming it. They're out there because they need answers we might be able to provide."

"You can stop lecturing me now. Just tell me the next move," he said, before taking another massive bite.

"This doesn't help us just yet," I said, holding up the cell phone. "We still need to find Lazio. Or get more out of the cop involved in the shooting."

"I thought Lowell told you to fuck off before I found you at Hanley's," he said.

"He did. But I'm wondering if maybe you could help with that. Maybe he's more open to chatting if a brother cop is around."

"I didn't know him much when I was on the job. But I'll make some calls, see if I can get a line."

"Don't reach out to Henniman," I said.

"Hey, if you want me to rein in my loathing of these protesters for the greater good, then you need to let go of whatever it is between you and Bill," he said.

"This isn't personal. Lowell freaked out when Henniman got mentioned outside the bar," I replied. "I have no idea why, but it doesn't seem like they're on the best of terms."

"Then he won't be my first call. But don't tell me how to work this," he replied. "Remember, you wrote about the arrests. I actually made them."

There was no point in fighting Frank on this. He wasn't going to listen, and I had bigger problems to handle.

While Frank was calling old friends and trying to track down Lowell, I'd need to try and win back a few if I was going to find Lazio.

Luis' phone at least presented an idea. If the lawyer was a golden ticket for Luis, it stood to reason he had the same agreement with Mathis as well. That would certainly explain some of his short jail stays.

I needed to get back in with his family, and that meant I needed to repair my relationship with Austin, Key, Dina, or maybe all three at once.

The TV spiked in volume, a breaking news alert about police bracing for increased demonstrations outside of City Hall.

Well, at least they wouldn't be hard to find.

***

I wasn't prepared for the sound.

The images of the protests had been ubiquitous on cable news for the past few years, the crowds filling streets in Cleveland, Baltimore, Chicago, Ferguson and New York all too familiar. I knew the cadence of the chants, but being there, it was like the difference between hearing the recording of a band and seeing them live.

What was happening on Broad Street in front of Newark's City Hall was about more than sheer noise, more than volume. It was a furious, constant, united front that burrowed in well past your ears and made you want to join the disaffected chorus. Each volley of "no justice, no peace" or "hands up, don't shoot" seemed to pinball between the high-rise buildings on the business-dominated north side of Broad, rebound back off the ancient storefronts across the street, then nestle its way inside you. It didn't matter if I agreed with them or not, the sound was grabbing me by the throat and making me at least try to understand.

There had to be three thousand people spilling across Broad Street, stretching out from City Hall's marble steps and splintering into smaller, clustered crowds across Green and into the major intersection at Church Street. I'd been standing on the edges of the demonstration for a half an hour, trying to figure out how I should approach or if I should approach. I'd been frustrated by police actions, stymied when seeking info by bureaucratic nonsense, but nobody had ever turned their gun on me. I wondered whether I was siphoning their anger to advance my own investigation.

Then someone got hold of a bullhorn on the steps, shouted for attention at a machine-gun pace, and I looked up and remembered we were there for the same reason.

Key was the center of the storm, as usual, her short frame only visible because she was teetering perilously on a folding chair, megaphone in front of her face. She was flanked by Austin Mathis. I scanned for the army of television cameras and tracked the light bath from Key's face to the source near the front of the crowd. Dina had to be nearby as well.

The roar of the protest slowly wound its way down to an angry murmur, everyone subduing themselves just for a moment to let Key have the floor. These movements didn't really have leaders – at least not in the top-down organized sense that would fit every conspiracy nut's fantasy about paid demonstrators -- but they had characters they rallied around.

"How long we been out here family? Three whole days?" she asked. "Three whole days asking for answers, and we ain't getting none, right?"

"No!" the crowd shouted back.

"Cops still won't tell us why Kevin got shot? Won't even acknowledge why we think they did it?"

No, they said again, louder this time, like they were in church answering a call-and-response hymn.

"No, they won't talk to us. But they'll sure come watch us, won't they?" Key asked.

She pointed to the outer edges of the street, about a half-block from either end of the demonstrators, and I noticed the hulking shadows. Lines of Newark cops, maybe county sheriff's deputies too, dressed in all black, bracing riot shields, helmets with plastic face guards flipped up.

The crowd members turned to face the police officers closest to them. The chant erupted naturally.

"Back up, back up, we want freedom, freedom, all these racist ass cops, we don't need 'em, need 'em."

The chorus bellowed for a solid 30 seconds, howling with enough fervor that you almost had to believe it was right. I was on the southern side of Broad, and there were a lot of black and brown faces in the line of officers next to me. Some stared blankly, their eyes flickering with nerves. Others had expressions twisted in anger or annoyance, jaws rigid, maybe waiting for a chance to respond to the cadence with something more tangible.

I knew that painting every officer out here, or anywhere, with such a broad brush was wrong. It was as inaccurate as it was unproductive. Saying every cop on the street was racist was as bad as assuming every person who got shot by the cops did something to deserve it.

But my fingers were tapping against my thigh to every word anyway. The rhythm of their aggravation was infectious.

I moved toward the crowd, walking quickly across the yawning stretches of asphalt at the edges of the group, then slowing as I got deeper into the tangle of chanting, shivering bodies. Real-estate became scarce the deeper I went, and it got to the point that I was twisting into little crevices between shoulders, bumping into and further annoying people who had already been whipped into a fury by the video of Luis Becerra's death and Key's booming rhetoric.

The crowd was overwhelmingly black and Hispanic, with a few white faces sprinkled in, probably the progressive types from the New Jersey Institute of Technology and Rutgers-Newark campuses in the Central Ward. Still, no one looked lost or unnerved to be there, the way I might expect an outsider to feel about being on a Newark street in the dark and surrounded by cops. In the other cities where this had happened, newspapers always seemed to quote out-of-town demonstrators, people who had made the pilgrimage to show solidarity. But I guess even when my city attracted national attention, it wasn't worth visiting. People didn't want to come here in the good times. They sure as hell weren't coming in the bad.

Eventually, my weaving and pushing became futile as I hit an unflinching line of demonstrators nearly 20 feet from the base of the steps, too far from the megaphone or the media pit to reach Key or Dina. I pulled out my phone and made one last useless call to each of them, as if they'd suddenly pick up in the middle of this after ignoring my attempts to contact them during the day.

I needed to get closer, convince them we needed to work together. But that wasn't happening until the crowd granted me permission. So, I stood there. Waited. Watched.

The video hadn't caused this march, it was just the spark that lit up the acres of dry brush waiting to burn. The quaking anger, the frustration I heard in the voices chanting and cursing on both sides of me, was the result of decades of feeling disenfranchised. Of feeling like you were always wrong, because the script said the other side was always right. That's the way it had been at the dinner table growing up for me, and that's how it started in the newsroom. The cop wasn't always right, just usually. I couldn't count how many times I heard an officer-involved shooting call come over the scanner and shrugged, knowing that the story would be over just as soon as I confirmed the suspect had a gun, or a knife, or that he'd looked at the officer funny.

A couple of hands went up at the left edge of the crowd, fingers pointing and unintelligible shouts following right after. I noticed a black town car peeking out at the intersection of Broad and Green, behind the police line. It slowly turned right as the crowd got louder. There was another town car behind that, trailed by an Escalade and a follow vehicle.

A motorcade. Either the Mayor or the Police Director was in the truck, maybe both. They were gone in a matter of seconds, disappearing down the part of Broad Street that had been rendered vacant by the protest.

I heard a "motherfucker" here and a "ain't even look at us" there, and it seemed the crowd had come to the same realization I did. The people they wanted to talk to weren't listening.

"You know what?" Key shouted into her megaphone, commanding the attention of her annoyed flock. "I'm seeing a lot of the same faces out here each night. Same people, hearing and shouting the same message. Nothing changes if we keep preaching to the same choir, right?"

No, the crowd shouted again, as forceful as before.

"Y'all think we need to take this somewhere else?" she asked.

I got jostled as a sea of fists rose in approval around me.

"Let's do it then," Key said, raising her megaphone up and pointing it where the motorcade had gone. The marchers immediately surrounding her cleared the way and Key vanished from sight, presumably stomping down the stairs to the head of the group. The crowd around me broke apart just a little bit, people moving at different speeds in the same direction. I used the space to try and hunt for Key and Dina, jogging a few steps each time a lane opened. I looked like a drunk running back trying to navigate an impossibly large football field, but I managed to get to the cameramen, all in a group with their on-air talent, trying to plot their next move.

Dina wasn't there. Of course she wasn't. We ascribed to the same doctrine as most newspaper reporters: if everyone is in one spot, you should probably be somewhere else.

Key had vanished from view, but I had to assume she was at the front of the surge of bodies moving east of City Hall. The crowd had spread out just enough that I could break into a run, so I took the space given, accidentally knocking a cardboard sign from someone's hands as I moved toward the police line.

The cops seemed to harden their stance as I got closer, hands traveling to the long batons at their sides, held at the ready so they could be easily thrust forward if necessary. I noticed the crowd slowing around me and managed to dart close enough to the front that I saw what was going on.

Key and Austin Mathis were nearly nose-to-face shield with a few of the officers, demanding to know why they were blocking the march. Dina was just to the left of them, her cellphone out and filming the argument. I'd always warned her to stay away from the police lines during protest coverage, cautioning that things could turn quick and she'd get arrested just like anyone else. You can't file or tweet from jail, I used to say.

But she hadn't listened, and once again, her coverage was the better for it.

Word traveled quickly through the crowd, and a chant of "let us through" began to boom into the night. I watched the cops' faces, looking for some tell about how this was gonna go, but they were all stoic, their minds gone to that fight-or-flight place that I was thankful I didn't have to visit every time I went to work. Still, there was no reason for them to be blocking the protest route. Broad Street was empty, and the police hadn't declared this an unlawful assembly yet, nor should they have.

Someone with stripes walked over from a trailer parked in the distance, a mobile command center. He whispered something to an officer at the end of the line. Heads turned one by one, his order sliding down in the tensest game of telephone you'd ever witness. The officers backed up slowly, a few steps at a time, their batons still ready and willing to damage if required. Once they'd opened a gap they felt comfortable with, the officers peeled off and re-clustered on the now empty steps of City Hall, re-establishing their line there.

A cheer came up through the crowd for their minor victory, and the march resumed, a series of the same chants bellowing louder than before as we headed toward Market Street.

I ran all the way out ahead of the crowd this time, spinning around and pulling out my cell phone like I was one of the younger marchers preserving the moment for Facebook. Really, I was just looking for the purple knit cap that would be perched on top of Dina's head. I found it behind an iPhone camera trained on Key's face, documenting the fury etched across it with each strained shout.

"That one will get a lot of retweets," I said, as I saddled up alongside her and slowed to the march's pace. "Greene will be thrilled."

Dina and Key both turned toward me. The protest leader rolled her eyes.

"I'm too busy for you, Russell," Key said, motioning to the crowd.

"I noticed you found a new favorite reporter," I shot back, as Dina moved away from us to get a better angle for her video stream.

"She's not my favorite reporter, but she's competent," Key hissed back. "Unlike some people."

"I feel like I'm the one who's supposed to be mad at you, but that's not the point right now," I said. "How long are you gonna stay pissed at me for?"

"How long you think I can stay pissed at you?" she asked.

I didn't know the exact answer, other than half past a long time. I turned to Dina, who at least did me the courtesy of putting her phone away.

"I called you," I said, splitting my gaze between Dina and where we were going.

Her hair was tucked away under the cap, and if she had makeup on I couldn't tell in the dark. We both hated the TV anchors who still dressed like they were going to work at a corporate law firm while pounding the pavement.

"Been a little busy," she replied.

Dina turned from me, walking backward but at the same pace as the crowd, holding her iPhone high. She wasn't even looking at the screen, not that she really needed to frame the shot well. The sounds and the size of the groundswell would tell the story in the 20-second clip she was about to send to her Twitter followers.

"What are you doing here, Russell?" she asked, her eyes still focused on anything that wasn't me.

"Same as you, I suppose," I said. "Trying to make sense of all this."

"You watched the video. You heard Austin's story," she replied. "What is there to make sense of?"

"There are a few things you don't know, Dina. That's why I need to talk to you, and Austin, and Key," I replied. "Hoping maybe we can all help get the full story out there."

She lowered the phone and typed something, a description to pair with the video, then met my gaze.

"Oh, now you want to share with the class?" she asked. "From what Key and Austin told me, you'd seen that video before. And then you tried to talk them out of going public. I was worried you might start to see things through a certain lens once you started this new job Russell, but I didn't think you'd go full native. Did you wear your Blue Lives Matter bracelet tonight?"

"That's not fair," I said.

"You lying to me wasn't fair. You using me to curry favor as part of whatever you're doing now wasn't fair," she said. "And you holding that video back, that was just wrong. Do you see what's happening here?"

She fanned one of her hands out toward the crowd as we advanced another block.

"You think this is a good thing?" I asked.

"You don't?"

"Dina, c'mon. I'm all about freedom of speech, but you know how fast these things can turn ugly. And besides, they're all out here protesting on an assumption. One that you reported, by the way. I don't have any proof that Austin's son died because of that video, and neither do you."

Our backpedal carried us past Market Street, but the crowd didn't follow. They turned right, heading north, and once I realized what that probably meant, I got worried.

The Prudential Center was only a few blocks away, and the Devils had a home game. That meant more cops, more out of towners, more potential for trouble. It was early in the season, and the arena known as "The Rock" would be packed. There would be traffic to stop, dissenting voices to rile up the crowd. And again, more cops.

"You think this is just about one shooting?" she asked, tucking the phone away and choosing to argue with me head-on. "You've covered this place long enough. When have you seen people get active like this? Talk about fixing the police like this? Never. This is about Kevin Mathis. It's about Luis Becerra. But it's also about a conversation that's long overdue."

"This is a conversation?" I asked. "All I see is yelling."

"That's better than silence," she shot back. "You're gonna tell me you would have handled this different?"

"Excuse me?"

"Switch places with me. Put your cop reporter hat back on for a minute," she said. "Tell me that if you got this video when you were with the paper, you would have held it back."

"That depends on.."

"No, it doesn't," she said, cutting me off. "Don't evade. Don't do all that straddle a line crap we hated at press conferences. Tell me you wouldn't have put the video out."

I wanted to say yes. I wanted to say I'd have done what she thought was the right thing. But I wasn't sure it was that simple. Maybe I just wasn't that brave.

I noticed two people breaking from the pack, sparing me from further self-analysis.

Two tall, lanky, black men, one wearing an olive green hoodie, were waving their hands in the air. I couldn't tell whether people were genuinely interested in what they had to say or simply looking for a break from the repetition of Key's bullhorn chants, but they were paying attention.

"Yo!" one of them shouted. "You wanna make these people listen? Then let's make them listen."

He pointed down the block and skyward, to the place where the search lights from the hockey game were waving across the night. Some of the crowd responded with an emphatic *yes*.

"Let's go then, people!" the same guy shouted. "Whose streets?"

"Our streets!" came the reply from a larger chorus than I expected.

They started jogging. People followed. The protesters that were branching out all appeared younger, a little more wild-eyed, ready to amplify their message with something more than catchy chants. I'd seen this happen before, the divergent approaches between the people who just discovered street protests and the people who'd been doing it long enough to know how to rock the boat without sinking it. This was what I'd been worried about.

Key crowed into her bullhorn, repeatedly urging the group to stick together, to stay peaceful, but her calls were drowned out by the rising, angry chorus.

Dina started running with the crowd, chasing the news. Key watched as more and more of her marchers picked up speed and stood in the street shaking her head, bullhorn slung down by her side.

As much as I needed to try and talk to Key or Austin while they were alone, I couldn't take my eyes off the crowd surging toward the arena. Dina would be in there, up close with the cops, with the people who were trying to stir this into more than a protest.

I took off. The crowd had already run into a police barricade at Market and Mulberry, where the cops usually cut off traffic in front of the arena. The chants swelled again as I closed the gap – "let us through, let us through" – but they were disjointed now, shouted in multiple directions at a bunch of different decibel levels.

As I got to the front, I noticed the scene at the barricade was tenser than the last brief collision between police and protester outside of City Hall. The chants may have been bellowing from the body of the demonstration, but the people at the front were screaming at the officers, middle fingers in the air. The word pig was used liberally.

This was how it would break down. Three days of peaceful protest, minimal arrests, tension but nothing terrible would be unwoven by twenty or thirty people. This was what would make TV. This was what would pulse across social media. These were the brief clips Fox News could focus on without worrying about things like context.

I couldn't tell you if their anger was justified or if they were simply there to cause trouble under the veil of civil disobedience. It had played that way before. Looters using protest as cover in Ferguson. Vandals hiding amongst crowds in Los Angeles and tagging cop cars while everyone else around them tried to send a message.

Idiots always start the fire, then slip away while the rest of us stand around and watch things burn.

The sound of glass shattering forced me to turn my head, and I spun to find the guy in the olive hoodie had hurled a brick through the window of the Devils' gift shop.

The noise was a starter's pistol, sending the crowd in two directions. Half of them peeled back, trying to get away from the bubbling chaos they hadn't signed up for. The rest surged forward, advancing on the cops, the barricades, anywhere they weren't supposed to be. I searched for Dina but couldn't find her, then moved forward, knowing where she'd have to be.

The sharp squeals of police sirens filled the street, drowning out the sounds of any additional damage the lead troublemakers were bringing toward the Prudential Center. I looked back down the parade route to see six, maybe seven, marked Newark cruisers headed our way. A longer shadow was trailing behind them, no lights, no sirens. But as it got closer, I recognized the shape of a school bus. The modern-day paddy wagon. The "in case we need to arrest all of you" vehicle of the Newark Police Department.

About two dozen people had chosen to take their anger out on the gift shop. Olive Hoodie was still at the front, laying waste to every window he could find, and others had started looting. Small things, mostly jerseys and tee-shirts, and clearly not for personal gain. A few of the shirts had Newark Police shields on them, holdovers from some charity event the team co-sponsored with the cops every year. The shirts were on fire in short order, a few people chanting "jail the killer cops" as orange lapped up the clothing.

The officers at the barricade held their line, batons at the ready, content to let the small splinter group have its fun. If the mass of reinforcements moving down Market were any indication, it wouldn't last long.

I weaved my way through a few retreating protesters and entered the main fray, as Dina stepped out of another cluster and trained her phone on Olive Hoodie.

"The fuck you filming me for?" he shouted, stepping toward her.

"I'm a reporter. This is a public street," she replied.

"Put that shit away."

"Can't do that," she said.

"I ain't asking you again," he said. "Put it away."

Dina shook her head no. I broke into a run as Hoodie advanced on her, but I didn't get there in time.

Dina put the phone away, but only so she could free up her hands to grab hold of Hoodie's left wrist. The dumbass had come in off-balance, and Dina's self-defense classes did the rest. She twisted, the same way she'd done to me in New Brunswick, bent him half over at the waist before he even knew what happened. Unfortunately for Hoodie, she didn't stop there, driving a knee into his chin that sent him reeling backward. The sleet on the ground did the rest, and Hoodie went tumbling head first into the pavement.

Dina stopped to admire her handiwork but didn't notice the other guy who'd helped Hoodie whip the crowd into a frenzy was coming up from behind. Thankfully, I was already running. He left his ribs unprotected as he wound up to punch her, making himself ripe for the best open-field tackle I'd laid on someone outside of a Thanksgiving morning football game.

Dina only noticed me when the idiot let out a groan as we hit the sidewalk. The force of the hit sent us rolling, and he wound up on top of me, trying to pin me down, leaving his weakened ribs vulnerable a second time. Dina's foot found a soft spot and he doubled over coughing.

"Did I look like I needed your help?" she asked, pulling me to my feet as Idiot #2 scampered off.

"I told you we needed to talk," I replied. "Figured that might get your attention."

She shot me a sideways look as we sized each other up, the burning hockey paraphernalia highlighting us in smoke as the rogue protesters kept doing damage nearby. Notepad clutched, stern look on her face, she'd turned into everything I foolishly thought she couldn't become. At home in chaos, maybe more so than I ever was. Meanwhile, I was breathing a little heavy after interjecting myself in her life again, eyes racked from lack of sleep, looking like I needed rescue and not the other way around.

"You OK?" she asked.

"Yeah, you?" I said, my hand unconsciously traveling to her shoulder.

She let it stay there, a small mercy, and nodded.

"We really do need to talk," I said.

She didn't answer, eyes traveling over my shoulder, so I turned around to find what she'd been staring at.

The cops had mobilized while we played Street Fighter. The detail that had been at the barricade when the fracas started was now backed up by at least three dozen additional officers, all in full riot gear. I turned back the other way and found the cruisers that had sped up Market were now empty, parked far behind another few rows of officers dressed the same.

"This is Captain Steven Cohen with the Newark Police Department. I am declaring this a violent congregation. You have five minutes to disperse," said a voice from a police loudspeaker. "If you do not disperse, you will be subject to arrest and other police actions, which may include the use of less-lethal munitions."

The unmistakable sound of a shell being racked in punctuated the message, immediately drawing screams from the hundred or so people who had been penned between the police lines. I was close enough to the front to see the noise had emanated from an officer producing a beanbag shotgun from the trunk of the car, but that information wasn't going to do anything to abate the panic already moving through the ranks.

People started to surge toward either police line, demanding to be let out, but the officers at each end either remained stoic or shook their heads. I heard one grumble "you had your chance," then turned my head to notice a little satisfied smile creeping out over his face. Most of these officers probably just wanted to see this end peacefully, but some wanted to use their toys.

The cops at the south end of the block stepped forward, chanting "move back!" and rattling their batons against their riot shields as the protesters found themselves huddled into a smaller and smaller circle. Dina and I got swept up in the wave as the perimeter shrank, ending up elbow to elbow with a mixed crowd of the people responsible for the gift shop looting, and the everyday protesters who just wanted to go home.

At this point, I doubted the police were making distinctions. I looked around for a way out, but found the two police lines had now met in front of the destroyed storefront, effectively boxing everyone in. Legally speaking, this wasn't how dispersal orders worked. The police needed to give you a chance to leave before they could affect an arrest. But rules and regulations tended to become unimportant once fires were set.

"Flash your press pass," I whispered to Dina. "They're not going to arrest a reporter."

"If they let me out I won't be able to see what happens."

"Dina…"

"Would you have left?" she asked. "Thought this was the right way to do things."

I looked up at the cops closing in, watched the panicked stares of the protesters stuck in the middle, then stared back at her and nodded.

At least we'd have plenty of time to talk.

***

As I sat shoulder to shoulder with Dina and a man whose next shower would likely be his first, I silently cursed myself for not writing that jail overcrowding story back when I was at the paper.

We made it out of the melee relatively unscathed by resisting the urge to resist arrest. The cops hadn't handled us too badly, though I felt like I strained something in my shoulder while trying to get comfortable in handcuffs.

I'm sure the people nearby trying to blink the last remnants of pepper spray out of their eyes or rubbing down muscles bruised by beanbag rounds would have traded places with me in a second. Dina and I got snatched up early, so it was hard to see what force was used and what was deserved. But I doubted the footage of mass arrests and the interviews that would come from the people sharing a cell with me would do much to improve police-community relations.

"This was what you were afraid of," Dina said, looking straight ahead at the chipped paint on the cell bars.

"What do you mean?" I asked.

"When Key reached out to me with the video, before I wrote the story, she told me you didn't want her and Austin to go public, but she wouldn't say why. At first, I thought it was just you being you, needing to control everything."

"And now you've ruled that out?"

"No, I'm not an idiot. I'm just saying maybe that wasn't the only reason."

"I don't have a problem with protesting Dina," I said. "I have a problem with people putting themselves in real danger because of a half-told story."

"Do not start telling me how to do my job again," she replied. "Everything in that article was accurate."

"Accurate, but incomplete," I replied. "There are some other pieces Key and Austin don't have."

"They hired you and you lied to them?"

"I didn't lie. I held back info. Hoping this wouldn't happen," I said. "There are some things I need to look into without every reporter on earth hovering over my shoulder."

"So you went to a protest where every reporter on earth would be hovering over your shoulder?" she asked.

"Well I was only looking for one in particular," I said, flashing a quick grin hoping she'd return it. She did not.

"I know you're not about to ask me for a favor," she said.

"Not a favor," I said. "Maybe more like … an arrangement?"

She leaned back a little and crossed her arms, accidentally jostling the guy next to her.

"I'm listening," she said, turning back to me.

"Key is freezing me out, which means I can't get to Austin. They trust you. I have a line on someone who might be able to fill in the blanks on connections between Luis Becerra and Kevin's deaths, but I'm not going to be able to find him without Austin's help. Which means I need your help."

"Is there a part where I get something out of this?" she asked.

"You get a source that no one else covering this story has," I said. "You get me. I won't hold anything back from you."

"Like you didn't hold anything back from Key?" she asked.

"You don't trust me?"

"I'm working on that," she said. "But until then, you're stuck with me. If I help you find this mystery person, I want to be there when you talk to him."

"Dina, this isn't about landing an interview," I said. "The stuff

I've had to do working this as a P.I. doesn't exactly line up with the *Intelligencer*'s ethics code."

"Well then maybe I can help you with that too," she said.

"Now you're going to tell me how to do my job?" I asked.

"You want my help or not?"

She held out her hand, and I looked at her naked ring finger longer than I should have.

"Friends?" I asked.

"Nope," she replied. "But I'll always take another source."

CHAPTER 13

Dina and I didn't work well together, and not just in the relationship sense.

She dropped by my apartment the next afternoon, after we'd been released on our own recognizance and taken a few hours to sleep on that wasn't a jail bench.

Her arms were filled with manila folders. Meanwhile my notes on the Mathis case were scribbled on Chinese take-out menus and what might have been the electric bill.

Dina laid out her folders across my coffee table, each one marked by the name of a different player in the mess we had agreed to wade into: Lazio, Lowell, Mathis. She opened them up to show printouts from LexisNexis containing home addresses and cell phone numbers, whatever records she could snatch from voter registration, and in Mathis' case, the rap sheet I'd read through days earlier. There were red lines through a few of the locations.

In the middle, she placed a cell phone. It had to be Kevin's, surrendered to Dina by Key or Austin Mathis sometime between our jail stay and now. Part of me wanted to ask if Dina had told Key we were working together, but the other was happy to reap the benefits of whatever story Dina had told to get the phone.

Key held grudges with a vise-like grip, and there was no use struggling until she was done squeezing.

I pulled out the burner given to me by Becerra's brother, eager to compare numbers and find the one that belonged to Eddie Lazio, but she pulled it back and shook her head.

"Nuh uh, ground rules first," she said.

"Ground rules?" I asked. "It's me, Dina."

"Your point?"

"Didn't we go over this last night?" I asked. "You help me, and you go where I go. You interview who you want. You get what you need for your story. I get what I need from Key and Austin since they hate me right now but trust you. Anything else?"

"Yeah. You don't pull anything like you did in New Brunswick. We're doing this the right way," she said. "No blackmail. No arm twisting. None of the nonsense that will make my editors heads spin."

"I don't have editors anymore," I said.

"Then you don't have Kevin Mathis' cell phone either," she replied, pulling the device further away from me.

"Look, I don't know where this is going to go, so I can't make blanket promises. Let's just play it by ear, OK?" I asked. "If we start getting into something that's going to cause you an ethical dilemma, we can figure out a way around it. But why don't we try working together first, and arguing second?"

She bit her lip for a second, then nodded, seemingly satisfied she'd gotten her point across for now.

"So, what's the plan?" I asked.

Not like I didn't have one, but deference was probably the path of least resistance with her.

"Based on what you told me last night, I'd guess it's the same as yours," she replied.

Our long night in jail had given me plenty of time to debrief her about Lazio, about my early morning clash with a drug dealer named

Levon who told me a cop outed Kevin Mathis as a snitch, about the burner phone given to me by Luis Becerra's brother.

I reached across the table to the folder marked by the lawyer's name, tapped the addresses she'd crossed out in red ink.

"Seems like you already figured out he's in the wind," I said.

"Yeah I called a few of those numbers. They were either out of service or old residences. There's a divorce filing in here too. Looks like Lazio and his wife split three or four years ago, but all her current addresses are in Maryland," Dina replied.

"So she's not gonna know anything."

"Not anything we need to know," she said.

I picked up Mathis' phone before she could play defense again.

"Well like I told you, Becerra's brother seemed to think our dead drug dealers had some kind of leverage on Lazio," I said. "I'm going to assume there's matching numbers between the two. Maybe one of them is our missing public defender."

She shook her head.

"Even assuming that we dive into that haystack and find the needle, it's like you said, Lazio's hiding," she replied. "You think he's going to come out and play if he starts getting calls from a reporter or a P.I.?"

"Fair point," I said.

"But what you told me about Becerra got me thinking … maybe him and Kevin weren't the only ones who had an extra special relationship with the public defender. Might be worth tracking down some of his other clients."

I rolled my eyes. Dina's diligence was bolstered by patience, another skill I lacked.

"Remind me again what you said about needles and haystacks?" I asked.

"And you've got a better plan?"

"Actually I do," I said, reaching for the folder marked Lowell. Her reflexes were up to par this time and our hands tangled, knocking the folder open and sending papers to the floor.

"Goddamnit," she said, jumping up and trying to re-organize the mess. She shook her head and walked past me, heading for my office desk.

"You got any paper clips? I need to put these things in order anyway," she said.

I ignored the question and focused on where she was going. The ring was still in my desk drawer, the one I'd meant to give her more than a year ago. The one I was either too lazy or hopeful to pawn.

She opened the drawer and I dug my hands into the couch cushion, praying her attention to detail didn't extend to the search for office supplies. I watched her rummage for a minute, yanking out a few pens and tossing a book of unused stamps out of the way. Something caught her eye, and I felt the color drain from my face, but she didn't look up. She fished out a small red stapler and came back across the room as I tried to compose myself.

"Russ?" she asked.

Shit.

"Yeah?"

"Can you pick up the papers you knocked over?"

Nagging never felt so good.

I scooped up the mess, happy for my reprieve, and handed them back to her. She started putting things in order as I scooped up the now empty Lowell folder.

"We don't necessarily need Lazio. We just need to know why he's a problem for Major Crimes," I said. "Henniman looked like he was going to have a heart attack when I name dropped the attorney. When I tracked down Lowell, it didn't seem like he and his squad boss were on the best of terms."

"You think tracking down a cop at the center of a controversial shooting that's national news is going to be easier than searching for the missing public defender no one cares about?" she asked. "Didn't you get your ass kicked the last time you tried talking to him?"

Well, we did have an inside track. One I hadn't mentioned, because I was sure it would make Dina's blood pressure soar.

"I think I have a way to get to him," I said. "Someone else has been helping me out with this."

"I'm not going to like this part, am I?" she asked.

"Nope."

"Who?"

"Frank," I said.

"Frank Russomano?" she asked. "Your old Major Crimes source? As in the same Major Crimes unit we think has a hand in all this?"

Reporters don't out sources, but sometimes you share that kind of information with colleagues, let things slip here and there. Especially when you trust that colleague. Or you're dating that colleague. Judging by the size of the ring I'd purchased around the time I told Dina about Frank, I didn't think trust was going to be an issue back then.

"You're really never going to fix that blind spot, are you?" she asked.

"Do you want to talk to this cop or not?"

"How much does he know Russ?" she asked. "And how much has he told Henniman?"

"He's not working with them Dina. He was the one who pulled me out of that bar fight in one piece."

"And if we get deeper into this, find something unflattering about the department, how long do you think it will take for him to switch sides?" she asked. "I know you trusted him back then, but you were also a lot more useful to him back then. You know how this story ends Russell, you're smarter than this. When push comes to shove, he's going to choose the department over you."

"You don't know Frank," I said.

"I know cops."

"Maybe not as well as you think."

She stood up and snatched Kevin's phone back while I wasn't looking.

"Well I'm going to the courthouse," she said. "Maybe I get lucky and get a line on Lazio. Maybe I wind up talking to him without you there."

"And what if I get to Lowell without you?" I asked.

"Did you even ask Frank to find him Russ? Do you know he's going to say yes?"

I did. But telling her that was only going to piss her off more. And I needed that phone.

"Alright, alright," I said. "Let's take turns running the show, like partners, fair enough? We go to the courthouse. If that doesn't work, then I call Frank."

She smiled.

"Was that so hard Russ?" she asked "Maybe if you'd listened more back then, we'd still be together."

Maybe. Or maybe I needed to pawn that fucking ring already.

***

Sifting through court records can be exhilarating or excruciating. It all depends on what you're hunting for.

Research a specific case, and sometimes you might want to consider bringing popcorn. For the crime aficionado, preliminary hearing transcripts have all the elements of a novel, with none of the suspense or pacing. You already know who got killed or robbed or wronged, but the fun is in hearing the why laid out from every possible angle: medical examiners, cops, victims, suspects.

But when you're digging up info on a specific person, especially a public defender who has handled the same kinds of low-level drug cases for the better part of a decade, things can get tedious. It's a lot of small print on computer paper borrowed from your elementary school, and it reads as dry as the textbooks from that time frame.

Dina had dragged me to the basement of the Essex County Courthouse, a musty backward-in-time library some of us derisively referred to as "the vault," to dig through Eddie Lazio's case load for the past four years. The polite woman at the records desk turned not so polite when Dina handed her a list of case numbers long enough to be spilled out on a scroll, and I shot my ex the same scowl as I flipped through another page of procedural drivel about a heroin possession case from 2013.

"We're learning so much," I said as she stared intently at a minute order from an arraignment, scribbling something in a notepad.

"You know this will go fasterwithout the play-by-play, right?" she asked.

It wouldn't, but I didn't have a clever reply for that one. So I went back to my endless stack of case files and hoped for the best.

All I could tell from the sea of tiny black letters on each page was that Lazio wasn't a very good lawyer. Most of his recent clients were sitting in cells on Doremus Avenue at the Essex County lock-up, the result of his inability to secure an acquittal or even a favorable plea on the most minute of drug charges. Public defenders don't have the greatest win-loss record, but Lazio's success rate was so far in the drain that I started to wonder if he was secretly working for the prosecutor's office.

This wasn't just a problem for Lazio. If most of his past clientele were locked up, that meant it would take a good long while to chat with them. You can't just show up and visit a prisoner. You need to get on their approved guest list. Which means sending them a handwritten letter, and hoping they want to sit down and chat. Once that happens, you're still meeting them in a county-controlled cell, where any number of sheriff's deputies or corrections officers can overhear or record you. Anything we said or asked would probably make its way to Bill Henniman's ears.

"I have a question," I said.

"Maybe it'll be answered if you keep reading," she spat back.

"You want me to go through another file that shows a Lazio client doing the near max sentence for a drug crime?" I asked. "You looked through Mathis and Becerra's files too, right?"

"Obviously."

She was never going to get tired of saying that.

"So then how do we sit here, flipping through record after record of Lazio effectively sucking at his job, yet he's the king of sweetheart plea deals when it comes to our two dead friends?" I asked.

Dina finally picked her eyes up from the paper she was studying, slid her reading glasses off, and met my eyes.

"We've both said we're pretty sure they had leverage on him. Whatever it was, it clearly gave him extra motivation to keep them out of jail," she said.

"So what? He suddenly becomes a better lawyer out of sheer force of will? Fear?" I asked.

She slid her chair near mine, the legs making entirely too much noise for the crypt quiet records vault. The clerk who already hated us issued a hush.

"Look," I said. "Almost all the cases we're looking at, Lazio gets saddled with a loser. Some hapless corner boy caught with a pocket full of rock or powder, stone cold, game over before it starts."

I pulled over one of Mathis' cases.

"Then here, with Kevin, look what you have. Dismissed LOE. Dismissed LOE again," I said, using the courthouse shorthand for 'lack of evidence.' "Then when he gets caught with painkillers, the hot button issue that we know no prosecutor can afford to slack off on, he gets probation or a stretch under six months. It's the same pattern for

Becerra."

Her head started bobbing, her brain laying down the same track as mine.

"Lazio wasn't the only one who wanted these guys out of jail," she said.

"You're thinking stuff got lost?"

"Or stuff got disappeared," she replied.

"That's a hell of a grenade to throw with no evidence," I said. "This is why we need to talk to someone inside Major Crimes. Someone like Lowell."

"You're not calling Frank," she said. "The more this looks bad for his old squad, the less I trust him."

"Then tell me how we're getting the goods on this lawyer, Dina?" I asked. "Because every client I'm pulling is either still in jail or in the ground."

"Not all of them," she replied.

Now it was her turn to tap her finger on a document, causing me to shift my chair in her direction. The metal-on-tile symphony caused another screech, and our vault warden looked up with an expression that said this was the day she'd lose her job for the chance to slap a customer.

Dina had a list of names on her notepad, defendant first and lasts copied from the mountain of paper she'd been sorting through.

"I've got at least four recent Lazio clients who are out and about. None of them were moving painkillers, but they all had some kind of drug rap and they all did less than a year. Not the same pattern, but maybe people worth talking too."

I scanned the names, and the second one on the list jumped out at me. Angel Trujillo. I pulled out my phone and punched his name in next to mine, finding an old clip that confirmed my hunch.

"Make it three. I knew I recognized that name," I said. "Angel

Trujillo is no longer with us. He got popped when someone lit up the Hotel Nile a few years back."

The Nile was the city's most infamous drug flophouse, one of several landmarks in Newark I recalled from a time I'd looked at it across crime scene tape.

"Shit," Dina said.

I thought she was simply reacting to the news but then I realized she had her phone out for the same reason. She pointed to the last name on the list, held up the screen and showed me a similar murder story chronicling the end of another Lazio client. Down to two.

"You ever wonder what people think when they Google our names and see them connected to nothing but dead people?" she asked.

"Don't look at me. At least I've got a Tinder profile," I replied.

She scowled. I hoped the idea of me single and free ticked her off, but she was probably just wincing at the lame joke. Or she knew I hadn't been on a date in six months.

I looked at the list again, and another name jumped out for the right reasons. Tyreke Best.

"You got his case?" I asked, tapping the name.

Even in the ocean of identical court documents, Dina had been able to keep things organized, and fished it out immediately.

I skimmed the paperwork, looking to see if there was an attached mugshot, and smiled.

"I think we got something," I said.

The sound of knuckles rapping against the table interrupted my celebration.

"Excuse me," said an older voice, and I looked up to find the Lady of The Vault glaring at us up close. "Are you finished with these? There are other customers who'd like to view them, and you've been here quite a while."

I checked my phone, noted the time and realized I'd spent two more hours than I'd ever wanted to in the basement of the courthouse. I wondered who would want to use the same mundane documents as a sleep aid, but when I looked past records lady, I quickly realized boredom wasn't going to be a problem anymore.

Two men in suits were waiting at her perch, one in blue the other in black, a well-dressed bruise. I didn't recognize them, but I had a pretty good idea where they came from.

"Dina, who are our new friends?" I asked.

She followed my stare and sighed.

"Left is Ritter. Right is Cole. New additions to Henniman's flock," she said. "They came into Major Crimes after you left."

"And now they want to look at Lazio's files," I said.

We looked at each other, then records lady.

"Yeah, we're done with these," I said.

But we'd stared too long. Frick and Frack made eye contact, clearly recognized the reporter and their boss' least favorite private investigator, and one pulled out a cell phone.

I stood up to leave, but Dina grabbed my wrist.

"You do realize those case files are going to get pulled in as part of some investigation once we leave, right?" she asked. "We're not going to get to look at these again."

"I trust your impeccable note-taking skills," I replied. "Besides, we don't need to. We can talk to Tyreke."

"You two are on a first-name basis now?" she asked.

We were. But I just knew him as Reek.

***

My phone rang almost as soon as we pulled out of the courthouse parking lot. The call was coming from a blocked number, and given the company we'd attracted in the records vault, I had a pretty good idea who wanted to chat.

"Hi, Honey," I said, imagining Bill Henniman growling on the other end of the line. "Sorry, not gonna make it home for dinner. Got a really interesting case."

"Not without your license you don't," the lieutenant replied.

Dina banked right onto Market and headed back to the heart of the city. It was a short drive to Reek's apartment, which would give me an excuse to drop Henniman's call in short order.

"How many times are you going to make that threat?" I asked.

"It's no longer a threat. This call is just courtesy," he replied. "I heard you got arrested last night."

"What does that have to do with anything?"

"Plenty. We have to notify the State Police's private investigations unit anytime someone with a license winds up in our custody. Usually it takes a couple of days, but I felt they should know about your case immediately," he replied. "Just wanted to give you a heads-up, they'll be checking on you soon."

The call shouldn't have come as a surprise. Still, the fact that the threat had become real was jarring. I doubted a minor arrest for failure to disperse would get my license pulled, but then again, if Henniman had enough juice to help me get my P.I. card, he certainly had enough juice to take it away.

"Do what you need to do Bill," I replied. "The way things are looking though, I doubt your recommendation will carry much weight with any cops in a few days."

"The hell is that supposed to mean?"

"I saw your goons at the courthouse. You know exactly what I'm looking at, and how it connects to you," I said. "If I were you, I'd worry less about my license and more about hiring a good defense attorney."

He laughed, which is not the response you want when your trading threats that can destroy careers.

"Whatever you think you know Russell, you don't," he said.

"Then why don't you help me fill in the blanks, Lieutenant? Why did you look like someone shit in your cereal when I mentioned Eddie Lazio to you the other day?" I asked. "Why did you send people to look at his case files?"

"I can't comment on an ongoing investigation," he said.

"You know I'm not a reporter anymore."

"If you don't cut the shit Russell, you're not going to be employed anymore," he replied. "I don't know what you think you're playing at here, what your angle is. But if you don't stop, people are going to get hurt."

"Is that a threat?"

"It's a warning," he replied. "And it's the last friendly one. Don't get in my way again."

He hung up. Dina pulled the car onto Martin Luther King boulevard and turned to me.

"Henniman is not happy with us," I said.

"That's a good thing, right?" she asked.

"What?"

"Weren't you the one who used to tell me if the people you write about are pissed at you it just means you're doing your job?"

"Yeah, that only works when you still have a job," I said. "Don't worry about it. Let's just focus on this."

She pulled the car to a stop outside of Montgomery Heights, a mixed-income housing setup meant to bring some life back into the city's once urban blighted Central Ward. Newark's heart wasn't home to as much mayhem as the south or west ends, and it wasn't run by any particular gang, but it was still plenty run down. Montgomery was supposed to bring a more middle-class feel to the area, if there was a such thing as a middle class in Newark.

When he managed to extract himself from his gangland days, Reek had chosen to settle down in the new complex. Most of his former Sex, Money Murder brethren stuck to the west side, where he'd introduced me to Hard Head. Geographically, the distance between his new home and his old stomping grounds wouldn't mean much on a map. But to Reek it probably felt like a different time zone.

He was the rare success story. The guy who got out of the life before it took too much from him. Reek had a kid, maybe 7 or 8-years-old, and from what I understood the two had a good relationship despite his absence when the boy was in diapers. The mom, his on-again-off-again-on-again-who-knows girlfriend, was also back in the fold and Reek had even told me he was considering snagging a ring for her. His life was on track. He'd helped me get the meeting with Hard Head because he knew I'd try to do it with or without his aid, and he didn't want me getting hurt. But most of the time, he preferred to leave his past in the past. Eyes forward and all that. Except now I needed him to look back, and I doubted he was gonna be thrilled with the idea.

According to the court filing, the case where Lazio had represented Reek was his final arrest from his Bloods days, a felony assault that the public defender managed to get pled down to a misdemeanor. The complaint wasn't too detailed, but I knew Reek had boxed a little when he was younger, and those fast hands were part of what helped him rise so quickly in his old set. Hard Head apparently respected people who could handle business without a gun. Reek wasn't an enforcer in the way most people might think, but his ability to solve problems with his brain or a beating had made him a valued employee.

He was past all that now. Or he would be. Until I started asking questions.

"Do you mind if I take the lead on this?" I asked Dina as we opened the black gate and crossed from the sidewalk into the Montgomery Heights' courtyard. "I've known Reek a while."

"He's your source," she said.

We moved up a set of short brick steps to a thin metal door. The windows still had the birdcages around them. Central Newark was improving, but not fast enough to dispense with the hallmarks of a rough neighborhood.

"Yo?" Reek asked from behind the door after I knocked.

"Hey man. It's Russ. You got a minute?" I called back.

"The hell are you…?" he started, then turned his head back toward his living room.. "No, no. Not you. Just watch your TV for a minute, Daddy'll be right back."

The door cracked open, and I saw Reek wearing a less-than-thrilled expression. A cartoon was flashing over his shoulder, and an excitable little boy was cheering on whatever was happening in the show.

"You got a phone, don't you?" he said, stepping outside. "My kid's here man, what do you want?"

He was wearing a black t-shirt with at least one stain on it, what looked like the aftermath of making lunch for a 7-year-old. The wind kicked up and Reek looked like he regretted the decision to step outside without a jacket, then did a double take when he noticed Dina.

"You bringing strangers by here now?" he asked.

"Dina," she said, extending her hand.

He shook it and laughed.

"Oh, the ex," he said. "Y'all back together now?"

"No," we said in stereo, finally agreeing on something.

"Right … if you two need a therapist, you might wanna head downtown," he said, before nodding his head toward the living room. "Can we make this quick?"

"You remember that thing I asked you for help with a few days ago? The shooting I needed to talk to Hard Head about?" I asked.

"Yeah, heard what you went and did with that information. Might not want to drive down Springfield anytime soon," he replied. "Levon ain't happy. And frankly neither am I."

"He was being an asshole," I said.

"Russ, I didn't think this required explaining, but if I help you out, get you in touch with someone for info, it's on you to not beat their ass," he replied. "Leaves me less inclined to do you any additional favors."

Reek crossed his arms and leaned back against the door, as if that was the end of the conversation.

"Well then how about you do me a favor?" Dina asked. "I promise I can keep him in line."

"She's the boss now?" he asked. "I can get behind that."

"I hate both of you," I said.

Reek wasn't paying attention to me anymore. He loved to shit talk, and Dina was demonstrating herself as a better sparring partner at the moment. I decided to let her drive.

"Russ is helping me look into the murder of a man named Kevin Mathis. He said you two talked about it before?" she asked.

Reek nodded. I watched to see if she would pull out her notepad, but she didn't. Get them talking first, go into reporter mode after.

"We now think it has something to do with a man named Eddie Lazio, a public defender," she said. "He represented you a few years back. We just wanted to ask you some questions about him."

Reek's smile quickly retreated, and it looked like a bad memory washed over his face. He turned back to me.

"You didn't tell me this shit had anything to do with that man," he said.

"The last time we talked, I had no idea it did," I said. "What's the problem?"

He pointed to the living room.

"The problem is named Jamel, and how I want to spend the rest of my day with him and not reopen some past bullshit," he said. "You know I don't like talking about the old days, especially when it can affect the present."

I didn't really know what that meant, but it sure as hell piqued my interest. Apparently Dina's too.

207

"Listen … Reek? Is it alright if I call you that?" she asked.

"Everyone else does."

"I don't know what you're worried about, but whatever it is, no one has to know we had this conversation," she said. "I'm not taking a notepad out. But we need your help. This lawyer, Lazio, might be in the middle of getting two people killed."

"There's no way that man ever killed anyone," he said.

"How do you know that?"

Reek turned back to me.

"You're really asking a lot here," he said. "And you already owe me one. What am I getting out of this?"

It was a fair question. Whatever Reek knew about the lawyer was clearly making him nervous, and I'd never known the man to get shook. In truth, I had no idea how helping us would really help Reek. He'd already been through the system, been marked up by the Newark PD on more than one occasion. If what we learned about Lazio helped expose Henniman, it would give Dina one hell of a story. It would certainly help me keep my license. But for Reek…

"When was the first time you got arrested?" Dina asked.

My eyes widened. The fuck was she doing?

Reek nodded his head toward his kid, met Dina with a look that said "Really, this, right now?" But Dina didn't flinch. Her eyes stayed locked onto his. She wanted her answer.

"I was 16," he said, punctuating the sentence with a long sigh. "Narcos were clearing a corner. I wasn't even involved yet, but I was there, got tossed up on a wall like the rest of them. Popped my shoulder."

"You think that was right?" she asked.

"I mean, I shouldn't have been with that crew. But they didn't need to jack me up neither."

"How often do you think something like that happens in this city?" she asked.

"More than it should," he replied.

"And if I told you that what you know about Lazio might help expose some bad cops doing bad things, clear room for some good ones to make decisions, what would you say to that?" she asked.

"I'd say you got some nice dreams and no sense of reality."

Dina shook her head and stepped in front of me, making clear this was now between them.

"Every time we ask about this lawyer, we're getting crap from cops. They nearly chased us out of a courthouse. There's a lieutenant threatening to wreck Russ's life. And I'm having a hard time thinking it's a coincidence that the same lawyer represented the two dead kids who have this city up in arms right now," she said. "Something bad happened here. And you might be the one who can help us figure out what."

Reek looked back toward his kid, wiping a hand across his face then running his fingers through his hair.

"Shit," he whispered, then turned back to us. "Guess those rumors weren't rumors."

We stayed silent. There weren't anymore questions to ask. Sometimes you just need to let the source make the decision on their own.

"This cannot come back to me, you understand?" he asked. "I've done my last dance with the NPD, and I don't need some sideways shit happening with my probation. I got out. I'm staying out."

"You trusted me once, Reek," I said. "And I promise you can trust her."

He turned back to his kid again, nodded.

"That case didn't last too long. He managed to get the assault knocked down, managed to drum up enough doubt about self-defense that the prosecutor didn't push the issue," he said. "But only after I did him a favor."

I saw Dina reach for her notepad but obviously thought better of it and stopped.

"Man was using. Pills. I tossed him a few oxy and suddenly he was working like the kind of lawyer you pay for," Reek said.

Oh fuck.

"Was he using in court?" Dina asked.

"Honestly, I don't remember," Reek replied. "But I asked around a little at the time, and apparently I wasn't the only one he played that game with. It was years ago, but judging by what you're asking, it don't sound like his ass found a 12-step program."

Luis Becerra and Kevin Mathis both sold pills, and Lazio had represented Reek years earlier. If the public defender was a junkie then, it stood to reason he was a junkie now. That meant hundreds of people had been convicted of crimes in Newark while receiving legal counsel from someone who snorted oxy while prepping motions. That meant hundreds of cases could wind up tossed if people started making appeals based on ineffective counsel, hundreds of arrests made by the Newark Police Department undone.

How many cases? How many lives altered? How many people sitting in jail cells who didn't belong there?

Now I understood the opposition we'd been getting. This wasn't just about Kevin Mathis or Luis Becerra, and it wasn't just about the overturning of wrongful convictions. There were criminals in Lazio's files too. Dealers, legit jumped-in bangers, people who could maim or kill.

Injustices might be set right if Lazio's truth got out, but the street would suffer too. People would walk out of lock-up and look to get their corners back. People would die.

It was a hell of a story. One a dedicated police officer, someone like Bill Henniman, might do anything to keep from being told.

CHAPTER 14

This should have been Dina's "I told you so" moment, but if there was a verbal eruption inside her, it wasn't showing as we shivered on the sidewalk near Reek's place.

My ex-girlfriend turned partner was chewing on her pinky nail, tapping a blank notepad against her thigh. She hadn't written anything down during our conversation with Reek. She didn't have to. It wasn't the kind of story you'd forget.

For Dina, it was the confirmation of a long-held suspicion: that something, somewhere in the Newark Police Department was festering and corrupt and needed fixing. For me, it was proof that I'd missed something, possibly because I'd refused to accept it was worth looking for. If I was the kind of reporter I'd thought I'd been back in the day, I might have noticed something like a half-high lawyer bumbling away hundreds of people's right to due process.

She was staring at her phone. So was I. We had to be feeling the same weight, asking the questions you ask when you find out something you're really not supposed to know:

Who do we tell?

How do we tell it?

Who's gonna get hurt?

Are we gonna get hurt?

How do we prove it?

I trusted Reek, and Dina seemed to believe him, but the word of a reformed gang member wouldn't carry much weight with her editors, nor did it answer the question Austin Mathis had hired me to solve. I still didn't know who killed his son, but we'd come a long way from that meeting where he'd suggested the shooter was a cop and I'd considered running out the front door laughing.

Dina was still down in her phone, tapping out what looked like a text message. Maybe she was talking to Key again, involving the activist like I'd begged her not to. Key was long past patience now, and if Dina told her anything that Reek told us, the protests would double in size and ferocity in the span of a few text messages and tweets.

Key had always believed the Newark Police Department was terminally ill, regardless of the facts of a given debate about the local criminal justice system. To her, the mere implication that the cops knew about a drugged-up defense attorney would be proof the tumor was malignant.

If Dina was going to break the rules, so would I. I pulled out my phone and sent a quick flare to Frank: "Need to talk. Urgent."

No need to elaborate. Either he already knew about this mess, at which point I'd need to concede defeat to Dina again and start reconsidering all life choices, or he didn't, and it was safer not to put anything in writing.

"What now?" I asked, as she continued to stare off. I followed her gaze toward the downtown skyline. She was looking at City Hall, it's gold dome, not too dissimilar from a mosque, meant to be a shiny symbol of progress or turnaround that you could see from the highway. Newark PD's former headquarters were next door, an older building with roman columns. Real hall of justice vibe.

Downtown was one of the few parts of the city that didn't look fucked up. At least not from the outside anyway.

And that was when I realized why she was quiet. Why she wasn't taking a victory lap around my shattered pretenses about the NPD.

Dina had grown up here, seen the city get poorer and bloodier over time, not sure which one drove the other.

She didn't want this to be true either.

"Dina?" I asked again, finally drawing her attention. "We need to make a move. Did you call Greene yet?"

The editor would salivate over this, a full on Pavlovian river. Whether that came from a desire to do accountability journalism or the chance to meet his page view goals was a separate issue.

"Not yet," she said. "We don't know enough. I don't want him telling us how to do the story before we know what the story is."

"Smart," I replied. "We do need more. Reek's a start, points us in the right direction. But it could take a while to find other clients, especially if we need to write them love letters in county lockup. Besides, that doesn't answer the question that really needs answering."

She turned to me, eyes narrowing slightly, knowing we were on a crash course for the same philosophical dispute again.

"We need to know what the cops knew," she said.

I nodded.

"You want to call Frank?" she asked.

"Yes."

"And you want my blessing before you do?" she asked.

I did. Even though I'd sent him that text, I felt kind of dirty about it.

"That's not happening," she said.

"He knows that unit better than anyone else."

"And that's the exact reason we shouldn't tell him about this," she replied. "You heard Reek. Lazio was getting high as far back as 2013. When Frank was on the job. In Major Crimes. He might have known about this, or at the very least, arrested some of Lazio's clients."

"Then why has he been helping me Dina?" I asked. "Just to cover his own ass?"

"Or to steer you away from figuring this out."

"That's not how it worked with us."

She spread her arms, as if she was summoning the whole city to argue with me.

"What is it with you? Always acting like the past is the present," she said. "When you were a reporter, you always knew the cops were right. That's how it worked. When this whole thing started, you knew Kevin Mathis was a drug dealer who probably got shot by a drug dealer. That was how it worked. You need to wake up Russ. Those neat little folders you wished everything fit into, they don't exist. Kevin was a victim, but he was also a criminal. Key is an activist, and sometimes she's an opportunist. Frank may have been a good cop, but that doesn't mean he's a good man. This city is complication after complication, and it's time you started looking at it for what it is."

I looked at my phone. Frank hadn't answered, at least not yet. I didn't have a card to play.

"What's your alternative?" I asked.

"You wanted to talk to Lowell, right?" she asked. "You seemed to think you had a rapport with him, that he wasn't all true believer, like Henniman?"

"Didn't seem like it," I replied.

"Then I think I can get us in a room with him, if you think you can get him talking again," she said.

"How?"

"By tracking down someone who owes us a favor," she replied. "Though I doubt she's going to be happy to see you."

***

Colleen Quinn looked like she was at peace.

Seated in the back of Montclair High School's auditorium with her hands folded on her chest, Collen's neck was rigid as her eyes traced the stage. Her oldest daughter was belting out her half of the female lead's signature number in *How to Succeed in Business Without Really Trying.*

The girl, the one whose college tuition I'd helped secure by sticking it to Colleen's ex back in New Brunswick, was quivering with energy as she attacked the crescendo to "Rosemary," nailing the whole thing, doing her best to cover up for the lack of power in the voice of the guy playing Finch. He was all nasal, no chest.

I was surprised by how much I remembered from the musical, which had been done to death by the drama companies in my high school and then again in college. But it was helpful in the moment. "Rosemary" was the penultimate number in the first act, which meant there'd be an intermission, which meant there'd be a chance for us to get Colleen alone.

I didn't feel great about it, and I was the guy who'd leveraged Colleen's problems with her ex to get Mike Lowell's name just a few days earlier.

Despite whatever was going on in Newark with her department, her city, Collen was removed from it in that moment. Wrapped up in her daughter's performance, giving her mind and attention over to someone else for a little bit. I guess this was what people who cared about things outside of their jobs did.

Once the curtains closed, we were going to try and corner Colleen in the auditorium hallway, near other blushing parents where she couldn't make a scene or shoo us easily. She couldn't leave either, lest she miss her daughter's continued journey through the Worldwide Wicket Company.

It was an ambush interview, one of my least favorite journalism tactics. It's that thing people do to celebrities when they're walking out of court or some other public appearance that has nothing to do with the questions you're asking. It's intrusive, and it's rarely effective. You do it to hostile politicians and people caught up in scandal who are almost definitely going to ignore you anyway.

You don't do it to sources. Or friends. But we were on a clock.

Dina and I had entered our natural state, arguing and exchanging withering glances, as we drove from Newark to Montclair. The battlefield on the trip up Route 280 was how to approach Colleen. Dina had filled in some blanks, like how she'd gotten Collen's cell phone number in the first place. Apparently after our night in New Brunswick, she'd approached the Internal Affairs boss, explained how she'd helped me deal with the alimony problem, then asked for nothing specific in return.

Just a friendly ear in the department now and then. I neglected to give Dina shit for benefitting from the whole New Brunswick thing, especially after the tongue-lashing she'd given me that night, because there was a different argument I needed to win.

Dina thought this would be as simple as calling her newest cop source. It wasn't.

The last time I saw Colleen she told me she was running an investigation that concerned Lazio. If that was true, she probably had a whiff of what Reek had told us, and she certainly wouldn't be taking calls from reporters. Face-to-face was the way to go, especially considering the approach I'd suggested Dina take with Colleen.

We needed to talk to Mike Lowell. He wasn't anywhere a public records search would lead us, and save for Frank, I was out of ideas on how to track YouTube's least favorite police officer. Colleen had to know where he was. She was investigating his shooting. She sure as shit wouldn't want us talking to him, unless she thought it was the only way to head off something worse.

"You ready for this?" I whispered to Dina as we sat in the last row.

216

"I know how to work a source, Russell," she replied.

"Not suggesting you don't," I said. "But this isn't how you normally operate. I barely ever bluffed back in the day, and you're not a great liar."

"Most people would consider that a positive attribute," she said.

"Most people aren't stalking an Internal Affairs cop and trying to squeeze them for information," I replied.

Applause erupted throughout the room, and I looked up to see the players departing stage left and right, signaling for intermission. Colleen stood up and turned toward the exit, spotting me almost instantly. Something between confusion and abject fury flashed in her eyes, and I thought about leaving and calling Frank right that second.

She turned away as soon as we stood up, huddling into a throng of equally excitable parents, barging her way into some inane conversation about how someone's kid shouldn't have been relegated to a chorus role. Safety in numbers. Not a bad plan, but she had to know we were too persistent for that.

Dina and I filed into the crowd, each pinning our arms to our sides so we could ride the wave of chattering audience members out to the lobby and stay close to Colleen. She kept checking over her shoulder, like she was in the slowest police pursuit ever recorded, but we stayed in her field of view.

"She doesn't look happy," Dina said.

"I'm sure you can charm her," I whispered back.

The doorway unclogged after a minute, as people split off toward the snack stands or the bathroom or out into the cold to sneak a cigarette before the teens reclaimed the stage. With the artery open, Colleen quickened her march, seemingly searching for the women's room as safe harbor. Maybe she hadn't noticed Dina.

I cut right and into an opening, flanking the IA boss through the lobby while Dina stayed on her rear.

The three of us were nearing the restrooms, and suddenly I was thankful for stereotypes. The women's line was twice as long as the men's, and Collen wound up stuck between two crowds trying to sidestep the wait as Dina filed in behind her. When she turned to move to the next clearing, I was already in her way.

"This is low, Russell," she said as we locked eyes.

"It's important."

"It's my daughter's fucking…"

She stopped, as the F-bomb drew more attention than she wanted.

"It's my daughter's senior play," she said. "You can't be here."

"I'll be gone in five. But I need to talk to you," I said.

"You think I'm going to fu…," she stopped, catching herself. "You think I'm going to help you with anything after last time? We had a deal. You broke it."

"You're not helping him," Dina said, finally announcing her presence. "You're helping me."

She realized she was surrounded, then groaned.

"You're both way out of bounds here," she said.

"I know, and I'm sorry, but this couldn't wait," Dina replied. "It's about Lazio."

Colleen blushed, looking past Dina and scanning the room. She wasn't the only Newark cop who fled to the burbs when the sun went down. Hell, she probably wasn't the only one with a son or daughter on stage that night.

"I can't talk to you about that," she replied.

"We know he was using," Dina said. "In court. During trials. You know I have to write that. I'm trying to give the department a voice in the story before I do."

"I don't know what you're talking about," Colleen replied, her poker face better than I remembered. "Just call media relations like you're supposed to."

She was lying. Dina knew that. I'd told her about my run-in with Colleen in the courthouse, that she was actively hunting for the public defender. But for whatever reason, Dina wasn't pouncing. Maybe it was the intrusive way we'd approached Colleen, the bruising nature of the whole thing. Dina was a good reporter, and she had no qualms about getting into rough situations, but we were admittedly doing a shitty thing to a good person.

Sometimes there are benefits to being the asshole.

"C'mon," I said, cutting past Colleen and hooking Dina's arm, just like I'd said I would if it went this way. "We tried. She can read about it in the paper tomorrow."

Dina tugged against me as I pulled her away. I didn't know if she was legitimately fighting me or playing into the act, but I didn't care. Sometimes you have to sell the idea that the source needs you more than you need them.

I wasn't moving all that fast, but I wasn't looking back either, hoping each step toward the exit would weigh on Colleen.

A rush of cold hit us as we slipped through the double-doors toward the outside, and just as I was starting to worry about my gambit not paying off, I heard heavy footsteps behind us.

"Outside," Colleen said, putting a hand in each of our backs and driving us toward the stairs. "Two minutes. And if I miss a of second of Act Two, I will find a way to make sure you both get ticketed every single time you even think about driving through Newark."

The courtyard outside Montclair High School was more like the center of a college campus. A lush lawn, stone benches and tall trees with muscular branches that stretched wide enough that they almost intertwined. The few parents still dawdling outside nervously lit second cigarettes, averting their eyes from others, maybe feeling dirty that their habits might make them miss any part of their kids' performance. Sometimes I was glad I quit.

"What do you think you know?" Colleen said, her breath leaping after her words like steam.

This was it. Dina had to push the issue. If she told Colleen the truth, that we'd only talked to Reek, that we only had the word of one dealer, she'd know the threat of publication was bullshit. I hated the idea of using fiction to draw out the truth as much as Dina did, but the only reality that matters is the one you publish. Given how the protests had started to turn ugly, the people needed answers more than Dina needed to worry about ethics.

"Five of Lazio's clients told us he requested drugs from them at some point during their trials. Painkillers, specifically. They are concerned he might have been high while representing them. Meaning his counsel was ineffective. Meaning they might deserve re-trials," Dina said. "The oldest case is in 2013, meaning he very well could have been abusing prescription drugs for at least four years while representing an untold number of clients. Obviously, you know two of his clients were killed in the past few weeks, both of whom he represented in cases where they were accused of selling prescription painkillers. One of them was killed by one of your officers, and I think that's something my readers need to …"

"Stop," Colleen said, wiping one hand across her face.

I looked to the right, saw some of the embarrassed smokers stubbing their cigarettes halfway through, worried they might miss the curtain raise.

"You can't print that," Colleen said.

"Are you saying it's not true?" Dina asked.

Colleen looked around again, seemingly relieved by the few stragglers moving away.

"Do you know where Lazio is?" she asked.

Now she was pumping us for information?

"What?" Dina asked.

"I'll take that as a no," she said. "I don't either. And that's why you can't print it."

"Colleen what are you…" I started, but she held a hand up.

"We are not on speaking terms," she said before turning back to Dina. "What do you want from me? Off the record, obviously. He already knew I was running an investigation about Lazio. Now you seem to have figured out why. What I don't understand is why you're here."

"How many officers knew?" Dina asked. "You run IA. You investigate cops, not public defenders. If you're looking for him, and you know about the drugs, that means you think somehow this connects to the department."

Colleen shook her head. I couldn't tell if she was disgusted with us, her agency, or both.

"I honestly don't know yet," she said. "And that's why you can't print this. Because I can't prove any of it yet. Not without Lazio."

"His clients…" I started.

"What did I just say about you talking?" she asked, glaring at me again before looking at Dina. "They won't talk to me Dina. Why would they? You think they're just going to admit to trafficking a controlled substance? Let's not pretend you came here to cough up your sources to me, so why are you really here?"

Dina looked at me, clearly uncomfortable. Arm-twisting Colleen was one thing. Being called out for it was another.

"Maybe we can help each other," Dina said.

Colleen laughed.

"Do you have any idea how many times I've said that to someone?" she asked. "How many times do you think I meant it?"

"Just hear us out," Dina said.

The Internal Affairs boss looked at me.

"He doesn't have a sterling track record with promises and

arrangements," Colleen said. "Though I guess you know that."

I'd never told Colleen about Dina, assuming they might cross paths professionally one day. I guess Dina let that slip in the source flirtation, used me as a punching bag to make for a common enemy. I was impressed. And pissed. But mostly impressed.

"If you want me to hold this story, we need some things in return," Dina said. "One, I want the exclusive when you find Lazio."

"If I find him we can stage the perp walk in your newsroom for all I care," Colleen replied. "You didn't come here for an easy request like that."

Now it was my turn.

"We need to find Mike Lowell," I said.

Colleen went to berate me again but I wasn't having it.

"I know, I know, you hate me. The last time we talked about him you got fucked over. And just for the record, I didn't give Dina that video. That was someone else you can spend the rest of your life staring holes through," I said. "But you and I both know where this is all going. Most of Lazio's clients were drug dealers, the kind of people arrested by Major Crimes. I'm sure you heard I went looking for Lowell. I'm sure you heard I got my ass kicked in the process. What you more than likely don't know is that between the looking and the ass-kicking, I had some words with the man. He doesn't seem like he's part of Henniman's brood. If you're looking for a way in, he might be it."

"Already tried that," she replied. "What do I possibly gain by letting you near him?"

"Best case scenario, he tells us what you want to know and then you have grounds to push a D.A. to subpoena him. Worst case, us knocking on his door and shouting Eddie Lazio's name sends him running your way. Either way, nothing comes back bad on you."

Colleen laughed.

"Isn't that what you said the last time I saw you?" she asked.

She looked around. We were alone now. Which meant her daughter was back on stage and she was stuck outside with us cleaning up a mess she didn't make.

"Shit," she said, searching through her purse. Dina had her pen and notepad out within seconds.

"He's in Seaside," she said, snatching the pad from Dina and scribbling the address. "If you two get him talking, you call me immediately. I doubt you're the only ones looking for him."

***

The drive toward Seaside Heights was unpleasant, and not just because you spent most of it staring at tail lights in beach traffic.

I'd made the trek with Dina more than once, back when we were the kind of happy couple who posted weekend pictures near the waves to Instagram, back when my biggest problem was grimacing at her music choices. Back before I'd let my failings at the Intelligencer spill into the rest of my life and turned into something of a festering asshole.

My brain hit pause before I could work too far down the list of excuses for me and Dina's collapse. I'd always blamed my exit from the paper and her decision to stay, in my job, for our split. But working alongside her again had stoked some old fires, reminded me just how clever she could be, how she had skills I always refused to recognize.

Back then, I'd treated her more like a sidekick than a partner. I couldn't get past the idea that she'd taken my spot and handled it every bit as well as me. Now I was the one struggling to keep up. She got Reek talking. She got me back in with Colleen and put us on track to find Lowell. My investigation would have been dead without her, and in the last few days she'd proven to be as good, if not better, than I ever was working the cops' beat.

Maybe there would be a time when I'd get to say that to her, but as I looked out the passenger side window, the angry white caps lapping at the Tom's River shoreline reminded me this was nothing like our summer drives. We were crossing the Mathis Bridge into Seaside Heights, a resort town and barrier island that effectively turned off once the fall got into full swing. By winter, the place was a husk, all vacated rental homes and sparsely occupied welfare motels. The town was ugly without sun. The mix of sand and days-old snow gave the beaches a leftover oatmeal complexion. The water was beyond uninviting once it got cold, each wave frothing at the mouth to break, slip back and wail on something a second time.

It was a good place to disappear, and Lowell certainly had a lot to hide from. As far as any protester was concerned, he might have killed Kevin Mathis for filming the shooting of Luis Becerra. Based on our run-in at Hanley's, he was on the outs with Henniman. The officer was on an island long before he'd actually fled to one.

The address Chelsea had given us traced back to a rental property owned by one of Lowell's cousins, something that Dina or I could have easily missed while scouring public records to find him.

Colleen warned us that other people might be looking for Lowell. If she knew where he was, I doubted she was the only cop who did. We rolled a red light at Ocean Boulevard and moved slowly down Sherman Avenue, searching for the address. The street had a nice view of some of the amusement park rides near the water, but the sight of an idle Ferris wheel with its gondolas being rocked by the wind wasn't exactly comforting.

Still, I would've taken that over the image of Frank's truck parked exactly where we needed to be.

"Shit," I said. "Pull over."

"What?"

"Dina, just do it. We got a problem."

She complied, putting the car in park, unlocking the doors. But we weren't going anywhere.

"That's Frank's truck," I said.

224

"What the hell is he doing here?" she asked.

"He promised to help me find Lowell a day or two ago," I said. "Haven't talked to him since I connected with you at the protests."

I neglected to mention the text I'd sent to him the night before.

"And now he's here without you," she replied. "Great source, that one."

Frank's presence, whatever the reason, was a problem. Maybe he thought he needed to butter up Lowell first, win him over without me there. Which made sense, considering what had happened the last time I'd approached the detective.

Or he'd gone there alone because he never had any intention of connecting us in the first place.

The sight of Frank trying to peer through the windows of what was supposed to be Lowell's hiding spot dropped a few places down the list of "Shit Russell Needs to Worry About" when a pair of Crown Vics glided past us.

Of course, they parked behind Frank's truck.

Of course, Lt. Bill Henniman exited the passenger side of the first one.

"What the fuck is going on here?" Dina asked.

I genuinely had no idea. I was even more confused when I saw Henniman throw his hands up in the air as he locked eyes with Frank, whose face was twisted somewhere between a scream and a snarl. I was too far away to hear what they were saying, but it sure as hell looked like an argument.

"I don't know," I replied. "Do you think Colleen warned them we were coming?"

"Seriously?" she shot back. "Your source is outside the home of the cop we've been searching for, without us, and you're questioning my source, who actually sent us this way?"

"Why else would they be here Dina?" I asked.

"I don't know, and honestly, I don't care right now," she replied. "How the hell are we going to get anywhere near Lowell with the Fraternal Order of Police on his lawn?"

She was red-faced. So was I. We were inches away from the interview that might have made her story, that might have answered Austin Mathis' questions, and now there might as well have been a forcefield around Lowell's house.

Dina looked at me like she was going to scream but she was interrupted by the sound of a car door opening. Neither of us had touched anything.

We turned around to see Detective Mike Lowell entering the backseat, his gun in full view.

CHAPTER 15

Lowell looked less like a detective and more like someone he might arrest as he piled into the back of the car. The gun was in his lap, the business end pointed between Dina and I.

His face was half obscured by the hood of a gray sweatshirt that bore the logo of what I assumed was a high school. He sat exhausted and stoic, eyes straight ahead, hunting for a space between Dina, the cops, me. Somewhere where there was nothing and no one looking to dredge up whatever it was that had him in this position.

"You don't need that," I said, my stare still locked on to his service weapon.

"You lied about who you were the last time we talked," Lowell replied, before nudging the barrel toward Dina. "And you convinced half the city that I murdered a kid. I'll decide what I need."

Dina placed her hands on the wheel, deliberate, slow, like the move was practiced. Given the occupation of the man in the backseat, maybe it was.

"We just want to talk," she said, eyes straight ahead.

"Yeah, so do they," Lowell replied, nodding his head toward the cops in front of his house.

Henniman and Frank were still embroiled in an argument, though I had no idea what was driving their fury. The lieutenant had backup, three guys in plain clothes. Two of them could have been the flunkies who'd found Dina and I in the courthouse, but I couldn't be sure. The oval shape shuffling behind them, face red from the cold or lack of circulation, was definitely Scannell.

"I know why they're here," Lowell said. "You two, I still don't understand."

"We'll explain, but how did you even spot us?" Dina asked.

I shot her a look that demanded to know why she was questioning the armed and disturbed police officer sitting behind us.

"They're outside of my sister-in-law's place. I wasn't staying there," he said. "There's a neighbor who leaves us their keys in case of emergency. One house back from where we're sitting. I had a feeling someone would come looking for me after you made me a national headline. Wanted to see who."

I looked up at the cops again. Frank and Henniman were still jawing, the lieutenant's hands waving like my Italian mother. Henniman's men were moving around the edges of the house Lowell was supposed to be inside, checking windows, perusing the mail. Scannell looked to be headed down the driveway in search of a back entrance.

"Why are they looking for you?" she asked.

"That's your question? Not, why are there five of them? And why do they look more than a little pissed that they can't find me?" he asked. "You already fucked me with that half-assed story, don't follow that up by asking shitty questions."

Something in Dina's eye twitched. I knew what happened when you questioned her journalism, because I was usually the one doing it and paying for it.

"Detective," I said. "I'm going to guess that being held at gunpoint is throwing her off a bit. We're not armed. We're not here for anything but a conversation. I think that might go better if you put the gun away."

Lowell looked down at the weapon, looked up at Dina's teeth

228

chattering even though the car's heater was whining with everything it had. I had on a poker face, but my hands were dug as far into the seat cushion as they could go, bracing for something awful.

"Goddamnit," Lowell said, shaking his head and sliding the weapon back toward his waist. "I'm sorry about that. You have no idea what I'm going through."

"Said the guy who shot an unarmed teenager," Dina replied.

"I didn't want to shoot that kid," he said. "You have to know that."

"I don't know that," Dina replied. "I know that he's dead and you're not. I know he didn't have a weapon. Those are the things that I know."

"That's why you're here? To argue over that video?"

"No, we're here to find out why you shot him," she said.

"He reached."

"For nothing," she said, turning to face him now, introducing him to the searing glare I'd learned to respect and fear as long as I'd known her. "You honestly think that's right?"

"I think it was legal," he replied. "Right is a different conversation."

Dina leaned back a bit, but I heard the same thing in his voice that I'd heard in the bar. The sick-of-death tremor.

"We know there's more to this," I said.

"You're goddamn right there is," he spat back.

"Then tell us," Dina said, doing her best to keep her teeth from grinding. "Those guys aren't scouring your off-the-grid address over a routine shooting. The city wouldn't be on fire for that."

"A lot more to this," he said again, not looking at anyone in particular.

I checked on our unwanted guests. Scannell and the flunkies were back, exchanging confused glances. Henniman and Frank seemed to have reached a détente, for a moment. I watched the two nameless cops move down the block, walk toward the porch of the home next to the one Lowell was supposed to be inside. Henniman and Scannell did the same, but they were moving our way. Frank stood still, looking down at his phone. Apparently, he wasn't allowed to play any reindeer games.

"If we tell you what we know, will you fill in the blanks?" I asked. "Because the minute those guys come this way, this conversation is over. If you've got a story to tell, now's the time to tell it."

Lowell looked to Dina.

"You can't use my name," he said. "But I'll give you what you need to set the record straight."

"I can't promise that," she replied.

"Then I can't stay in this car any longer," he said, starting to slide left.

"We know about Eddie Lazio," I said, stopping his movement. "We know he was buying drugs from clients. We know the kid you shot was one of his clients. We know another one of his clients wound up dead not long after, and we know why that might make Henniman do some desperate things."

Lowell went to reply, but Dina cut him off. It was full court press time.

"Which means you also know exactly why people might think you shot Luis Becerra for reasons that have nothing to do with any use-of-force policy," she said. "You know that, once this gets out, the half of the city that doesn't think you're a murderer will change its mind. You know that Lazio being a junkie means hundreds of arrests made by your unit could be overturned."

She paused. I didn't know if it was for effect or to catch her breath. But Lowell looked like he wanted to hear the rest of what she had to say.

"We also know Henniman has tried to stop us from looking too closely at this every chance he got. It sure as hell looks like your unit is trying to clean something up," she continued. "If you're not involved, if you want there to be a story that says you're not involved, you need to help us."

His face was slack, unmoved.

I looked back toward Henniman and Scannell again. They'd struck out at House #1, but mercifully, an older woman had opened the door to House #2 and was giving them an earful about something.

"Clock's ticking man," I said. "I don't want to be here when they come this way, and you don't want to be sitting with us."

"I didn't know about Lazio," he replied. "Not until after."

Henniman was done at Door #2. He was moving up the block again. He'd be parallel with us soon.

But if we stopped Lowell from talking now, who knew if he'd start back up again later. Besides, if we pulled out, they might try and stop us. Our best move was not to make one, at least for the moment.

"We kept a list for targeted enforcement. Dealers suspected in shootings, robberies. You know what the bosses say, can't arrest your way out of the drug problem. So, we focused on the ones doing the most damage," he said. "Becerra. Mathis. Those names didn't mean anything to me until a few weeks ago. Suddenly, they were on that list."

I checked Door #3. Scannell was looking at the windows again, as if he'd suddenly gained X-ray vision that hadn't helped him the first few times.

"We were supposed to bring both of them in, notify the Lieutenant if we saw them. It seemed odd, but I didn't ask any questions. That's why I was after Becerra the night …"

He stopped himself, shook his head, craned his neck, like he could escape what had happened.

"The night things went bad," he said. "After it happened, I wanted to know who he was. Wanted to understand. Ten years on, and I'd never fired my weapon. I needed to know what he was running from that was worth all this. You've seen his record. No outstanding warrants. Nothing violent. It didn't make sense. I started asking why we were so hard up for him. The other detectives didn't know. Most guys in my unit don't question Henniman. People who do don't last long."

I knew that song.

"It took a few weeks, but I finally got someone talking. Scannell. He wouldn't wipe his ass without Henniman's permission. But he gets real talkative after a few bourbons. Told me I'd done good. That Mathis and Becerra were a problem, that they knew something the lieutenant didn't want known. They'd been giving pills to Lazio whenever he worked their cases, and apparently they'd gotten to bragging about it. Told more than a few people that they had a get out of jail free card. That they had something to trade if we ever jacked them up."

"They were threatening to use Lazio against the unit?" Dina asked.

"Maybe it was just shit talk. Maybe they'd made a direct threat. I don't know. What I do know is Henniman wanted them off the table, and I did half his job for him," Lowell replied. "I did not know about any of this shit when I pulled the trigger. I thought he had a gun. That's it."

"But if Henniman was afraid they'd use what they had on Lazio to cut a deal if they ever got arrested, why would he want them in custody in the first place?" Dina asked.

She knew the answer. She just wanted Lowell to say it.

Easier for them to get lost that way.

I checked outside again, searching for Henniman and Scannell. The other two, the nameless detectives, were working our end of the block. They were closing in.

I didn't have time to hear the end of Lowell's story.

"You two need to finish this somewhere else," I said.

Dina followed my gaze, noticed Lowell's former friends were heading our way.

"Shit," she said.

Lowell started to fidget, like he was going to bolt.

"You want the truth out, you need to stay with her," I said, my hand moving toward the door.

"The hell are you doing?" she asked.

"Henniman will be good and pissed if he sees me here. Should distract him long enough for you two to get moving and end this," I said. "Just make you sure you tell the story the right way."

She smiled.

"The way you used to do it?"

I smiled back. Hopefully, it wouldn't be the last time we shared one of those moments.

"Nah, your way's working just fine. I couldn't have broken this story," I replied. "But if they shoot me, I expect a glowing profile."

I hopped out of the car and cut straight across the street, staying out of Henniman's view just long enough. I moved down the block in a crouched walk, about eye-level with the rear-view mirrors of each parked car, until I was only a few feet away from Frank.

I stood up slow, making each step deliberate, causing the snow to crunch to announce my arrival.

Frank turned first, his face half alarmed, half amused.

"The fuck?" he asked.

The sound caught the attention of the rest of the class. Henniman was already wincing from the cold, so it didn't take long for his face to return to its natural snarl. He came charging across the street, brought the rest of his search party with him.

I'd expected him to be pissed.

I hadn't expected him to be the second Newark cop to point his gun at me in the span of an hour.

CHAPTER 16

Outnumbered. Unarmed. Staring at four faces that looked like they could care less what happened to me as long as it meant they would walk off the street in one piece.

Luis Becerra's decision to run suddenly made a lot more sense.

I backed up slow, hands high in the air, keeping Dina's car in my peripheral vision. The vehicle was crawling backwards out of the spot, trying not to raise any attention. But any and all parties interested in the detective in her backseat were focused on me now.

Henniman was maybe 15 feet away, eyes bulging, body in a shooting stance. The two cops from the courthouse and Scannell had their backs turned to Dina, oblivious to their slowly escaping prey. Frank was off to the left, a blank expression on his face.

Part of me hoped he was just thinking of a way to get me out of this.

The rest of me knew that was bullshit. He'd chosen his side, and it was opposite from mine. It was the only reason he'd have been here.

"I told you to stay away," Henniman said. "You have no idea what you're fucking with here."

"You pointing a gun at me gives me a pretty good idea," I replied.

Dina has eased into a K-turn now, still creeping so slow that the tires barely made any noise over the winter beach wind. They'd be gone soon.

"See, I get what brought you and hungry hungry hippo down here," I said, pointing to Scannell. "You wanted to have a little chat with a certain detective. He's not here by the way. Left about an hour ago."

If Bill knew I was lying, his face didn't show it. But he was still too focused on me. A flash of red lit up the corner of my field of view. Dina's taillights.

"Do they know why they're here though?" I asked, nudging my head toward the unnamed detectives. "They know what you drug them into?"

I looked at Frank. His face wasn't moving but his palm was resting on his chest, thumbnail slicing along the edge of his neck.

No, not his neck. His throat.

Was he waving me off? Was he still with me?

"You know what? I think me and Russell need to have a private conversation," Henniman said, turning to his underlings. "You three keep looking."

Then he turned to Frank.

"And you, go home. You're retired. This isn't your problem anymore."

Henniman started to advance on me, arms still locked, gun still ready.

"Frank?" I asked.

He didn't say anything.

"Frank, what the fuck?" I asked again.

He shook his head and looked away from me. He'd bailed me out with Scannell, but Scannell was an asshole. Henniman was the department, through and through. Frank wasn't going to choose me over them.

The lieutenant stepped behind me, barrel keeping me frozen, as Frank started to walk toward his truck.

"So it was all bullshit?" I asked. "All that stuff you used to tell me about doing what was right, instead of just what was right for the department?"

He kept walking. Henniman started shoving me toward Lowell's driveway, gun now in my back.

I marched as ordered, staring a hole through Frank's spine, or whatever he had that passed for one, as I moved.

Dina had been right. Key was right. I'd put my trust in the people I was told to respect instead of the people I actually knew, and now I was getting marched out of sight at gunpoint for it.

The rage was keeping me focused, but it was also keeping me focused on the wrong things. My best source leaving me high and dry was a motherfucker, but it wouldn't make a difference if Henniman was taking me somewhere quiet for the purpose of keeping me quiet.

The driveway had been lazily shoveled, if at all. We trudged through patches of uneven snow, neither of us entirely steady. I searched for a patch of ice, something to slip on, something to create separation. But a twitch like that might make Henniman fire. Even if it didn't, I had no car and nowhere to run to, except toward a block filled with guys taking orders from the Lieutenant. I was gonna have to talk my way out of this, but Bill had always been the one snake I couldn't charm.

We entered the backyard, where the snow got up to ankle-depth. Some patio furniture sat caked in white, and Henniman shoved me toward it.

"You wanna be involved in this mess?" he asked. "Then here's your chance. Cause there's only two ways you leave this backyard."

"You're gonna shoot me like you shot Kevin Mathis?"

He slapped his free hand against his head.

"You are a fucking idiot," he said. "Tell me where Lazio is and this stops. You get what you want."

"What I want is for you to answer for what you did," I replied. "It's just us now, Bill. You don't have to put on a show, pretend you're the last one defending some blue line. If word spread about Lazio, then the last few years of your career, your unit's arrest log, it would all go up in smoke. You wanted to protect it. Mathis was a threat. So was Becerra. Now they're dead. It's a pretty simple story."

"Where's the lawyer, Russell?" he asked. "You're either a cooperating witness or a suspect. I don't care much which."

"Suspect?" I asked. "The fuck are you gonna arrest me for?"

"Interfering with a police investigation, for one."

"That would never stick."

"You're probably right," he replied. "But plenty of guys saw you and Scannell go at it the other night. Most of them say you threw the first punch. Assault on a peace officer, now that's something that can stick. That's something that you do time for."

The threat had teeth. There were probably more than enough people inside Hanley's that would sing whatever song Henniman played, and Scannell would have credibility. His internal affairs jacket was clean now. Thanks to me.

I scanned the buildings nearby. Looking for a window. A witness. Help of any kind.

But there was nobody. I wasn't getting out of this.

"I don't know where Lazio is," I said.

"Then you know someone who does," he said. "I'm trying to help you, dipshit. Give me something."

"You're trying to help me?" I asked. "What kind of shit is that? You want to ruin me? Ruin me. But if we've got all our cards out, at least tell me what this is. At least own it."

I'd gotten too worked up. Moved forward. Balled up my fists.

The gun rose up to meet me.

I'd given him a reason.

"Last chance, Russell," he said.

One last look at the buildings. Nothing in the windows. No one.

237

Then I turned to the driveway and saw hope.

"You want me off the board, then we can do it in front of a judge," I said to Henniman, letting my hands climb slowly as I turned my back to him. "But you're not ending this here."

Something clicked as I looked away. It sounded like he was snapping his handcuffs off his belt.

"This has been a shitty week," he said. "But this just might make it worth…"

He didn't finish his sentence. His voice cut off, and I turned to see a muscular arm laced across Bill Henniman's throat. A hand palmed the back of his head, compressing the lieutenant's neck in the trap. He'd be out in seconds. It was a blood choke. One of those self-defense moves Frank had taught me back in the day.

He was a lot better at it than I'd ever been.

"The fuck are you doing here?" I asked him.

"I believe the words you're searching for are 'thank you,'" he replied.

"Thank you," I said. "Now what the fuck are you doing here?"

"I should put you out all the same, especially with all the shit you talked out front," he said. "But we don't have time. They're cleaning up."

"Who is … what?" I asked.

"I heard your conversation. The lawyer, right? The one the Becerra kid's brother told you about," he said. "Henniman is looking for him. Same as he was looking for Lowell. If one's missing, they'll go hunting for the other."

"What are you saying, Frank?"

"Lowell's father was on the job. I called him to get a line on this place. I wanted to talk to him before you did, get the truth of it, but his father seemed to have a pretty clear bead," he said. "The lawyer, all the cases that would go away, the reasons someone like Bill would want people like Luis Becerra and Kevin Mathis out of the picture. They want, no, they fucking need, this to go away. You think Henniman

238

brought three extra cops to have a friendly chat with Lowell?"

Lowell certainly hadn't thought so.

"They're clearing the table, Russell. You want me to tell you that you were right? Fine, you were fucking right," he said. "But if they find Lazio before we do, then none of this shit matters. There is no story to tell. We need to find him. Right now."

I had no idea how to find Eddie Lazio

But based on what Lowell told us in the car, I might have had a line on someone who could make the lawyer find us.

***

I sat in Frank's passenger seat at the corner of Springfield and Littleton, recounting all the shitty, risky things I'd done to get this far, wondering if the answers I sought were worth the shitty, risky thing I was about to do.

In less than a week I'd manipulated Dina, manipulated Colleen, fought a drug dealer, fought a cop, been arrested, exploited the broken hearts of Luis Becerra's brother and mother and probably lost my P.I.'s license thanks to Henniman.

All that to get maybe a step from the man whose drug addiction might have gotten two people killed, who might have opened some of Newark's cops up to their worst impulses in the hope of protecting arrest totals and crime declines.

Eddie Lazio was within reach. I knew who he was now. What he really was. An addict in hiding. One I could lure out by using his own desperation against him. The guy sure seemed like he deserved to be led by the nose to his own demise, but that didn't mean I had to feel good about it.

I could see Levon, the drug dealer who'd taken over Kevin Mathis' business, through the windshield. He was wearing the same Brooklyn Nets cap as the last time we'd crossed paths.

Dina and I had engaged in a dissertation length text message

239

exchange over the course of my ride in Frank's car. Trying to determine what else was needed to go public. Trying to figure out what it might take to get Colleen or someone else to move on Henniman. Lowell's story was good. It certainly gave Henniman, or one of his cronies, proper motive to want Kevin Mathis dead. It put the Major Crimes unit in the center of a cover-up that might have left who knows how many suspects, guilty or innocent, under the ineffective and drug-induced counsel of Eddie Lazio. We had the beginnings of proof of a scandal. But Lowell's word wasn't enough. We both knew it. We needed the lawyer, and Lowell genuinely didn't know where he was. The same went for Colleen.

In the middle of that, Key had sent out one of her text message blasts. There was another protest scheduled for that night. Back at City Hall. The same place the last one had exploded into tear gas. With no answers to their questions, Key's crowd would be itching to scream and hiss in the faces of the police officers who had grown less patient as the week of civil disobedience had worn on. Someone was going to push things too far, take the city in a direction it couldn't turn back from. People were going to get hurt.

This needed to end. For the city's sake, and my own. While I was thankful for Frank's rescue, choking out the Major Crimes lieutenant would have consequences. By the time Henniman had woken up, he'd probably directed his guys to search for both of us. Given them license plate numbers, vehicle descriptions, home addresses, known associates. We were in their city, working their turf. It was only a matter of time before they caught up to us, and I needed to let the world know who they were before they put us in handcuffs. Or worse.

But if the last dominoes were going to fall, I'd have to knock them over and make a lot of noise doing it.

If we wanted to find Eddie Lazio, painkiller addict, our best bet was to dangle painkillers in front of him. His number was somewhere in the cell phone Austin Mathis had given us, and it matched one in the burner I'd taken from Luis Becerra's brother.

But the number was useless without the right person to call it. Someone who would have something Lazio would want. That person was Levon.

Based on our last interaction, I doubted Levon would want to do me any favors, but I had a card to play. One I couldn't play if Frank walked up there with me.

"That him?" Frank asked, reaching for the door handle, looking through the windshield to the spot I'd been staring at.

I grabbed his wrist harder than I should have and he tensed up. Maybe his adrenaline was up from the clash with Henniman but something seemed different in him, charged. Not the pulsing anger I'd seen when he'd first come to help me, more like a coiled rage at the idea of another scandal scarring his beloved agency.

"Yeah," I replied. "But it's probably better if I handle this on my own."

"I helped you get this far," he said. "I want to see how it ends."

Always the fucking detective.

"Frank, he's a dealer. You were a cop. You kinda stand out around here," I said.

"Because I'm white?"

"No, because you have a cop moustache and you're wearing a suit," I replied. "Besides, this guy is even less of a fan of the badge crowd than your garden variety dealer. Remember what we talked about when this all started?"

His face twisted up in concentration. It had been a long week. I gave him the minute to catch up, to think back to the diner.

"This is the guy you called me about?" he asked. "The one who said a cop wanted him to lie about someone being a snitch?"

I nodded.

241

"I told you that was bullshit," he replied. "How do we know anything he even says is reliable?"

"We don't. But he's a drug dealer and we're hunting a drug addict, and we don't have a lot of time," I said. "Now unless you've got a better plan."

He shook his head no, then tapped his hand to his holster.

"If anything goes wrong…"

"Yeah, if you hear anything that sounds like me being killed, feel free to ride to the rescue," I replied. "Otherwise, just stay here."

The wind hit hard as soon as I got out of the car, one of those straight through your body gusts that reminds every muscle it's tired and every brain cell that being outside in November is stupid. I hadn't been sleeping much, which is what happens when you spend a week getting arrested and beat up.

I moved toward Levon, wondering if getting shot wasn't the worst outcome after all.

The Brooklyn Nets cap turned my way when I got within fifty feet. His expression changed as he stepped off the stoop where he'd set up shop, somewhere between confusion and a bad memory. He said something to the tall guy with the linebacker build to his right, and the heavy moved for me while Levon stood perched with his arms crossed.

"You got balls coming back here," he shouted. "Maybe not brains, but balls."

"Would you believe me if I told you I was here to help?" I asked.

"No."

The linebacker threw a forearm into my chest. I stumbled back from the blow, let out a cough. Guess he didn't believe me either. I'd managed to march into a shadow between the streetlight and the overhead beam of the apartment where Levon was standing, hopefully out of Frank's view. Things were nowhere near bad enough for him to come charging in and blow our last lead.

"Guess I … deserved that," I said, each word struggling to charge past the sudden tightness in my chest.

"You deserve a lot worse," Levon said. "And it's coming."

His feet entered my doubled over field of vision. Guess he'd left his stoop fiefdom to come down and hang out with the little people. I came a little further out of my crouch to see what was tucked into his waist band. The gun he'd been too smart to carry the last time.

"Came prepared," he said.

"You can shoot me in a few minutes if you don't like what I have to say," I replied.

I rose slowly, looking back and forth between Levon and the guy who nearly caved my chest in, waiting to see if another blow was coming. After spending a few seconds unmolested, I decided to press my luck.

"You remember the thing we talked about last time?" I asked.

"You mean last time when you sucker-punched me?"

That was not an accurate description of the events. But I didn't like the odds of the guy without the gun fact-checking the guy who was packing.

"What I mean is, I think I can get rid of the man who was causing you a problem," I said.

I was expecting a reaction that didn't come. Levon was looking at Forearm Guy, maybe thinking about having him beat on me again when he should have been listening.

"We need to make this a private conversation?" I asked. "I'm assuming you didn't tell your friend here about it."

Now Levon was looking at me. Good.

Unfortunately, he was also moving toward me. Bad.

The uppercut he threw was wild, ugly, the kind of punch offered by someone who hadn't thrown too many successful ones. But it surprised me enough that I stumbled backwards and into the light just in time for the follow-up body shot that doubled me over again.

Frank had to have seen that. Tick Tock.

Levon pulled me in close, grabbing me under the shoulders of my jacket.

"You want me to mention the cop in front of big boy, or you wanna talk?" I hissed in his ear.

He let go, turned to the heavy, who looked he wanted to hurt me way worse than Levon could ever hope to.

"Take a walk," Levon shouted. "I need to teach this bitch a lesson on my own."

"Levon," the big man replied.

"I said I got it," Levon said. "Walk."

The big man rolled his eyes. I imagine he did that a lot around Levon's overconfident ass. But at least he was walking away.

"You got one minute to tell me what the fuck you're talking about," he said.

"The cop who told you to spread word that Kevin Mathis was a snitch. I think I know who he is. I think he's involved in some nasty shit. And if you do me a small favor, I think I can get him in jail and out of your life," I said.

He laughed, a hyena yelp.

"You think I'm gonna do you a favor?"

"Fine, then don't consider it favor. Consider it self-preservation," I replied. "The guy is looking for you. He's cleaning up the mess he caused. The mess you unwittingly became a part of."

"The fuck do you…"

I felt my wind coming back, which was good, because the more I talked the less Levon would.

"I think the cop who came after you killed Kevin Mathis. I think he's trying to cover it up. You being dead would help with that," I said. "You do this favor, and he goes away before he makes you go away.

244

Sound fair?"

"Depends on the favor," he replied.

I turned around to look for the truck, for Frank, but it was too dark to see if he was still inside.

"Kevin had a specific customer I need to find," I said, pulling out the cell phones that once belonged to Kevin and Luis. "The numbers are in these. He's a pill head, the kind who wouldn't just come down to the corner. I need you to call him and get him somewhere I can find him."

"Oh, you mean the lawyer?" he asked.

"How the hell do you know about that?"

"Man, Kevin was always running his mouth about that shit. And besides, this is Newark. How many customers you think we got worth making deliveries to?"

It occurred to me that I hadn't known about Lazio when I first approached Levon. It occurred to me my life could have been a lot easier.

"You can find him?" I asked.

"Find him? Shit I already know where he is, or where he will be to pick up," he replied. "I took over supplying him as soon as Kevin got capped. I can have him at the Hotel Nile in an hour. But how's this get that cop off my ass?"

I reached for my phone, slow, nodding at Levon so he knew I wasn't trying anything. Once he confirmed Henniman had leaned on him, things would get a lot less complicated.

"This the cop who came after you? The one who made you tell people Levon was a snitch?" I asked, as I searched for the picture.

"Yeah," Levon said, a sudden tremor in his voice.

I looked at him. He wasn't looking at me. Or the picture. He was looking over my shoulder.

Right where Frank Russomano was standing.

CHAPTER 17

I stared at Frank, trying to figure out who, or what, I was looking at.

He was in the same suit I'd seen him wear at a hundred other crime scenes, standing just out of the bath of a streetlight, lips slightly upturned, a smile that could drop into a scowl before you blinked.

His eyes were pensive, like always, scanning the situation. My face. Levon's face. Trying to read what we'd been talking about.

I knew his tics because he was the cop I knew best in this city. My source. My friend, even though I wasn't supposed to use that term.

But if what Levon was saying was true, then he couldn't have been any of those things. If what Levon was saying was true, he was the guy who told a drug dealer connected to one of the most powerful gangs in Newark that Kevin Mathis was a snitch.

Which meant he wanted Kevin Mathis dead.

Or that he'd killed him all by himself.

Frank stepped closer. Maybe he wasn't sure why Levon was staring at him like he'd forgotten how to speak. Or maybe he was, and that was just as bad if not worse.

"You alright there, Russ?" he asked, looking past me at Levon.

I nodded. Levon nodded. Talking didn't seem like the best move yet, not until I got the tremor in my throat under control.

"This our new friend? He have a way to find the lawyer?" Frank asked, tapping his watch and snapping his fingers in my face. "Cause the clock is ticking."

Well, he was calm. That was good. Maybe that meant he didn't remember Levon, or didn't think Levon recognized him, or didn't realize what was going on. Or it meant he was a sociopath who'd been lying to me from the start who I'd allowed to worm his way into my investigation because I'm a fucking idiot and Dina warned me and goddamnit and...

"Yeah. Yeah," Levon said, the swagger returning to his voice. "I can get your boy in a place where you can find him. But who the fuck are you?"

Damn. The kid was playing it off well. Better than me. And nothing had changed in Frank's face when he said it. Each side kept up their pretense, like their lives depended on it.

Maybe they did.

Whatever panic they were suppressing had made its way into me threefold. I needed a cigarette. No, I needed a drink. No, I needed to sleep for a week.

"He's a friend," I said, turning to Levon mostly so I didn't have to look at Frank. "Just someone I work with. He's trying to help me out on this thing. Figure out who killed Kevin."

"Yeah, whatever," Levon said. "No offense, but I ain't that sentimental about Kev. I just wanna know what this kinda intel is worth to y'all. You are interrupting my business after all."

Frank laughed. I laughed, cause what else do you do when one guy who wants to kill you asks for a bribe from another guy who likely wants to kill him?

"Wrong question," Frank replied. "Now, what's it worth to you? Because that's the right question. Maybe Russ failed to mention it, but I'm ex-NPD. So, it's less, 'you help us, we give you something,' and more, 'you help us, you don't lose anything.'"

"How's that?" Levon asked.

"If I make a phone call, how long do you think before you wind up in handcuffs? An hour? Two?" he asked. "Or you make a phone call, get us what we need, and we're out of your life before the night's over. My way sounds simpler."

"That's some bull…"

Frank moved fast, pulling something from his hip. Levon and I both flinched, but it was just a cell phone.

"What'd you say his name was Russ? Levon? That 'V" capital or lower case?" he asked. "Just want to make sure my friends spell it right."

Something was different in his voice. He sounded cocky now. Like he knew he was only a few steps from erasing whatever he'd done.

"Alright. Alright," Levon said, pulling his own phone out, taking a few steps back. "I'll make the call."

"You can do it in the car," Frank replied.

"What?" I asked.

"He's coming with us, Russ," he replied. "This guy coughs up a high-end customer and we leave him out here, and he what, just behaves cause he's really a wonderful person underneath the du-rag and shitty haircut? The minute we leave he's going to warn the guy off. Ain't that right Levon?"

"Fuck you," Levon replied.

"I'll take that as a yes," Frank said. "Oh, and drop whatever you're carrying."

"Excuse me?"

Frank had the gun out before Levon could say anything else.

"Wherever it is. Toss it," he said, before turning to me. "C'mon man. This is almost over. Get your head in the game."

It was almost over, but the story was headed for a worse ending than I'd hoped. Frank had done something terrible, even if I wasn't exactly sure what that was or why. Levon and Lazio might have been the only two people out there who could connect him to it.

Now all three of them were about to be in the same place, and Frank would be the only one with a gun.

***

We were driving East across MLK, a ride I'd taken countless times before on Newark nights, racing toward a scene Frank would have been standing at.

It made me think back to when this all started, when I'd sat behind the wheel of the Cutlass blasting At The Drive-In, feeling excited, feeling the adrenaline crackling in my blood as I rushed to sit down with Austin Mathis and Key a week earlier.

That vibe I couldn't find anywhere else. The feeling I was chasing something I wasn't supposed to catch.

Except now I'd caught it, only to figure out there's a chasm between writing about life-and-death situations and being in one.

Back in those days, when I'd light up a smoke and turn the radio up to an earsplitting level, I'd watch every street corner and stare down every passer-by wondering about their story. Like the people in the city were just characters for my next piece. Most of the time, that was all they were. Shadows that I filled in with motives and shot counts and stable or critical conditions as relayed by the cops and city officials.

Sometimes they died. Sometimes they lived. But they did it on the page or on my computer screen.

They didn't crumple to the ground in cell phone videos, and their mothers didn't look at me the way Luis Becerra's had.

They didn't fight for what they believed in just to see their pride and passion distilled down to a 30-second YouTube clip and a litany of arrests for unlawful assembly, like Key.

They didn't trade punches with me in the West Ward then end up hostages in the back seat of a truck, like Levon.

They didn't make me question if the Newark I'd seen was the Newark that was actually there, like Frank.

For a man who'd taken a drug dealer prisoner, assaulted a police officer and possibly committed murder in the span of a few days, Frank was exceedingly calm. He pointed at the now defunct Queen of Angels church as we drove, spitting jokes about a lewd conduct arrest he'd made where he had to chase a suspect onto the altar and nearly broken a crucifix in the process.

Maybe he felt untouchable. Maybe he felt like he could piss off Jesus. Maybe he was right.

As far as I could tell, I was the only person who knew Frank had a role in this. Now there was a chance I was about to help him cover it up.

I should have known better. If I was as good as I thought I was back in the notepad days, I'd have questioned his appearance at Hanley's the night Scannell handed me my ass. I'd have kept better tabs on him when he turned sour on me after the Becerra family brought up Eddie Lazio.

Some reporter. Some trained observer. I'd been walking around with my eyes closed. I hadn't just let the fox in the hen house, I'd told him where the fucking hen house was.

Dina warned me. Key warned me. Hell, maybe even Henniman did. I went looking for heroes and villains in a city that only bred survivors. Now people were gonna die because I was an idiot, because I'd tried to tell a story I didn't understand.

"What are we doing?" I asked, the words leaping out of me as involuntary as breathing.

"I don't understand the question," Frank replied.

"Yes, you do. What are we doing when we find Lazio?" I asked.

Frank turned to me, looking at me the same way I'd looked at him when Levon made me question everything. Like he was staring at something far in the distance, squinting to get the whole picture, scanning to figure out if I was friend or foe.

"We question him. We confirm what Henniman was hiding. Then he answers for what he did," Frank replied.

"You mean killing Kevin?" I asked.

"Woah, what?" Levon shouted from the backseat.

The truck slowed to a stop at the intersection of Clinton Avenue, braking less than gentle at the bottom of a hill. The Hotel Nile, the drug flophouse where Levon said we could find Lazio, was on the left. But Frank turned right.

"We need to have a conversation, Russ?" Frank asked. "Cause you seem like you want to have a conversation."

"Might not be the worst idea. May not want our new friend hearing what I have to say," I replied.

Frank nodded. He took us up Clinton, banked right and crossed the McCarter Highway before rolling under the train overpass that ferried the 9-to-5 crowd in and out of downtown, keeping them safe and sound from the real parts of the city. He pulled over in a mostly empty park-and-ride, letting the car idle, the engine's growl drawing the attention of the few people shambling around the quiet streets in the shadow of Newark-Penn station. They were either workers heading home from the bakeries and lunch spots in the Ironbound, or homeless creeping back to the train station, the city's largest unofficial shelter.

"You stay here," Frank said, turning and pointing at Levon. "You're not gonna like what happens if you don't."

He glared at me as he moved to exit the car. At least I was putting some distance between him and Levon, so one thing was going right. Frank slammed the door shut, and I noticed the key fob for the truck was still in the cupholder.

Levon looked confused when I threw it to him.

"What the fuck is going on here?" he asked.

252

"I honestly don't know," I replied. "But it's probably better if you're not part of it."

I slipped out the passenger side door and shut it fast before Frank could get around and see what was happening.

"What happened to you?" he asked, not even looking at me, walking further across the gravel lot and into the wide-open space between us and the nearest building. "How many years did we work with each other without question? How many beers? How many stories?"

"Things were different then," I said.

"Yeah I know that, Russ. I own a fucking television. No catchy chants. No lives mattering. You left the paper before it was cool to come after my tribe on every little thing we ever did. But I thought I knew you better," he said. "What happened to the guy who told me he wasn't like the rest of the reporters in this state? That he understood the job. I gave you access other people would have killed for. Info on any and every homicide you asked about, info on cops who went too far. I trusted you when other people wouldn't. Just this week I saved your ass at least twice. All that, and I have zero credit in the bank with you? You're still challenging me here in the eleventh hour? What am I missing Russ? What changed between then and now?"

I followed him further into the cold, stepping past him, keeping my back turned. I needed to draw him further away from Levon, but I also needed this conversation. I needed to know exactly how wrong I was all this time.

"You know what worries me? That entire rant right there. And maybe you don't remember, but you're the one who taught me that," I replied. "If someone starts defending themselves before you even accuse them of anything, it probably means they did something shitty. Maybe not the thing you think they did, but something. You told me that. And when I started thinking that way in interviews, it was a lot easier to weed out the assholes on Broad Street or in the department."

253

"So, what is it you think I did Russ?"

I wasn't ready to ask that question. Not yet.

"I mean, I just saw you kidnap someone. You're not a cop anymore Frank, and yet you put that kid in the backseat of your car at gunpoint," I said.

"Kid?" he asked, throwing one hand up in the air in disgust. "That's a grown man who makes his living dealing poison to children. The fuck do you care about him?"

"Doesn't mean you get to stick a gun in his face."

"So now you're one of those? You've seen what we're up against. We don't have time to play patty cake with drug dealers."

"We can't pick and choose who we treat like human fucking beings Frank," I shouted. "Kevin Mathis was a drug dealer. Luis Becerra was a drug dealer. Now they're both dead behind what I thought we were trying to expose. That is what we're trying to do here, right? Or did you go see Lowell without me for some other reason?"

I turned around, looked at the car. We were a good distance away, far enough that if Levon had slipped out of an unlocked door we might not have heard it. But I had no way of knowing if that was the case.

"I told you why I went down there. You saw Henniman snapping at me. I saved you from whatever he was about to do to you. And you're still questioning it," he said. "If you want out, if you want me to finish this myself, just say so. I don't know what the fuck's gotten into you, but the man responsible for all of this is a few blocks away. We can get him. We can end this. Or we can stand here screaming at one another."

"So now you think Lazio killed Kevin?" I asked. "I thought it was Henniman. The department covering the whole thing up so they didn't see hundreds of arrests undone. Now you think a junkie public defender dropped a rough-and-tumble dealer like Kevin?"

"All I think is that talking to Lazio is our best chance to figure out what really happened here, a chance we're gonna lose if we don't get over to the Nile soon."

Finally, we agreed on something. But I wasn't gonna tell him that.

He moved closer to me, slow. Put his hand on my shoulder and softened his expression. It was the way he'd talked to me when we first met and I got heated while chasing a story. Back when he was teaching me how to see the city. Maybe he was just teaching me to see it the way he did.

"Russ, we have a chance to do something really important, right now. Right here. Something we couldn't do years ago. We can find a truth that stops these protests, that fixes the department without destroying it. We can actually change things, the way we couldn't when we were just counting up the dead back in the day," he said. "You can tell a story that really matters."

"OK," I replied, nodding but far from in agreement.

There was a story to tell, but it was someone else's.

He started leading us back to the car.

I slipped my phone out while his back was turned, scrolling through my messages for the right contact, responding to someone I should have trusted more than I'd ever trusted Frank. Someone who'd always put the city first, even when it seemed otherwise. I sent a time and a place and a name that would hopefully draw the right reaction.

Frank opened the driver's side door and shouted "Fuck" so loud that it echoed against the rowhouses that lined that part of the North Ward.

"What?" I asked.

"He's gone," Frank shouted, glaring at me as I got into the passenger seat.

I must not have looked surprised enough for his liking, because his hand started traveling to his waist.

"Why'd you let him go Russ?" he asked.

"Why'd you want people to think Kevin Mathis was a C.I.?" I shot

255

back.

Frank closed his eyes, let out a long exhale, like I'd lifted a weight off him just by showing my cards.

Of course, now that meant the stakes were real. He raised the gun slow.

"Didn't I tell you to drop this when you first came to me Russ?" he asked.

"Wouldn't be much of a reporter if I did that."

"You're not a goddamn reporter anymore."

"And you're not a cop anymore either," I replied. "Though I didn't think you'd end up a murderer."

"You're never going to understand this."

"And I don't want too. But I can't let you make this any worse than it already is," I said. "Because that's what's about to happen isn't it. That's why you've been so hot to find this lawyer. He dies, the scandal dies, and the band plays on?"

Frank didn't say anything. He kept looking at me, then the gun, then me again.

"You need to walk away Russ," he said. "Don't make me do something you don't deserve."

"Kevin Mathis didn't deserve it," I replied.

"Kevin Mathis was a piece of shit," he said.

"Kevin Mathis was a screwed-up kid with a father whose life has been ripped apart because you and Henniman cared more about your fucking pride than..."

His knuckles pushed the rest of the sentence back into my mouth. Frank always had fast hands, but the shot he delivered to my teeth was so quick that I had barely even seen his arm move. My head rocked back into the passenger side window and I felt something in my neck jam.

"Get out, Russ," he said.

I rubbed at my face for a minute, hoping the buzz in my head or the water in my eyes cleared before he delivered a follow-up jab. Thankfully, neither came. The shot left me woozy, but able to talk, which was probably useful than throwing a punch at close range with Frank.

"And let you go through with this? Absolutely not," I replied. "Besides, you know what happens if you let me go. So, either shoot me or start the car."

"You know what I'm going to do to Lazio," he said. "You really want to be a witness to that?"

"I'm banking on the fact that you don't want me to be a witness to that," I said. "It's like you said, we have a chance to do something really important here. Maybe for you, that's keeping a secret buried. For me, it's keeping you from taking another life. You don't need Lazio dead Frank. You need him gone. We convince him to disappear, flee the state, flee the fucking country. I don't care. But no one else has to die. We can figure out the rest later."

"How am I supposed to trust you to keep your mouth shut about any of this?" he asked.

"By proving to me you did a terrible thing for the right reasons, that you really had no other choice," I said. "You already killed one man Frank, do you really want to kill two more? You can convince me, or you can shoot me, but those are the only ways this ends."

Frank kept staring, searching my face for some kind of answer, but he wasn't going to find it.

He started the car. I checked my phone, seeing the reply I wanted.

Hopefully I'd done the right thing.

Hopefully I'd live long enough to find out.

***

The Hotel Nile felt familiar, even though I'd never been inside.

I'd lost track of the number of times I'd mentioned the place in an article, but between raids and shootings and stabbings I had to have put the hotel's name in close proximity to the words "killed," "slain" or "injured" on more than a few dozen occasions.

A four-story brick face apartment complex with architecture so caked in grime that you knew it was built before the riots, the Nile was one of Newark's oldest and saddest constructs. It was a haven for people lost so far down the spiral of addiction that their entire lives consisted of sleeping, shooting and scoring. It was common practice for someone to rent a room on the same floor as their dealer – at least for the day or two they could afford it-- just to make sure they had an immediate line on a fix. Sometimes the rooms were stacked five or six people deep, a full-on shooting gallery.

The city knew the place was a giant scar, and they occasionally made a show of rousting the building and perp walking the hollowed-out husks that dealt and doped and frequently died inside, but they never moved to shut it down. No nuisance abatement lawsuits. No injunctions. Nothing that might actually change anything.

Frank once told me that the department brass thought it best to keep all that misery and malfeasance confined to one place, for fear of what might happen if it all spilled out into the daylight. More street dealers. More end users stealing because there was no place cheaper to confine them aside from jail.

Of course, that logic only held up if you dismissed the people inside the Nile as beyond help. If you thought their crimes disqualified them from the basics of human decency.

I really should have seen this all coming.

Frank rolled the car to a stop across the street from the apartment complex. Not hard to find parking outside a building where almost no one can afford a car. The wind picked up, rattling the barren branches lining the block, kicking up plastic bags and other debris in a scratchy howl, the disaffected cry of everyone who'd died inside that building.

Maybe they knew another was about to join their ranks.

Frank hadn't spoken on the ride over. Not that I'd felt too talkative either.

The Sig Sauer looked heavy in his hands. I didn't know how many guns Frank owned, and I had to wonder if that was the one he used to shoot Kevin or if it was on its maiden voyage of unnecessary bloodshed.

"So it's that simple?" I asked.

He didn't respond.

"You never killed anyone when you were on the job," I said. "How did this become so easy for you?"

"You think this is easy?" he asked. "You think I wanted to do this?"

"Who forced you Frank? You're the one with the gun."

He shook his head, laid the weapon down flat in his lap. I thought about reaching for it, and then I thought about getting shot. He was out of my weight class. Talking was the only way out of this.

"I need you to explain this to me Frank. For fuck's sake we're sitting outside a flophouse. You're about to go in there and shoot a man in cold blood and one way or another, I helped you. I deserve an explanation," I said. "I deserve to know why you're doing this. Or why you're doing it again."

"It wasn't cold blood," he whispered, staring straight ahead out the window, eyes trained on nothing.

"Kevin Mathis was unarmed Frank," I responded.

"That's not what I mean," he replied. "I mean it wasn't the plan. No one was supposed to die."

"And yet here we are."

Frank held his hand up and fanned his fingers out as if to say stop.

"I'll explain. Not because you deserve it, but because you were right before. I need you to understand this," he said. "Because otherwise I have to shoot you. And I wholeheartedly do not want to do that."

How humanitarian of him.

I nodded. I tend to get quiet when people promise to kill me.

"You talked to Lowell right?" he asked. "So you know all about Lazio, the drugs, the very real risk of god knows how many dealers and bangers and shit heels pouring back onto these streets."

I nodded again, still rendered mum by the aforementioned death threat.

"Henniman reached out to me a month or so back, maybe more. Explained the situation. How Becerra and Mathis were running their mouths. How it was only a matter of time before everything went to shit," he said. "We agreed they needed to disappear. But that was it. We wanted them out of Newark. Out of the state. If they happened to get dead the way every other drug dealer in this city does, wonderful. But otherwise we were just going to convince them to leave, that whatever card they thought they could play wasn't worth it."

He cleared his throat, ran his thumb across his neck.

"The thing with Becerra and Lowell, that just happened. He didn't know what was going on. I know how it looks, but they just happened upon him on another bust. The shoot looked legit to me, and no amount of protests or chants or news stories is going to change that. The kid reached. Lowell fired. It had nothing to do with all this."

I wouldn't have believed that last part if I hadn't talked to Lowell. Whatever had crawled inside of Frank and Henniman wasn't infecting the young detective yet. He was the kind of cop whose story I'd gone into the business looking to tell.

Or at least I hoped he was. I'd once thought the same of Frank.

"Once his running buddy died, Mathis went to ground," Frank said. "I worked some old C.I.'s, and Henniman had a few of his people do the same, but no one could get a line on him."

I didn't ask him who the "few" were. I didn't really have to. Scannell and the faceless detectives we'd run across in Seaside had to have known about this.

"But you found his supplier," I said. "Levon."

"They weren't the best of friends," he replied. "So, I bent his ear, let him think Kevin was a snitch, hoped that story would either make the kid listen to reason or send him running out of the city."

"And you didn't care if it got him killed?" I asked.

"It didn't."

"It could have."

"And it didn't," he said.

Only because it had reached the wrong ears. I thought back to my conversation with Hard Head, the Bloods O.G. who knew Kevin Mathis well, who knew the rumor Frank started was bullshit. Kevin was "no angel," the dismissive term used by too many newspapers to describe too many people who'd died the same way Kevin had in recent years, but he deserved better than he got. A gang leader had placed more value on his life than the ex-cop sitting next to me.

"So why is he dead Frank?" I asked. "Despite your most reckless efforts, your lie didn't send him running and it didn't cost him his life, so why is he dead? What did you do?"

"I found him. Once I applied the right pressure, the same C.I.'s who led me to Levon eventually were able to point me at the place on the West Side where Kevin stayed sometimes," he said.

I didn't want to know what the "right pressure" was.

"I tried to talk to him," Frank continued. "It didn't go well."

"It didn't go well?" I asked. "That's it? That's all you have to say?"

"What do you want from me Russell?"

I wanted him to give me a reason. Some shred of anything that made this less than 100 percent his fault. I wanted him to tell me Mathis had a gun. Or he'd turned toward him. That he presented an imminent threat to life and safety. I knew part of that desire was born during all the time Frank and I had worked together, drank together. But that was only part of it.

My brain was still playing by an outdated set of rules. The one that said Frank had to be right, somehow, even with everything I knew. That the cops looked like me and the robbers looked like them, and those roles were immutable no matter how much time and space we all traveled through. Even now I couldn't shake free of that.

"He ran," Frank said, the story finally starting to spill out of him without me prompting. "Didn't even give me a chance to ask a question. He just took off when he saw me. Probably assumed I was police or ex-police, and I guess after what happened with his friend, there was nothing left to be said. Maybe he thought I was after that video. We didn't even know about that, which is still the craziest part in all this, at least to me. I went after him. I honestly didn't know what I was gonna do. Like I said, this wasn't planned. But when I caught up to him in Woodland Cemetery well … you know that place Russ. How many times did I get called out there for a murder? Someone Kevin Mathis' age, who'd lived Kevin Mathis' life, winding up dead in that same spot. I'm not religious, but maybe it was a sign. He was going to die in that neighborhood one way or the other. At least this way, I stopped him from telling a story that would have caused who knows how many people to die the same way, fighting over the same bullshit stakes."

I didn't even know how to begin to respond to that.

"We understand death better than most people, right?" he asked. "Me investigating it. You writing about it. Sure, there's natural disasters, car accidents, acts of God. But mostly, people die how they're supposed to. Especially here. Kevin Mathis had an expiration date. I just moved it up a little for the greater good. Eddie Lazio? Same thing. You said you wanted to see this through with me, so you could keep anyone else from dying, right? Well so do I. That's what this is. Lazio dies, and the wound closes. Lazio lives, the story gets out, and it's open season. Cases overturned. People back out on the street who shouldn't be. The department's reputation destroyed."

There it was. The thing that this was really about. Through all his altruistic bullshit, this was about worship of an institution. Adherence to a dogma that had been written from one point of view. A tome I'd added to over the years.

But I had one more story to tell. And to tell it right, I had to get into that room.

"No one else dies," I said.

"That's up to Lazio," Frank replied.

"No, that's up to me," I said. "Dina doesn't have the whole picture yet, but I can give it to her. And if I do, then this has all been for nothing. You killed Kevin Mathis for nothing. You want me to keep your secrets. You play by my rules. Convince Lazio to leave, but no one else dies."

Frank nodded. I nodded.

We got out of the car, headed to one last crime scene together.

CHAPTER 18

I wanted Eddie Lazio to look more menacing.

Even if it was indirect, the man was responsible for at least one death and a host of legal injustices. He also struck the match that burned down whatever shaky truce Newark's police and residents had been operating under.

But when he opened the door to the apartment Levon had directed him to and stared up at Frank and I with wet brown eyes, he just looked sad.

The public defender wore an ill-fitting tee-shirt and faded straight leg jeans indicative of mid-life surrender, both of which accentuated a bloated mid-section. His thinning hair was splayed in different directions, like a cartoon character hit by a bolt of lightning. His face was a mask of disappointment and confusion.

"Where's Levon?" he asked.

Confronted by two strange men in a building known for violence, he didn't care who we were, just who we weren't. We weren't the men who could feed his demon, so we didn't matter.

I'd wanted him to be malevolent, arrogant. Someone else I could blame for the turn the city had taken. But he was just another domino toppled on its side, one life careening into the next until the tiles smacked Kevin Mathis and Luis Becerra into the ground and under it.

"Levon's making himself hard to find," Frank said. "And if you're smart, you'll do the same."

He brushed past Lazio, taking command of the room like he always did. Whatever remorse Frank had been feeling, or pretending to feel, was gone once he took a look at the man whose life I was trying to save. Based on his rants in the car, he was probably looking at Lazio the same way he'd looked at Kevin. A drain. A problem. A catastrophe waiting to happen who wouldn't be missed. The kind of name I used to toss away in the bottom of law & order briefs that nobody cared to read, and I honestly cared little to write.

"Who are you?" Lazio finally asked as Frank swept the room.

The public defender didn't look like a threat, not to me and especially not to Frank, but my ex-source wasn't taking any chances. He was pulling open drawers and checking under surfaces, probably hunting for weapons. Not that Lazio was in any shape to do anything, even if he had a gun or blade tucked away somewhere.

"Who are you?" he asked again, voice lacking any authority. He sounded like a scared child.

"Just sit down, Eddie," I said, placing a hand in the small of his back, trying to guide him toward the bed. "This will all be over soon."

I looked at the clock. It'd be over in about five minutes, maybe less, if my text message had accomplished anything.

If it hadn't, I was still right. It would be over soon. But in a lot bloodier fashion.

"You fucked up," Frank said, turning toward Lazio, hand at his side but weapon still holstered. "And you need to pay for it. My friend and I have different views on what that might entail."

"What are you…" Lazio started.

"Kevin Mathis. Luis Becerra," I said, hoping to snap the lawyer out of his self-involved spiral and back into the mess he'd made. "You know who they are. You can't be that far gone."

His eyes went wide. Even in this sad state, he knew what happened to them. What it might mean for him.

"No," he said. "No. I didn't…I won't…I went away."

Frank shook his head in complete disgust, looking past the car wreck on the bed and toward me.

"Oh yeah, this is going to work out just fine," Frank said. "How long do you think this guy lasts outside this room?"

"Frank…"

"Answer the question, Russ," he said. "You wanted me to convince you? Well you need to convince me too. How long until this idiot gets picked up somewhere? Only reason he got away with it this long was because he was hiding in hell's armpit. How long does he last outside?"

That wasn't the amount of time that mattered. I checked the clock for the one that did. Three minutes.

"I don't know. Maybe we get him some help, clean him up. Get him out of the state so if he does fuck up he's way off Internal Affairs' or anyone else's radar," I replied. "I'm not the one trying to cover shit up Frank, I don't have all the answers. All I know is we can't do it your way."

Lazio started to whimper and shake. He looked like he might cry, or vomit. Maybe both.

"I didn't want any of this to happen. It wasn't supposed to…"

"Shut the fuck up," I shouted. I'd spent more than enough time listening to Frank's justifications downstairs. Crouching down, I got right in Lazio's face, stared straight into the black holes behind his drooping eyelids.

"You're getting out of Newark, and out of New Jersey, right now. And you are not coming back. That's it. That's all there is to it," I said. "People died because of you."

"No, but…I didn't…I have kids here," he replied. "I can't just…"

"Enough," Frank said.

266

I turned around, less than surprised by the sight of the Sig Sauer. Frank's gun and I were becoming entirely too familiar.

"I told you it was his choice, Russ," he said. "Now he made it. Move."

The wall clock was on a dust-covered dresser behind Frank. One minute. Hopefully.

"You really want to do this. Look at this guy. It'd be murder. Point blank," I said.

"What's the other option here? He walks. He gets caught. And then how many more murders, shootings, happen in the fallout?" he asked.

"You don't know that," I said.

"Yeah. I do," he replied. "And so do you. I'm not asking you again. It's pick a side time Russ."

I looked at the wall clock again, staring intensely, hoping I could somehow will that minute to move into the next. The time didn't change.

But the chants started early.

Frank turned toward the window as he tried to identify the source of the low roar. I knew the cadence, the rhythm, even if I wasn't sure of the exact words being used. They'd be close enough soon.

"What the fuck is that?" he asked.

"My side," I replied.

He lowered the gun and reached for the shades, but I didn't have to follow Frank to know what he'd see when he drew them back.

A crowd had gathered, hopefully as large as the one from a few nights earlier outside City Hall, with Keyonna Jackson at the front, megaphone in hand. The protest would draw media, police, eyes. The city's shareholders all in one spot, able to bear witness to the shadows that had put them at odds in the first place.

Key would have to swallow one more lie, but at least this one had a purpose. The message I'd sent in the parking lot around the time Levon escaped was a response to her group blast about the night's planned demonstration. I'd told her the officer who fired the fatal shot in the video would be here, at this time and place, hoping I'd earned enough trust over the years to overcome our recent disagreements.

She deserved to be here. She'd started all this anyway -- pushed and argued and taunted me toward taking Kevin Mathis' case, one I would have otherwise ignored. She'd pushed for the release of the video that I wouldn't have, sparked action in a city that otherwise tended to stay silent when it should have been screaming.

"What did you do?" Frank asked, his back still to me.

"Ended this," I replied. "Whatever happens in this room, people are going to know, Frank. Burying things is how we got here. If you shoot him, if you shoot me, it doesn't change a thing. This is all going to come out."

I hoped Dina was in that crowd too. This was the story she'd been searching for all this time. She needed to be the one to tell it.

"You...you son of a bitch," Frank said, voice rising in volume and rage as he stepped back from the window. He wasn't facing us yet, but his hand was already traveling south. "Do you have any idea what you've done?"

"I didn't kill anyone," I replied. "And I'm not starting now. You can only make this worse from here."

"I don't know about that, Russ. We're still the only ones in this room," he said. "And you know what they say about history, who it gets written by."

He reached, started to turn. I made my move, however suicidal it was, racing toward Frank and his way too fast gun hand, putting my body between him and Lazio.

The weapon was up before I'd closed the distance, trained on me.

Frank looked like he was searching for something, hoping maybe there was still some part of me that would fall in line with his hopelessly broken line of thinking.

It was only one second of hesitation, but it was enough. Because I knew exactly who I was looking at now.

Everything that had gone wrong in the past week coursed up my hip, into my shoulder and through my fist, uncoiling in a desperate haymaker that caught Frank clean on the jaw.

The blow staggered Frank, and the sight of the gun sweeping toward the ceiling seemed to wake Lazio from his withdrawal haze. I saw the public defender leap up and race toward the door as I tried to wrestle Frank in the opposite direction.

I reached for his wrist, trying to gain control of the gun. We locked eyes again, but the hesitation was gone now. Frank was in the fight, and that meant I was in serious trouble. He jammed an elbow into my chest, created some separation and fired a wild shot at the fleeing public defender. I couldn't see where the round went, but I didn't hear any screams of pain, just the sound of the door flying open.

A chorus of shrieks started outside. Cops would flood the room in seconds.

But until then it was just me and Frank. He took a step toward the door, then stopped, probably doing the same math I just had. Lazio was gone. The cavalry was on its way. This was all but over.

He charged, raising the gun too high to shoot, then bringing it down in a swooping motion toward my face. He missed, but the swing forced me to backpedal, and that was enough to give him leverage. Frank was on top of me in seconds, pinning me down and reigning blow after blow, the same way Scannell had outside Hanley's. But he was in better shape. He knew how to throw a punch, and he knew how to make it count. Teeth rattled. I felt cuts opening and blood leaking. My vision started to blur. The cops weren't going to get there fast enough.

"You made a choice, Russ," he said, ending the barrage, placing an arm across my throat, pressing the gun to my face. It was still hot from the last shot. I felt skin sear on my left cheek. Not that it would matter in a few seconds.

"They won't believe the junkie," he said. "And they're not going to get a chance to talk to you."

He was wrong. Key's crowd would make too much noise. Dina would find a way to get something in the paper. The story would be told.

He was going to answer for this. Even if I wasn't gonna be there to see it.

"Goodbye Russ," he said.

"Put it down!" screamed a voice I never thought I'd be happy to hear.

Frank still had me pinned. I couldn't see anything. But I recognized that agitated growl.

Bill Henniman.

"Frank. Put the gun down," Bill screamed again. "Now."

"Bill, I…"

"Now, Frank!"

Frank looked at me, then the gun. He seemed like he was weighing his options. He didn't have many. With the gun still pressed against me Frank let his head sink down to his chest. For a second, I thought he was crying. Then he let out a half-smile.

"Well shit, Russ," he said. "Guess I'm gonna give you one last story after all."

"Frank!" I shouted.

But he was already moving, pulling the gun back and spinning toward Henniman's voice.

He reached. They fired.

CHAPTER 19

I flipped open a copy of the *Signal-Intelligencer*, spreading it across a table in the back of Hobby's as I waited for some comfort food. There was no need to hunt for the article I wanted to read. It was splashed across the front of the old broadsheet.

It was the best story I'd ever been a part of. The kind of piece a cop reporter dreams of writing.

But my name wasn't where I'd ever have expected it to be:

By Dina Colby
Signal-Intelligencer **Staff**

The shooting death of a former Newark homicide investigator was linked to a widening corruption scandal that could lead to the retrial of hundreds of defendants and has reignited calls for federal oversight of the state's largest police department, according to multiple city officials and law enforcement sources.

Frank Russomano, 55, was shot and killed by city police officers late last week after a confrontation inside the Hotel Nile in the city's Central Ward. Officers were responding to a report of gunfire near the scene of a large-scale protest and found Russomano pointing a weapon at someone inside the building, according to Acting Police Director Anthony DeMaio.

Moments prior to the shooting, Russomano had been involved in a clash with Deputy Public Defender Edward Lazio, who is now the subject of separate investigations by the Essex County Prosecutor's Office and the New Jersey BAR Association, according to three law enforcement sources. Investigators believe Lazio was abusing prescription medication while trying cases for at least two years, which could prompt new trials for hundreds of defendants, the sources said.

The sources spoke on condition of anonymity because they were not authorized to discuss the case.

Russomano is also suspected in the shooting death of 20-year-old Kevin Mathis, whose death fueled a number of demonstrations throughout downtown Newark in recent weeks, the sources said. Mathis and another man, Luis Becerra, were both former clients of Lazio who had threatened to expose his drug use, according to the sources and interviews with the victim's relatives. Becerra, 19, was shot and killed by a Newark police officer several weeks ago.

Newark Mayor David Giambusso called the situation "horrific" in a statement released last night but urged residents not to blame the entire department for a scandal that appeared to be limited to a few detectives.

"We will do everything in our power to root out officers like this," Giambusso said in the statement. "But in this time of tragedy, we need to remember the majority of the city's officers are here for only two purposes: to protect and serve."

Other city officials did not share Giambusso's restraint. Six members of the city council have publicly called for the department to enter a "consent decree" with the U.S. Department of Justice, ending a years-long investigation into the department's practices. The DOJ has been considering federal oversight for years, after a scathing petition from the state chapter of the American Civil Liberties Union.

Russomanno admitted to killing Mathis in order to quash the Lazio investigation, according to Russell Avery, a former Signal-Intelligencer reporter now working as a private investigator. Avery was hired by the Mathis family and was in the room when Russomanno was killed.

Several law enforcement sources confirmed portions of Avery's account, though a Newark police spokesman declined to comment on the matter.

It went on from there, with plenty of blustery reaction quotes from Key and politicians and the police union president who was "stunned" by the entire situation.

I read the story over again. Then a third time. We'd done it. Though, honestly, she'd done it. Or at least finished it. This was the kind of story the police department couldn't ignore. Between our investigation causing things to spill over inside the Hotel Nile and Dina having the sourcing to tie each senseless death into something meaningful, someone was going to have to pay for what happened here.

Not Frank. He'd chosen his own escape route. But the city and the department's brass would have to answer for letting him off the leash now.

A waiter brought over a steaming bowl of matzoh ball soup. I paused before I dove in, half because of the heat, half because I had to wonder what Dina was doing at that moment.

She was out there somewhere, running down her follow-up piece. We'd exchanged the required "are you OK?" texts in the hours after Frank nearly killed me, but I hadn't seen or heard from her since she'd interviewed me for the story. She was busy, sure, that was part of it. But the length of time between text message replies told me something else too. I recognized the cadence, the pattern of responses.

She'd text me again when I knew something. I wasn't her ex anymore, just a source.

I didn't love it, but I respected it. At least things were clear.

Made it easier for me to pawn that ring.

The soup swirled as I attacked it. Luckily, I happened to be reaching for a napkin when the table lurched, launching a wave of burning liquid in my direction. The weaponized lunch fell short of my face, landing on the newspaper, turning part of Dina's article into a garbled inky mess.

I looked up to find Key smirking as she wiggled into the booth across from me. There was plenty of room, no need for her to deliver a knee strike to the underside of the table. She winked at me, then leaned over the bowl to check what I was reading.

"Wormed your way back onto the front page?" she asked.

"Looks like we both did," I said, running my finger along one of her react quotes lower down in the story. "But she used mine first."

"Your mother must be so proud," Key said.

"My mother reads the *New York Post*," I replied. "Causes a lot of hell when I visit for Christmas."

She let out a snort that might have been a laugh and called over to the waiter, ordered a #5 before the poor guy could even start trying to make small talk.

"I'm surprised you had time to meet up," I said after dispensing with the last of the soup. "Figured you'd have more people in the streets than ever before."

"I'm an activist, Russ. I got more moves than protest," she replied. "Besides, feds seem like they actually care about this so-called investigation now. Been reaching out to community leaders like me, trying to find people who have had ... unpleasant ... experiences with the NPD. If they're listening, we'll talk. I only take to the streets when I'm out of other options. They plug their ears again, well ... I won't have too much trouble messing up traffic on Broad Street."

The waiter was back, dropping off Key's sandwich with a nod and no words.

"Something's been gnawing at me though," she said. "That night, when you were in that hotel room…"

She stopped to bite of a hunk of the sandwich, Russian dressing dribbling from her lip.

"If I didn't show up, make enough noise that all those cops and reporters had to stand up and pay attention … what were you gonna do?" she asked.

"What do you mean?"

"You know what I mean," she replied. "If not for the sold-out crowd outside that building, your boy probably shoots that lawyer, and this whole tale, everything about Kevin, becomes by and large conspiracy theory unless you step forward to tell it. I wanna know what would have happened if it came down that way. Would you have put yourself all the way out there? Would you have done the right thing, turned Frank in?"

Tough question. One I hadn't really had the balls to ask myself. Maybe one day I'd find that courage.

"There's a reason I called you first, Key," I said.

"That's not really an answer."

"Well, it's the only one I got," I said. "Frank … I hate what he turned into. But he got that way by making unilateral decisions. By thinking he knew what was best in a situation that affected this whole damn city. The way I helped things go down, at least the city got a part in making the call. You. Dina. The protesters. The cops that weren't involved in all this shit. The story got told by the right people. That's all that matters to me."

Key took another bite of her sandwich, nodded. Maybe she was satisfied by the answer, or maybe she was just too enthralled by her lunch, but she didn't offer a follow-up.

We sat there quietly for a few minutes, watching the room. Two uniform cops came through the door, their squad car parked in a loading zone outside. Just about the only way you could find a parking spot near Hobby's around lunchtime. One of them looked at our table, elbowed his partner. They both gave me a once-over, but their faces didn't betray their thoughts.

I couldn't tell if they wanted to hit me or thank me. But that confusion didn't bode well for the future of my suddenly reeling P.I. business. People had been keeping their distance since Frank fell.

Henniman hadn't spoken to me since he saved my life. Between the shooting and the investigation into the whole Lazio mess, I doubted he'd be sending me work anytime soon. Colleen was taking my calls again, but now it was me struggling to pin the Internal Affairs boss down for a lunch date, not the other way around.

My client well, at least the well-paying cop kind, was drier than the bottom of my short-lived soup bowl.

"Key?"

She tossed the last piece of rye crust onto her plate, gave me her attention.

"You got any work for me?" I asked.

She lifted a napkin, the cloth getting caught in her overgrown nails. Key was never one for grooming, but she'd really let herself go from the days and nights in the streets.

"Course I do. One in particular," she replied. "But the last time we had this conversation, Austin Mathis had to wait days and days for you to decide it was worth it. The people who go through me to hire you aren't always your favorite people on earth, and the people they usually have issue with are the kind with badges."

In the last couple of days, I'd watched a man with a badge I'd once considered a friend try to kill a witness and consider killing me.

In that same span of time, I'd watched a man with a badge who detested me save my life.

Maybe it was time to stop judging police and protesters, and just start judging people.

***

Kevin Mathis' memorial had grown since the last time I'd seen it.

The number of balloons and posters wishing for him to rest in peace and power had increased exponentially. There were stuffed animals now too, some holding candles whose wicks had long ago burnt out.

But for all that, there was no one there mourning him.

Maybe it was the time of day I'd shown up. Maybe it was sheer luck. Or maybe Kevin Mathis was just a name now. A life reduced to a bit player in the larger fiasco that had enveloped Newark in the past week. The latest in a line of dead who might be replaced by another dashboard camera video, another chant, another city. Another tragic mistake or another kid who should have stopped resisting, depending on who you asked.

I crouched down at the center of it, looked around to see if anyone was watching, and started thumbing through the cards at the base. The handwritten messages that went more than a sentence or two.

In the week I'd spent investigating Kevin Mathis' death, I'd learned little to nothing about his life. At least nothing outside his court records.

There was a message from a neighbor at the base of the memorial, a posthumous thank you for all the times Kevin had watched their dog. The note behind that one was from an uncle, about how his younger cousins would miss their favorite babysitter.

Somehow, I was surprised. As if I couldn't imagine there was more to Kevin than the things that added up and led to his death. The mistakes that put him in the crosshairs.

I thought back to the first time I'd seen the memorial. When I'd nearly mixed it up with the group of kids on the street corner, the anger coursing through the oldest one in the hooded sweatshirt.

"You was just saying what they always say," he'd shouted at me. "Like how he lived just had to be why he died."

It was the lens I viewed things through that Key had always judged me for. The lens, in part, shaped by Frank. Maybe it would die with him.

I thumbed through the other notes for a few more minutes, reading the extremely condensed history of the rest of Kevin Mathis' life. I got so focused, I almost failed to notice the footsteps coming up from behind.

I turned to find Bill Henniman moving slowly, hands jammed in his pockets, head down. He slid up next to me and stared at the memorial, mouthing something under his breath. When he closed with the sign of the cross, I realized he'd been praying.

"You're religious?" I asked.

"After this week, I figured I might start again," he replied.

"Not the worst idea I've heard," I said. "Don't think I could sit still long enough to get through a mass though."

"Somehow, I feel staying silent would be a larger issue for you," he said.

We stood there for a minute, both showing something approaching respect for the makeshift memorial. Eventually, I proved his premise right.

"Did you follow me here?" I asked.

Henniman turned to me, then rolled his eyes.

"What? I'm just saying, you're developing a habit of being wherever I am," I said.

"So that's how you thank me for saving your life?" he asked.

I was still struggling to reconcile our last two interactions: Henniman threatening to arrest me, and Frank coming to the rescue. Frank shoving a gun in my face, and Henniman taking his friend's life to spare mine.

"I guess," I replied. "Though I still can't understand why you did that."

Henniman looked up at the angry cloud cover and shook his head. Another long exhale followed.

"How is it you were smart enough to unravel this whole Lazio mess, but stupid enough to ask that question at the same time?" he asked.

"He was your friend," I said.

"Was," he replied. "Yours too, at some point. Then he wasn't. Then he was a suspect. Armed and dangerous, a threat to you, Lazio and who knows how many other people. I did what I had to do."

"So you knew Frank killed Kevin Mathis?"

"I didn't say that," he replied.

"Then why were you there that night, Lieutenant? Hell, why were you in Seaside earlier that day?" I asked. "I don't understand you. You stopped me from looking into this at every turn. You threatened my business. You tried to arrest me. But then with everything on the line, you killed one of your own to save me, put a magnifying glass on yourself, your unit and your department in the process. Why?"

Frank crouched down at the memorial, reached in between two dying bouquets to snatch a polaroid of Kevin. He was younger in the photo, maybe 15. Smiling. Life hadn't done any damage to him yet.

"I didn't shoot this kid. No one in my department did," Henniman said. "But we helped him get dead. I asked for Frank's help when this all started, when Mathis and his running buddy made themselves liabilities, threatened to put Lazio's shit in the streets. I thought … no, I hoped, that I could keep the lid on everything and run them out of town. I was afraid of the same things Frank was. Mass jail releases. People who needed to be put away back out on the street, hurting people who would have otherwise gone on living their lives. And yeah, maybe I wanted to spare the department from the federal shit storm that was about to rain down on it. But no one was supposed to die."

He held the picture closer, like he was examining it.

"Frank got lost. He got confused about what we were supposed to protect and who we were supposed to serve. He chose the agency over the citizens. I can understand that. Hell, I've done that. But nobody died," Henniman said, now turning the photograph so I could see Kevin's smile. "I have no love for this kid. And regardless of what happened the other night, I don't like you all that much either, Avery. But he shouldn't be dead, and he is, because I let Frank go too far. I wasn't going to make the same mistake twice."

"Are you sure?" I asked.

"You're standing here, aren't you?"

"No, I'm grateful for that, believe me. But if you could have stopped Frank without all the news, without the rest of the city knowing what Lazio was into … you would have, right?" I asked, aware how much I sounded like Key grilling me the same way.

Henniman crouched back down, placed Kevin's photo in its right place. I wanted an answer I wasn't going to get. I wanted to know Henniman saw the same things I did in the past week or two. Systemic issues. A stacked deck. A criminal justice system focused more on minimizing damage than preventing it.

"I really don't know, Russell," he said. "I just know I'm sick of going to funerals."

He turned from me and headed back for his car, in search of a world that made sense to him. I hoped he didn't find it. Not because I wished ill on him, but because I wanted to know the past few days had meant something. That Newark had received a diagnosis and that the disease could be treated before it became terminal.

Kevin Mathis died before I took his case, but I was complicit anyway. I'd ignored the problems that put him in the path of a bullet back when I'd been tasked with chronicling the city's ills. Too busy convincing myself that I was the smartest person in the room. Too busy ignoring all the voices eager to prove that I wasn't.

I pulled out my phone, searched for Key's number. She did say she had a case for me after all.

I agreed with Henniman on one thing.

I was sick of funerals too.

ACKNOWLEDGMENTS

A lot of people breathed life into this book. All I did was write it down.

The five years I spent at The Star-Ledger changed me as a person, a journalist and a writer. I'm not who I am today, and this book probably doesn't exist, without the patience and guidance of editors and reporters like Mark Mueller, David Giambusso, David Tucker, Steve Liebman, Chris Megerian, Peggy Ackermann, John Appezzatto or Robin Wilson-Glover.

Bashir Akinyele, Donna Jackson, Hykine Johnson (RIP), Ronald Rice Jr., Ras Baraka, Deborah Jacobs, Anthony Ambrose, Thomas Fennelly and Samuel DeMaio – thank you for the different perspectives you gave me on a complicated city and for helping me chronicle its real and fictional iterations. Some of you might feel awkward being listed in the same space, but maybe that's the point of this whole thing?

To the law enforcement officers and Newark locals I can't name because you don't reveal sources – you know who you are, you know how you helped, you know I can't ever thank you enough for it.

To Jim and Donna, for believing, for not pushing me toward something more practical when I decided I was gonna write for a living, for driving me to every basketball practice and track meet and show at Dock Street. Some parents just say they'll be there for you. Mine have been showing up since Day One and never stopped.

To Mike Queally, my kid brother, best friend and original beta reader back to the days when I was trying to write "prose comic books." Thanks for reading everything, thanks for letting me get all the bad ideas out so we could get to the good one. Thanks for keeping me grounded, even if you never actually hit me for saying I was "the voice of a generation" like you promised.

Many of you either read LINE OF SIGHT in its various iterations or read drafts of other pieces of fiction that helped me figure out how to write it, so if I forget anyone, I am extremely sorry. But for your time and thoughts, I am forever indebted to Patricia Cole, Saba Hamedy, Allie Singer, Anthony Sellitti, Fran Gerrish, John LoCasto and Jason Katz.

To Rob Hart and Todd Ritter, for sending the elevator back down. The two of you didn't simply guide me in writing this book -- though your influence and advice are tucked into plenty of these pages -- you pretty much raised me as far as fiction goes. From the first flash piece at Shotgun Honey to saving me from stepping on landmines while querying agents, I will never be able to cover the tab I owe both of you. But I'm gonna spend a long time trying.

To my agent, James McGowan, I'm glad we took a chance on each other. Thank you for believing in this book and fighting to make it real.

To my editor and publisher, Jason Pinter, thanks for giving Russell Avery a home. Hopefully, this isn't the last time you walk into his office.

Jenny Tsay, I assume you read this whole list wondering where you were, so please understand I just wanted to make sure everything started and ended with you.

You are everything I could have ever asked for in a lover, best friend and tag-team partner. Whether it was printing out the first few chapters of early drafts of LINE OF SIGHT, listening to me try out different short stories for readings or just letting me ramble through some plot element as I tried to figure out what was in Russ' head (or my own), you often showed me you believed in this thing more than I ever did. You pushed me back in the room to write when I was frustrated, and maybe more importantly, you pulled me out and shoved me into a beach chair when you knew I needed it. I can't do this stuff without you, nor would I ever want too. I love you more than the most and can't wait to spend the rest of time sharing a habitat with you and the pup.

ABOUT THE AUTHOR

James Queally is an award-winning crime reporter for the *Los Angeles Times*. Throughout his career, Queally has covered hundreds of homicides as well as national use-of-force controversies. His short stories have appeared in *Thuglit, Crime Syndicate Magazine, Shotgun Honey* and more. *Line of Sight* is his debut novel. Follow him at @JamesQueallyLAT.